THEN SHE WAS SCREAMING, AGONIZED AND HOPELESS.

It went on and on until she thought she wouldn't be able to stand it for another second. Then it grew louder.

She heard Willow cry, "Buffy!"

Then she was burning up, standing inside a firestorm that ate away every inch of her being. She writhed as flames whooshed around her, burning through her lungs, her vocal cords, her ears.

She trembled, freezing, in utter silence. She looked left, right; but where she was, endless blackness stretched in all directions. She tried to move, but she was frozen to the . . .

to the . . .

to nothing.

She was utterly, vastly *nowhere*.

Somewhere, very far away, she heard a voice she once had known very well. With a laugh, it spoke:

"I have won."

Buffy the Vampire Slayer™

Available from ARCHWAY Paperbacks and POCKET PULSE

Buffy the Vampire Slayer adult books

Available from POCKET BOOKS

BUFFY THE VAMPIRE SLAYER™

BLOODED

Christopher Golden and Nancy Holder
An original novel based on the hit TV series
created by Joss Whedon

AN ARCHWAY PAPERBACK
Published by POCKET BOOKS
New York   London   Toronto   Sydney   Singapore

AN ARCHWAY PAPERBACK *Original*

An Archway Paperback published by
POCKET BOOKS, a division of Simon & Schuster Inc.
1230 Avenue of the Americas, New York, NY 10020

™ and copyright © 1998 by Twentieth Century Fox Film Corporation.
All rights reserved.

All rights reserved, including the right to reproduce
this book or portions thereof in any form whatsoever.
For information address Pocket Books, 1230 Avenue
of the Americas, New York, NY 10020

ISBN: 0-671-02134-6

First Archway Paperback printing August 1998

10 9 8 7 6

AN ARCHWAY PAPERBACK and colophon are
registered trademarks of Simon & Schuster Inc.

Printed in the U.S.A.

To Tom.
I'm sorry there are no monkeys.
—C.G.

To the memory of my father, Kenneth Paul Jones,
and the happy memories of our years in Japan.

—N.H.

The authors would like to thank: our agents, Lori Perkins and Howard Morhaim, and Howard's assistant, Lindsay Sagnette; also, our editor at Archway/Minstrel, Lisa Clancy, and her assistant, Elizabeth Shiflett. Our gratitude to Caroline Kallas, Joss Whedon, and the entire cast and crew of *Buffy*. Thanks to our patient and supportive spouses, Connie and Wayne, and to our children, Nicholas and Daniel Golden, and Belle Holder, who remind us daily what it's all about.

PROLOGUE

The front row of the old Majestic Theatre was filled with corpses. Glassy-eyed, their throats ripped out, the dead had the best seats in the house.

But the final curtain had yet to fall, and as far as Buffy Summers was concerned, until it did, there was no telling how the show would end.

Time for a little improv, she thought.

She'd have been way more confident about the whole scene if not for the fact that she was without a clue as to what the hairy, loud-mouthed, badly-in-need-of-Weight-Watchers vampire—who called himself King Lear, of all things—had done with Xander and Cordelia.

A single spotlight shone down from the balcony on the heavy red velvet curtain that hung across the stage. The Majestic was ancient, but still beautiful despite its state of disrepair. Kind of like Mrs.

Paolillo, who had subbed as Buffy's English teacher for three days the week before. Dust spun in the beam of the spot, and the rest of the theater was dark.

Amazingly, the Majestic had existed as a venue for musicals and stage plays until two or three years earlier and had never been transformed into a movie theater.

"I . . . well, I do suppose you realize that this is a trap?" Giles whispered behind her.

Buffy rolled her eyes. "Come on, Giles, give me some credit," she said, sighing. "I may not like being the Chosen One, but I've been Little Miss Vampire Slayer long enough to know when I'm being set up."

"Yes, um, quite right then," Giles mumbled. "It's only that . . ."

"Only that there are four majorly ravenous bloodsuckers in the balcony above our heads?" Buffy whispered.

"That would be it, yes," Giles replied. "Remind me again why I persist in joining you on these excursions. You do seem fully capable of handling them on your own."

Buffy reached into her Slayer's bag and handed Giles a large wooden crucifix and a long, tapered stake.

"One hundred people surveyed, top five answers on the board," Buffy quipped. "Number one answer: Giles has no social life!"

Despite the tension that filled the darkened aisles of the theater, Buffy had a half-smile on her face as she turned to look at Giles. He sputtered, cocking his head the way he did when he wanted to look as though he were majorly offended. Rupert Giles was her mentor. As her Watcher, he was responsible for the Slayer's training and general well-being. As her friend, he had to put up with all kinds of teasing. Starting with the fact that he was Sunnydale's high school librarian—so totally the honey-magnet occupation of all time—as well as a bit of a stiff, especially if you thought Bryant Gumbel was just all crazy.

But Giles was her uptight Englishman, and Buffy wasn't about to let anything happen to him. Which meant that in about two seconds she was going to have to knock him on his woolen-clad behind yet again.

"Giles, down!" Buffy snapped.

Her smile disappeared as the Slayer went into action. She was all business as she stepped forward, bumped Giles with a hip to send him stumbling into a row of wood-and-metal folding seats, and held a sharpened stake above her head.

It was rainin' vampires.

The first one came down on her stake. He weighed close to two hundred pounds, and she started to buckle under his falling corpse. She'd planned to fall, roll, spring up again. But she didn't need to bother. The second the stake pierced his heart, the vamp exploded in a shower of ashes. Two others came down at the same time, and one of them tagged her arm, grabbing the fabric of her blouse as he landed. A button popped at her neck and her sleeve tore.

"Ooh!" she grunted. "You are not my friend."

Buffy launched a kick at the vampire's jaw that snapped its head back hard. She followed with a roundhouse kick at its solar plexus. The other one came at her from the side, and she ducked and used the vamp's own momentum to send him flying into the seats. The one who had ripped her blouse came after her again, snarling.

Buffy snarled back. She blocked his attack and drove the stake up through the vampire's ribs and into its heart.

"That was silk," she snapped, and turned her back on him even before he turned to dust.

A few rows up the aisle, Giles cracked his heavy cross across the head of the vampire Buffy had thrown into the seats. As she watched, her mentor staked the vamp in fine style for a guy who was fortysomething going on seventysomething and, well, not the Slayer. Still, Giles knew his stuff. Knew enough to teach Buffy more than the average red-blooded American high school girl ever needed to know about fighting vampires, demons, and the forces of darkness.

But, hey, who wanted to be average, anyway?

Well, actually, Buffy did. But they'd been over that so many times that bringing it up again would be like making an O.J. joke. It was over, but not way over, like, say, Keanu. No, it was more like Travolta before *Pulp Fiction:* just waiting for the perfect wave.

"You seem a bit rusty, Buffy," Giles said, straightening his tie. "Which leads me to wonder if I've been too lenient of late."

"Am I the only one who's noticed you're still breathing?" Buffy asked.

"Hmm?" Giles said, focusing on Buffy again. He did have a tendency to get distracted. "Of course not. And I do thank you for that, very much indeed.

It's simply that I'm concerned that against a more powerful vampire, your technique might require—"

"Giles," Buffy said.

He prattled on. "—a bit more of a—"

"Giles!" Buffy shouted.

She ran for him, but too late. Another vampire had leaped out from the balcony above them and fallen on him. Buffy felt her adrenaline surge as she considered the horrible idea that something awful might actually happen to somebody close to her. It had happened before.

Fortunately, Giles was quicker on the uptake than his absentmindedness seemed to indicate. He fell under the weight of the vampire, but even as Buffy reached for the bloodsucker, the vampire did that extremely rewarding dust-detonation thing. Giles had managed to turn the broken end of his large wooden crucifix up, and the vampire had impaled himself on it.

"You did remember that I said there were four of them up there, didn't you?" Buffy asked as she helped Giles to his feet.

"Hmm? Oh, yes," Giles replied as he wiped the dead-again ash from his glasses. "Just a bit distracted is all."

"Maybe you should work on your technique," Buffy said.

"Yes, well, you do have a point," he conceded. "But perhaps we should concentrate on finding Xander and Cordelia before this Lear fellow decides they've outlived their usefulness as bait," Giles replied.

Buffy grimaced, eyebrows knitted. She was plenty

focused; nothing was more important than getting Xander and Cordy out of there safely. That's why she and Giles had split up from Willow and Angel to begin with. But she was nervous and angry, and sarcasm helped her with both feelings.

"Haven't you ever heard of whistling in the dark?" she asked.

With a sudden, metallic whoosh, the curtains began to draw open. Buffy and Giles moved quickly down the aisle toward the stage. The Slayer was careful not to pay too much attention to the not-so-grateful dead in the first row, right in front of the orchestra pit. She'd seen more corpses than a serial killer, but it never got any easier.

"Why am I always the life of the party?" she whispered to herself, and grimaced at her silent answer. *Because I'm always the only one still alive!*

There was a second curtain at the back of the stage. Buffy figured the layout of the Majestic was a lot more complicated than the auditorium at Sunnydale High, where they'd held their recent talentless show. But even that stage had four or five curtains. It looked like they were going to have to go onstage, maybe take the spotlight, even, if they wanted to find out what Lear had done with Xander and Cordelia.

On the other hand, it wasn't as if the huge bad dude didn't know they were there. Which gave her an idea.

"What are you waiting for, Lear?" she shouted. "The audience is here!"

Giles stared at her like she was, well, her, and Buffy had to admit that, though she enjoyed taunting pompous vampires who looked like Santa's evil twin, doing so when said obese, bloodsucking actor-guy was holding some of your friends hostage was generally a not so specially good idea. But she'd figured with an ego like Lear's . . .

"'Attend the Lords of France and Burgundy!'" came the deep bass voice of Lear. The vampire strutted onto the stage in full Shakespearean costume.

Buffy might have laughed if not for the lives that hung in the balance. Instead, she looked at Giles for some kind of understanding. After all, the only Shakespeare she knew was that rock-and-roll Romeo flick with Leo and the girl who played Angela on *My So-Called Life*. Well, that, and the one Mel Gibson did. Her mom had insisted on renting that one. Not bad. "Lear's first line in King Lear," Giles whispered to her.

Buffy watched Giles for a moment as he muttered to himself as though he were trying to remember song lyrics. On the stage, Lear walked into the spotlight, staring out at the "audience" but not even glancing down at Buffy and Giles.

"'I shall, my liege!'" Giles shouted suddenly, making Buffy jump. On stage, Lear smiled.

"'Meantime,'" Lear smiled smugly, so pleased with himself he was practically drooling, "we shall express our darker purpose.'"

At that cue, the second curtain began to draw apart behind the corpulent vampire, and Buffy couldn't stop the gasp that escaped her lips as she saw Xander and Cordy. They were both gagged, and locked into a wooden contraption that snapped down over their wrists and necks, leaving them completely helpless. Maybe it had been a stage prop, once upon a time. But right now, it was all too real.

The worst part was, they were awake. Buffy could see their eyes, and though both of them had seen a lot since the Slayer had come into their lives, she could tell that they were terrified.

"Oh, my," Giles murmured.

"'Is man no more than this? Consider him well,'" Lear roared madly.

A chill ran through Buffy. She'd thought Lear was just a cruel moron. But that was wishful thinking. The only thing worse, in her opinion, than a fat, slobbering, undead, bloodsucking show-off was one who was also completely out of his head, a few bricks shy of a mausoleum.

She saw rustling behind Xander and Cordelia, where the backstage curtains hung. There were other vampires there, she knew—others who followed Lear. But she didn't know how many.

A quick glance at Xander's face, at the fear in Cordelia's eyes, and Buffy realized it didn't matter how many. But what could she do? How could she get to Lear before he could get to the rack Xander and Cordy were trapped in?

Suddenly, Giles began to applaud.

Willow followed Angel up the stairs that led to stage left. They had discovered a tunnel that ran under the stage from one side to another, which would allow actors to move from side to side without disturbing the stage crew. She'd been certain they'd find some vampires in it, but, so sad, no joy.

Not that there was any shortage of vampires. From stage right they'd seen at least six of them, lurking behind various curtains and off stage in the wings, working pulleys to open curtains and move props.

Willow shivered. She hated vampires. Well, present company excluded, of course, despite the fact that Angel had tried to kill her once. Well, tried to kill them all. But that hadn't really been Angel, that . . . made her head hurt to think about.

Angel glanced back at her as if he could read her mind, and she offered him a helpless, why-me smile. Frankly, she didn't know why he'd agreed to let her tag along. She didn't have a clue why Buffy even wanted her around when it came to stuff like this. Giles knew his stuff, and he was the Watcher, after all. Xander at least could fight. Angel was Buffy's boyfriend, and, there was that whole thing about him being a vampire—but the only good vampire they'd ever heard of.

Not to say Willow hadn't held her own before, for at least seven or eight seconds. She had. And she wanted to be there, in a kind of Three Musketeers solidarity thing kind of way. But once the research was done, she'd already served her purpose in the little cadre of Friends of Buffy that Xander affectionately referred to as the Scooby Gang.

Willow, sad as she was to admit it, was Velma. The brainy but relatively useless one. And she hated being Velma.

She sighed as she followed Angel into the rows of curtains that hung in the wings at stage left. Willow had a stake, but that was more for protection than offense.

There was a thump ahead of her, and the curtains swayed. Angel peered around them, his serious, soulful eyes—and wasn't that ironic, soulful?—making her feel a little safer. He motioned for her to follow.

Clawed hands grabbed him around the throat and drove him hard to the floor. The vampire on Angel's back was leaning forward, trying to rip out Angel's throat, when Willow moved in to stake it. She didn't see the willowy blond vamp girl coming at her until the last second, and then she got the stake up just in time to have it knocked from her hands. The vampire girl reached for Willow, but she ducked, pulling the curtains between herself and her attacker.

That bought her three whole seconds. Then the vampire girl was there again, smiling at her—until the one who'd attacked Angel body-slammed her to the ground. Only when Willow saw Angel going after them did she realize what had happened.

No second-string vampire was going to take Angel out of the game.

Willow shook herself. *Sports analogies,* she thought, *I must be in shock.*

Angel made short work of the two vampires. But there were at least two others, possibly three, making their way across the stage behind the backstage curtain. Onstage, things had gotten way tense. Buffy had to do something, or Lear was going to kill Xander and Cordelia.

Willow and Xander had been best friends since forever. She just couldn't let that happen. She looked down at a pile of old, dusty props. Flagpoles, broomsticks, wooden swords, chairs, a wooden cart . . . a three-foot metal crucifix.

With two quick strides, she bent to pick up a wooden sword and threw it to Angel.

"Help Buffy," she said.

Angel looked at her, frowned, glanced at the curtains moving as the vampires came across the stage—obviously too terrified of upsetting their master to disturb his performance—and then he ran out on the stage, holding the wooden sword in front of him as though he knew how to use it. Which, given the fact that he grew up in the eighteenth century, Willow figured he probably did.

Willow picked up the huge metal crucifix. She was Jewish, of course, but she figured that, hey, whatever worked. It was heavy, but the weight felt good in her hands. She tried to make herself feel tough, tried to look mean. Tried to be more like Buffy.

It all happened quickly for Buffy. One second, Giles was applauding, and Lear had a supremely pompous, pleased grin on his face. He was playing them like a total media harlot, and their job was to adore him. Giles's applause had him so slaphappy, Lear actually stepped forward and executed a deep bow.

Idiot.

Buffy took three strides, put her foot on the armrest of a front row chair, and did an aerial somersault to land behind the obese vampire on the stage. She'd put herself between her friends and death.

That was where she belonged.

That was why she was the Slayer.

"No curtain call for you, Urkel," she sneered. "I may not know Shakespeare, but I'm pretty sure this is not his proudest moment."

Unfortunately, Lear was faster than he looked. He

batted the stake from Buffy's hand, grabbed her by the throat and lifted her high off the stage, fury burning in his eyes.

"Everybody's a critic," he growled.

Buffy grabbed his wrist, kicked him hard in the face, and Lear dropped her, howling in pain and humiliation. She scrambled to her feet, trying to stay between Xander and Cordelia and the raging vampire. Problem was, she had no stake.

"Buffy!"

Angel's voice. Behind her.

Lear dove for her, Buffy sidestepped, brought a knee up into his ample belly, and spun around behind him. She chanced a look up. Angel had smashed Xander and Cordelia free, and they were already moving to help Willow hold off three other vamps who'd come from backstage. Then she saw what Angel held in his hands. A long wooden sword. He threw it to her just as Lear barreled at her again, all pretense at sanity gone. Buffy had to jump to grab the sword's hilt in the air. When she came down, she dropped to her knees, and turned the point of the sword straight for Lear's oncoming girth.

The sword slid into him, and Lear staggered, a step forward, a step backward. She hadn't pierced his heart, at least not completely.

"Giles!" Buffy shouted. "Stake!"

"'Fortune, good night,'" Lear croaked. "'Smile once more. Turn thy wheel.'"

The vampire collapsed forward onto the stage, wrenching the sword upward in his chest. He burst into a huge cloud of ash, a spray of dust that flittered to the stage and then was still.

In the front row, Giles tsk-tsked. "King Lear," he

said. "King of melodrama is more like it. Had to overplay it, right to the end."

"Oh, wonderful," Xander said with his usual sarcasm. "I hope I gave my performance just the right note of terror for you, Giles."

"Okay," Buffy interrupted. "Enough with the dramatic metaphors, now. It's getting a little tired."

"So am I," Willow agreed. "Good thing it's not a school night." Cordelia and Xander exchanged a glance.

"Think the Bronze is still open?" Cordelia asked.

"Perchance," Xander replied, feigning a bad Shakespearean accent. "Prithee escort me, thou fairest maiden."

"Whatever that means!" Cordelia snapped. She rolled her eyes and strutted up the aisle and out the door. Xander followed.

"You're welcome!" Buffy called.

"Come on," Angel said, sidling up next to her and putting his arm around her waist. "I'll walk you home. The streets of Sunnydale aren't safe after dark."

Twenty minutes later, Willow was almost home. Giles had offered her a ride, but she'd sort of half-lied and told him she had a way home. Which was true. Walking was a way.

She wanted to walk and think and come down off the adrenaline rush of playing Slayerette, which was, like, one of the Slayer's backup singers. Or whatever.

It was intense and cool and all of those things. It was also necessary. Since Willow knew that Sunnydale was built on top of the mouth of Hell—which made it kind of a hot spot for things that went bump in the night—she kind of felt like she had to do something about it. Like Spider-Man always said, "with great power comes great responsibility."

And Willow knew better than anyone that knowledge was power.

At the end of the day—or night, as it were—Willow didn't really mind being backup. She could sometimes be effective backup, like tonight. Which was fine. At least she wasn't the Slayer. Willow couldn't even imagine the pressure of being the Chosen One, whose job it was to save the world from the forces of darkness.

The spectre of SATs was enough to give her nightmares, and those weren't until next year.

If the pressure of being the Slayer wasn't enough, there was that whole staying-alive thing, too. Trying not to get as dead as the guys you were killing. Who were already dead. Or undead. So staying alive was sort of important.

"I need sleep," Willow said to herself.

Which was when powerful hands grabbed her from behind and swung her sideways into the brick side of Mona Lisa's Pizza. With a gasp, she whirled around, facing her attackers. They were two guys, their faces shadowed. Both were tall and muscular, one in a jeans jacket, the other wearing a dark blue sweatshirt.

Attack, she told herself, but she just stared at them helplessly. She couldn't even make herself scream. She was frozen on the spot and she just stared at them.

With a low, mean laugh, the one in the jeans jacket laughed and took a step toward her. It was then that Willow collected her wits and started to run.

"Oh, no, you don't!" he said.

Thick arms trapped her and drove her to the pavement. Willow's head hit the ground too hard, and her wrist was trapped beneath her.

She felt something in her wrist give way, just before the darkness claimed her.

CHAPTER 1

Monday morning. The words alone were enough to send tremors of fear shuddering through even the most stalwart of students. And the adults thought they had it hard!

Still, despite the awful Mondayness of it all, it was a gorgeous morning. Bird song filled the air. The scent of flowers floated in from a nearby garden. The sun shone brightly down, sparkling on the windows of Sunnydale High. It was almost enough to make you forget you lived in the Hellmouth.

Almost, but not quite.

Fortunately for them, most of Sunnydale High's students didn't know they lived in the Hellmouth. In blissful ignorance, they went on wasting their lives— a full-time job for a teenager, especially if you wanted to be really good at it. Kids were boarding down the sidewalks—which was illegal even if skateboarding had never been, was not now, and would never be a crime—and palavering about their weekends and their homework and doing all those fun teen-things that most high school students got to do on a much more regular basis than the Chosen One.

As for that Chosen One, Buffy was quaking with fear. A little. As much as the Slayer ever quaked. But it wasn't vampires or demons that had her sweating the day ahead. Uh-uh. This was *much* worse.

Math test. Today. No studying. Bad equation. And it wasn't like she could show up with a note from the vampire community. "Please excuse Buffy from her test today. She was busy out on Slayer-patrol last night, keeping the world safe from dead folks." Yeah, that'd go over big.

No. She was doomed.

"And how would *you* like *your* stake?" she grumbled.

"Buffaleeta!" Xander cried, screaming up beside her on his board. He braked and hopped off, then brought his foot down onto the front and flipped it into his grasp in exactly the same way Buffy stomped crossbows into battle position. Despite her math tremors, Buffy grinned. Her buds had most definitely picked up a few tricks from watching her. Which was good, given the fact that being her friend put them in danger on a regular basis.

"Heya," she said. "Where's Willow?"

He inclined his head, arched an eyebrow. "Fine, and you?"

"My bad." She made a little I'm-sorry face. "It's just that you two usually show up on school days as a matched set, like Salt-N-Pepa or something."

Xander smiled, looked aghast. "I hope you mean the condiments, my MTV-challenged friend, because there are three bodacious ladies in Salt-N-Pepa."

Buffy narrowed her eyes. "So sue me, I'm a little too busy to videe the big weekly countdown. You know what I mean, anyway. You guys always come to school together."

"Joined at the hip, like Siamese twins. That's me and Will. Sadly, I had an errand to run this morning, thus causing my solo-ness."

"An errand?" she pressed, intrigued. Who did errands before sunrise? Besides vampire minions, that is? "Like what, Boy Wonder? You had to drop your bat cape off at the cleaners?"

"That would be my Robin cape." He looked at her sternly and wagged his finger at her. "Tsk-tsk, Slayer. How are you going to get invited to all the cool parties if you can't keep your pop culture minutiae straight?

"Actually," Xander drawled, "the blame for my lateness rests firmly on the shapely shoulders of the conniving Catwoman!"

"Not Catwoman?" Buffy gasped. "That cheap hussy!" She arched an eyebrow as he had done. "We done with the Batman shtick now?"

He pointed slightly to the left of the swarm, at that familiar figure with the trendoid clothes, accent on upscale, and every single brunette hair exactly where it had been ordered to be.

"And speaking of cheap hussies," he said, "there's mine."

Cordelia Chase turned, registered their approach, and launched herself in their direction. It was clear she had something that she considered important to discuss.

"Now my morning is complete," Buffy said, sighing. "A Xander spouting nonsense, a math test, and a chance to be insulted by the why-are-you-dating-her-again girl, all in one day. How can one simple girl have so much?"

As Cordelia drew near, Buffy saw the concern on the girl's face and rolled her eyes. "It's probably my fault that she broke a nail or something."

"It's just that crazy life you lead," Xander drawled.

"I need to talk to you guys!" Cordelia said hurriedly, glancing around, obviously hoping she wouldn't be spotted talking to them by any of her friends.

"Cordy," Xander greeted her brightly, "what's the haps? Crush any young male egos yet today?"

"No." She grimaced at him.

"Well, no need to fear, the day is young," he said cheerily.

Cordelia rolled her eyes. "Whatever." She turned to Buffy. "Listen, I just want to know if there are any bizarre events planned for next weekend—you know, like if it's Curse of the Rat-People Night or anything. I have plans next Saturday, and I do not want them ruined just because some monster who's been trying to kill the Slayer for a thousand million years decides that would be the perfect night to rise from its grave."

"Yeah, Buffy, break out your Calendar of Dreadful Events, just make sure that night is clear for Ms. Chase, would you?" Xander snorted, and glanced at Cordelia. "Do you think Buffy plans these things?"

Cordelia squinted at Buffy with intense irritation. "You know, when you first came to Sunnydale, I tried to bring you into the elite circle. But no, you had to hang with the losers. Don't you ever wonder what might have been?"

It amazed Buffy that after all this time, Cordelia still had the ability to hurt her feelings. But she did have that power, and she also had the skill. Because yes, Buffy did wonder what it would have been like to be popular at her new school. She missed having lots of friends and getting invited to the good parties and all the same things she had started missing once she found out back in L.A. that she was the Slayer. It was an occupational hazard, and not one any seventeen-year-old girl would cheer about.

But she knew Cordelia was specifically referring to the fact that Buffy had dared to be nice to Willow when Cordelia had, frankly, treated her like dirt, publicly humiliating her and bullying her. By being friendly to Willow and asking her for homework help, Buffy had sealed her own fate as an outcast. As for that other "loser," Xander, he came with the package, since he and Willow had been best friends since preschool.

And if achieving popularity would have required dissing them in the least, then Buffy wasn't missing a thing.

"Is it me, or did someone erase your short-term memory?" Buffy asked her. "Specifically, all that stuff about you dating one of those losers?"

"Hello!" Xander protested. "Isn't there a kinder word?"

Cordelia glared at him. "No."

"Once you regain your soul, you'll find you regret harsh words such as these," Xander shot at Cordelia.

Cordelia looked startled, and then she clenched her teeth and narrowed her eyes at Xander. "Ha ha. You are so completely anti-hilarious."

"But I'm a great kisser," he said, raising his chin and smiling proudly.

After a moment's pause, Cordy smiled. "I'll let you know when you've hit 'great' status."

"And you'd know," Xander said pleasantly. "You've tried them all."

Cordelia huffed and stalked away.

"Oh great *sensei,* tell me how you did that," Buffy pleaded as they watched her disappear back into the throngs. "So I can do it, too."

Xander made a show of stretching and putting his hands behind his head. "It's all in the timing, Ms. Summers. She lunges, you parry." He grinned. "And then you thrust."

"Do not even go there," Buffy said, and shook her head as they began walking again. "It's best I don't hear any more. I still don't understand what this thing is between the two of you. Somehow you get through the chinks in her armor."

"Or the cracks in her makeup. Did you notice that she had on just too much foundation? You're right; it does make her look like a cheap hussy. You should talk to her about it, Buffy."

She chuckled slyly. "Maybe. The right place, the right time . . ."

"She'd stew for at least two classes," he assured her. "Better yet, ask Giles to do it. She'll really go nuts."

Buffy smiled, but halfheartedly. She hadn't failed

to notice that Xander had riffed off her own life while he was teasing Cordelia. His crack about Cordelia's regaining her soul had obviously been about Angel, and the horrible guilt he had suffered after regaining his own soul.

Xander's wit could be just plain silly, but it could also be cutting at times. Especially with Angel. Of all of them, Xander reserved his hardest comments for Buffy's undead boyfriend. Actually had the guts to call him Dead Boy, even though Angel despised the name. In fact, Xander called him that specifically *because* Angel hated it so much. Xander was jealous of Angel, no question about it. But Buffy knew that when the mouth of Hell coughed up something nasty, Xander would risk his own life for any of them, including Angel, despite all they'd suffered at Angel's hands.

Buffy's wandering mind was halted when she spotted Willow sitting on the bench where the three of them often met.

"Well, if it isn't our willowy Willow," Buffy said, and pointed.

Willow was wearing a baggy coat thrown over her shoulders and, as usual, she was bent over a book. She used to read science books, Net guides, that kind of thing. However, since meeting Buffy, her reading material tended toward dusty, heavy, leathery encyclopedia-sized doorstops about demons and monsters. Either that or she was surfing pagan Web sites on-line. With the death of Jenny Calendar, Willow had struggled to do even more than her fair share. And her fair share was often a lot more than anybody else's.

It's too bad Willow isn't the Chosen One, Buffy

thought; she did a heck of a lot more research on the wonderful world of Slayage than the actual Slayer. Imagine, a girl who could kick monster butt while reciting all the legal vampire holidays from memory. Giles would love it.

Too bad nobody had a choice about who was a Slayer, who was a Watcher, or who chose the wardrobe for Seven of Nine on *Star Trek: Voyager*. Poor thing had to be in serious pain.

"Will, hey," Xander called, waving. "I called you yesterday for a 911 rescue attempt on my biology report but you never picked up the pho—" Xander trailed off and he touched Buffy's hand.

Buffy's lips parted. She rushed to Willow and dropped down beside her. "Willow, what happened?"

Willow's face was mottled and bruised. Her left cheek was crisscrossed with deep scratches.

And her left hand was in a cast.

Buffy's mind raced back to their night at the theater. Willow had been fine when they'd split up.

"Willow?" Xander sat on her other side. "God. Did you have an accident?"

Willow tried to smile but it made her mouth hurt. She thought about trying to make a joke, but nothing about this was funny. So she told them the truth.

"I got mugged."

"By vampires?" Xander cried. He grabbed at Buffy's Slayer's bag. "Quick. Give me something sharp, Buff."

"Nothing supernatural," Willow assured them. "I was walking home alone."

"Didn't Giles give you a ride?" Buffy interrupted.

"Oh, well, I kind of wanted to be alone. I had some thinking to do," she added sadly.

"You could have been alone in your bedroom," Xander chided her. "And you can think there, too."

Willow swallowed hard. She didn't know why she was so embarrassed for them to see her injuries, but she was. Her first impulse after the attack had been to call them both, but something had made her put down the phone.

"Who was it?" Buffy demanded, her thinking apparently running along the same lines as Xander's: it was payback time.

"I don't know," she replied meekly, and half-protested as Xander closed her demonology book and set it on his own lap. "I was just walking along and these two guys—regular ones, I think, not vampires or demons—jumped me. They took my watch and twenty bucks."

She glanced at Xander and felt a rush of sadness. "I'm sorry, Xander. It was the Tweety Bird one you gave me for my birthday."

"Darn. And that promo's over at Burger King." Tentatively he examined her cheek, cupping her chin very gently. "Oh, Will . . ." he began, and she could hear the frustration in his voice. Xander wanted to help, but it was too late for anyone to help.

"Did they break your wrist?" Buffy asked.

Willow shook her head. "It's a bad sprain. From when I fell weird." She realized she was near tears, and fought hard to hide them. "After all these times I've watched you practice falling with Giles, and seen you in action, you'd think I'd know how to do it."

"It's an acquired skill," Buffy said kindly.

"Take up skateboarding. You'll get lots of practice," Xander added, obviously trying to lighten the moment. But he wasn't smiling. His dark eyes were serious and his mouth was set and angry.

"Willow, why didn't you call us? Tell us?" Buffy asked.

Now Willow did smile. She was lucky to have such great friends. Although, of course, in Xander's case, she still wished he was more than a friend. But she'd been wishing for that longer than Buffy had been the Slayer. And, well, there was Oz now.

"It was . . . I don't know," she said. "I felt . . . like not talking."

"I understand," Buffy told her, and Willow figured she did. After Buffy had been killed by the vampire known as the Master, she had bottled up her feelings for a long time. All her fear and frustration had poured out in a long crying session in Angel's arms.

"Listen, I hate to do this," Buffy said, grimacing, "but it's almost time for class, and I promised to check in with Giles before first period. Will, are you going to be okay?"

"Sure, Buffy," she said in a small voice. "Go on ahead."

Buffy looked unhappy about leaving Willow, which touched Willow deeply. She had never had a friend like Buffy. Buffy was brave, and strong, and no dumb mugger would ever take her down . . .

"Aw, c'mon, Rosenberg," Xander said, as a tear trickled down her cheek. He pulled her against his chest, kissed her on the top of her head. "It's okay."

"No. It's not. Because this kind of stuff is going to keep happening to me," Willow said, letting the tears flow as Buffy disappeared into the building. "I'm useless, Xander. A liability. Half the time Buffy has to risk her life to save me, and—"

"—and the other half, she has to save me," Xander finished, trying to get her to meet his eyes.

Willow was miserable. For so long, she had wanted Xander to hold her, and now he was just being nice. Just pitying her. He would never pity Buffy.

"Maybe you should ask her for some fighting tips."

"Huh?" Willow sniffled. "I could never be like Buffy. I see those vampire guys and I totally freak out. I hate being Velma."

"Come on!" Xander protested. "Velma's the coolest! The smart chick always saves the day—as long as she doesn't lose her glasses. Hey, look, at least you're not Daphne. Now Daphne was useless."

"So who's Daphne?" Willow asked, allowing herself a small smile at Xander's waxing philosophical about Scooby-Doo.

"Please!" Xander snapped. "Cordy, of course. What, you thought *I* was Daphne? See, I figure Angel and Buffy are Shag and Scoob. Giles is Freddy."

"So who are you?" Willow asked, shaking her head in confusion.

"Me?" Xander asked, then his eyes dropped and a deep sadness came over his face. "I'm afraid I'm not even first string, Will. To my everlasting shame, I'm . . ."

He took a deep breath.

"I'm Scrappy-Doo."

Willow started to smile, just a little, but it felt good. Then Xander stood, held up his right fist and shouted, "Puppy Power!" and Willow laughed so hard that the pain of her injuries came back full force. A few more tears slipped down her cheek, from a combination of amusement and discomfort.

"Ah, Will . . ." Xander murmured.

"Hey, hi," a voice said.

Hastily Willow dried her tears and looked up. It was her boyfriend, Oz. He was a senior at Sunnydale High, and his band, Dingoes Ate My Baby, played a lot down at the Bronze. He also happened to be a werewolf.

Willow saw the concern in Oz's eyes and it cheered her up a bit.

"What happened to you?" he blurted.

"I fell," Willow said quickly, mentally begging Xander not to contradict her. She was embarrassed about not having been able to defend herself. Actually, not even trying to defend herself. But the Scooby Gang knew about that part. "I was doing a chore—a chore of housework—I was painting the house—which is a chore—and I fell off the ladder."

"Whoa. Bummer," Oz replied, nodding sagely. "Painting the house, though. That's impressive." He took her backpack from beside her feet. "C'mon. The bell's going to ring. I'll carry your stuff for you."

"Okay." A bit unsteady, she stood up. She looked uncertainly at Xander, who was smiling faintly like a big brother, nodding his approval. Even though she really liked Oz, part of her still wished Xander would get jealous. Maybe he even was jealous, in a way. But only because they were so close, Willow knew. Not because Xander felt anything . . . anything romantic for her. Not like he did for Buffy.

But Oz didn't lust after Buffy. Nope. He seemed to like Willow just fine. And he was pretty cute . . .

The three of them entered the school and started down the hall.

"Oh, my God, Willow, what happened?" Cordelia piped. She was flanked by two of her Cordette wanna-bes, who stood just so, smirked just so, and were just . . . not. It was kind of sad, really, to want to be someone else so badly, or so Xander thought. Of course, there had been many moments in his life when he had wanted to be someone else: someone suave, someone rich . . . someone with a car.

Also, someone Buffy would seriously adore. As long as he didn't have to be Angel. 'Cause, y'know, being dead had to kinda suck. No pun.

"Good morning, Mistress Cordelia," Xander intoned, extra politely, as if they had not spent an hour this morning being more than polite to each other. It was their shtick around the Cordettes, not being a cute couple, so that she wouldn't lose her hard-won status as a stuck-up snob.

He looked hard at Cordelia, trying to ESP her a message: *Don't you dare be mean to Willow.*

"Did you fall off your trike, or is this just some tiresome bid for sympathy?" Cordelia asked, gesturing to Willow's face and arm.

"Don't," Xander said, and Cordelia looked mildly shocked.

"Or were you trying to use a new masque, and . . ." She frowned at Xander. "What?"

"I know your species culls the weak and the aged," Xander said, "but they obviously don't have any rules about the thick-as-a-brick. Willow's off-limits today, Brunhilde."

"Well, I was just, I . . ." Cordelia clamped her mouth shut.

"You were just on your way to the library with us," Xander said meaningfully, "to check the calendar for special gatherings of the crazed and possessed."

"Are you speaking English?" one of the Cordettes asked, sneering.

"It doesn't matter," Xander told her. "I'm talking Cordy's language. Am I not?"

Cordelia gave her hair a toss. Clearly, she had recovered from the momentary shock of someone pushing her off her venom-powered steamroller. "It doesn't matter. I don't have time for your weirdness. The buses are leaving for the museum in five minutes."

Xander thought a moment. "Oh, the field trip!" In all the worry over Willow, he had completely forgotten about their break for freedom. "What a sweet surprise on a Monday morning!"

"Especially for Buffy," Willow concurred, cheering a little. "If we pay extra specially close attention to the exhibits, so we're late getting back, then Miss Hannigan will have to postpone the math test."

"Oh, good heavens, I see what you mean," Giles said to Buffy as they approached Xander, Willow, and Cordelia. "Poor Willow."

"You were supposed to give her a ride home," Buffy snapped at him.

"Oh, dear." He was stricken. Giles was good at big-time guilt. Maybe it was a British thing. "She was so insistent about other arrangements . . ."

"Being insistent never does *me* any good around you," Buffy huffed.

"So, Giles, Buffy. Field trip," Xander said, as they approached.

"That's right!" Buffy clapped her hands. "I'm saved." She thought a minute. "Am I saved? How long is this field trip?"

"I think it will be long enough," Xander said with a wink.

"Yes. Quite. There will be a lot to see, from what I've read of the exhibit catalog," Giles said, and gestured for them to keep moving.

"You can buy the exhibits?" Cordelia asked.

"On your mark. Get set," Xander said.

"No. The catalog merely describes the exhibits. I've been anticipating this for months, actually. It's a traveling exhibition about the art and culture of ancient Japan." Giles smiled excitedly. "Such a rich and varied history."

"History." Buffy grimaced. "Oh, joy."

"I believe you'll find it a nice change of pace," Giles insisted. "For all of you."

"Yeah, uh-huh. Reading little plaques about a bunch of old stuff." Buffy yawned. "Wake me up when it's over."

"I just had a thought," Xander said. "Wait, where'd it . . . ah, there it is! Seems to me that a museum of that size would have a large number of closets."

"God, you never stop, do you?" Cordelia sighed.

"Me an' that bunny," Xander agreed.

They all started for the exit, where the bus was waiting.

"So," Cordelia said to Xander. "Lots of closets?"

Chapter 2

The museum was one of the things Sunnydale's mayor always crowed about; one of the things he claimed made Sunnydale more than just another Southern California paradise.

However, none of the truly unique things about a town whose original Spanish settlers called Boca del Infierno—the Hellmouth—seemed to make it into the tourist brochures the Chamber of Commerce kept putting out.

Yet, somehow, even with a decent museum and a picturesque downtown that looked like something Spielberg stole from Frank Capra, tourists managed to bypass Sunnydale for the most part. *Lucky them,* Buffy thought. She and her mom hadn't just visited . . . they'd moved here!

The exception to the tourist rule seemed to be when an upscale exhibit came to the Sunnydale Museum of Art and Culture, or the Sunnydale

Drama Society put on a decent play. There were art galleries—like her mother's—and an annual Renaissance Faire and a whole host of other things for the aging Baby Boomers to do. But for teens, the ultimate consumers?

Nada.

Or at least so close to nada that it didn't matter. The Bronze could get boring if you went there every night. At least, Buffy thought so. But when you'd lived in L.A., it was hard to imagine having to cross into the next town just to go to a movie made this year. Sunnydale was no L.A. It wasn't even L.A.'s little sister.

As the bus pulled into the museum's parking lot, Buffy sighed and let her head rest against the window.

"Suddenly, I'd rather be Slaying," she muttered to herself.

And that was saying something.

"Hey, hey!" Xander said. "What's this I see?"

Buffy glanced up at that familiar, goofy grin, and couldn't help but smile in return. Xander had turned around in his seat and was looking down on Buffy and Willow, waving a finger in their faces like a stern parent.

"I don't recall giving permission for glum faces today," Xander chided. "Okay, so the museum is not the coolest place to be visiting on a Monday morning. Okay, so on our last merry outing to these hallowed halls of pots and pans, we ran into a particularly attractive and exotic young lady who had a . . . all right, I confess, she had a thing for me." He smiled modestly and touched his chest.

"And turned out to be an ancient Incan mummy, and sure, I was way too young for her," he added.

Xander tilted his head to one side, leaned over the back of his seat so his face was only a foot away from Willow and Buffy. His smile was manic, impossibly wide.

"But think of the hideous alternative to this trip." His eyes flicked toward Buffy. "Maaaaath teeeest!" he moaned in a ghostly voice.

"Mister Harris!" a voice snapped from the front of the bus. "Do you mind?"

"Ah," Xander sighed, an apologetic expression on his face. "The Professor has spoken. I must behave. Or die trying." He spun and sat down in his seat.

Buffy looked at Willow and grinned. "Mister Harris!" she mimicked.

Willow covered her mouth to hide her smile. Buffy was relieved. Will had been on a major blues trip all morning. Not that she could be blamed. The extreme number of muggings in this burg was another aspect of Sunnydale that never got much press.

"Did a little research for ya last night," Willow said under her breath.

"The über-scholar," Buffy replied.

They were riffing off Mr. Morse, the teacher who'd yelled at Xander. Buffy's usual history teacher was out on medical leave. Nobody knew exactly what was wrong with her, but of course, all the really good gossip ran toward the loony bin angle. For the past several weeks, they'd had to put up with Mr. Morse instead.

He was a little, bespectacled guy with a comb-over that did more to accent his increasing baldness than disguise it. Mr. Morse obviously thought that most of his students were morons, and didn't do much to hide his opinion. He began each history class session by plopping a huge stack of books on his desk and announcing, "I did a little research for ya last night" as if it had been a major favor and weren't they so totally fortunate to have him for a teacher.

Uh-huh.

On the other hand, Xander was right. The alternative to the museum caper was even nastier than said caper. Miss Hannigan might be nicer, but Buffy would take a Carnival Cruise with Mr. Morse if it meant missing a math test.

Okay, well, maybe not. But the museum wasn't half bad in comparison.

The bus screeched to a stop and Buffy followed Willow as they filed off. She glanced up and saw Giles, who gave her the patented Giles earnest nod as he helped Morse shepherd the wayward students toward the museum's entrance. As Buffy and Willow passed, Giles put a protective hand on Willow's shoulder. Buffy felt a sudden rush of affection for the proper British librarian. For her Watcher.

Buffy rarely gave him credit for all he'd done for her. Mostly, in fact, she gave him grief. But Giles had taught her a great deal, enough to keep her alive—most nights. Buffy smiled at him. She wouldn't want anyone else in her corner when it came down to the last round.

She only wished it didn't come down to the last round quite so often.

"Y'know, this place is actually pretty cool," Buffy admitted, glancing around as they walked through the museum. She scanned the ancient artifacts and weaponry from cultures throughout history and across the world as they passed from one exhibit to the next. "I just don't know how they manage to get all this stuff. I mean, the zoo has a few hyenas, and one saggy old grizzly, and that's about it. But this place is almost as good as the one we used to go field-tripping to back in L.A."

"Yeah," Xander agreed, "Sunnydale is just like L.A. Without the celebrities, the movie studios, the chic eateries, the attitude, the incredibly gorgeous females . . ."

Willow and Buffy glared at him.

". . . who are so completely unreal. Plastic. Horrible creatures, really," he said quickly.

"Are you brain-dead, as if I have to ask?" Cordelia chimed in as she caught up with them. "L.A. rocks."

"Ah, speak of the mannequin, and she appears," Xander snapped.

Buffy shook her head. Ever since Xander and Cordy had started sneaking off to grope together in the shadows, she'd been expecting them to act all couply. But they were just as vicious with one another as ever. Maybe more so, at times. Ah, love.

"Actually," Willow said softly, "we're pretty fortunate to have such an excellent museum. This place is world-class. Sometimes we get exhibits on tour that don't even stop in L.A. "

"See, now that's what *I* don't get," Buffy replied. "I'm asking, why? What's so special about Sunnydale?"

"You're asking *us?"* Cordelia said, staring at her in disbelief.

"Definitely the nightlife," Xander volunteered.

Buffy just gave him the Jack Nicholson eyebrow,

and he shot back with puppy-dog eyes and an I-can't-help-it shrug.

"Which nightlife are you talking about?" Willow asked, and glanced knowingly at Cordelia.

"Oh, please!" Cordy sneered. "Can't you people just cold shower for thirty seconds?"

"Yeah," Xander said, making a show of siding with Cordelia. "You people are so smut-oriented. *I* was referring to the ever-popular, much-anticipated Curse of the Rat-People Night. Wasn't that what you were referring to, Cor? The specialness of this very special little town?"

Cordelia seethed in silence.

"Seriously, Willow," Xander continued, "why does Sunnydale rate?"

"The best and most common of reasons," Willow replied. "Money. The museum's endowment is huge. Apparently a lot of rich people come from Sunnydale, and even the ones who leave are generous enough."

"And no doubt sold their souls for those generous riches," Xander said. "Like those frat boys who almost fed Buffy and Cordelia to their worm-monster god-guy last year."

He smiled brightly at Buffy. "Just think, there are probably several more secret organizations you'll have to bust up to save all the town's virgins—and other people—from certain death."

"Let's hope not," Buffy sighed, then noticed that Cordelia's cheeks were turning pink.

"And we move on," Xander suggested.

They passed into the visiting exhibition hall, which was a labyrinth of rooms filled with art and artifacts from ancient Japan. Almost immediately,

Buffy became fascinated, despite her earlier grumbling. The culture of ancient Japan was so different from Western culture of the period, and even more so from the Western world of modern times.

In the second room, they came upon Giles examining what appeared to be a tiny plastic garden.

"Ah, there you all are," he said, as though he'd been desperately searching for them. "Isn't this a marvelous exhibit?"

"Maybe not the word I would have picked, but it's pretty cool, yeah," Buffy admitted, joining him in craning over a miniature curved bridge and tiny evergreen trees. "What is it?"

"Hmm?" Giles hmmed, then glanced back down at the tiny garden. "Oh, right. Quite impressive, actually. It seems that Sunnydale was, at one time or another, the sister city of Kobe, Japan."

"Wait, isn't that where they had that big earthquake?" Xander asked.

"Indeed."

"Wow, that's a weird coincidence," Willow said. "I mean, with us having *our* earthquake and all."

"My thinking precisely. That parallel is what has captivated me," Giles explained, pushing up his glasses in his Giles-is-thinking way. "You see, I'm not entirely certain it was a coincidence."

"I don't get it. And I really don't get what this has to do with your big Chia Pet there," Buffy said, already glancing around at other exhibits in the room.

"This is a friendship garden," Giles said impatiently. "The people of Kobe planted and groomed a real Japanese garden here in Sunnydale, recreating one just like it in their city. Apparently, after the earthquake in Sunnydale, the garden was abandoned and all of its vegetation simply withered and died. Quite unnaturally, in fact. It seems that local authorities went so far as to bring in botanical specialists, but no one could explain it."

"So this happened right after the Hellmouth opened under Sunnydale," Xander said. "And your thinking is what, vegetarian vampires?"

"Well, it's merely conjecture, of course . . ."

"Giles, your conjecturing is a little like the oracle at Delphi. Spit it out," Buffy said.

They all stared at her.

"What?" Buffy asked. "Come on, Willow is my history tutor! I do know some things."

From across the room, a whiny voice said, "I heard that, Summers. Let's hope you know enough to pass this semester."

Buffy gave Mr. Morse a purposely fake smile and batted her eyelashes at him, hoping he got the sarcasm in her reaction and suddenly terrified that he'd miss it. Pip-squeak would probably think she was flirting with him.

She sighed and glanced at Giles. "You were saying?"

"Well, it does strike me as odd that the garden died in the wake of the earthquake, and that Sunnydale's sister city had an earthquake not long afterward."

"Wait, you think that the Hellmouth somehow caused an earthquake halfway around the world by, I don't know, infecting another city through some friendship garden?" Xander asked incredulously.

"Well," Giles said stodgily, "when you put it that

way, it does sound a bit dodgy, but it does still seem an odd confluence of events, wouldn't you say?"

"Is this going to lead up to me having to kill something?" Buffy asked.

"No," Giles replied, with an odd look. "I can't say as much." He murmured, "For certain."

Buffy grinned happily. "Then, oh, yeah, Giles. Definitely super-odd, the um, conflue-thing. Can we see what else is here now? Mr. Morse threatened to test us on this field trip, and I can't afford to miss a thing."

"By all means, do," Giles said, obviously a little disappointed that his theory hadn't interested them more. But he got over it quickly, and was soon lost among the artifacts once more.

They'd lost Cordelia early on, but soon Buffy, Willow, and Xander also drifted apart, each gravitating toward different displays, different rooms in the maze of the exhibit. From time to time they'd cross paths and share information.

Xander quickly became interested in displays about the samurai and the art depicting their legends. There were reproductions of traditional samurai garb and information about the privileged life they led.

"Man, these guys had it good," Xander said when they met up.

"Yeah, sweet life," Buffy replied. "Someone gave 'em trouble, they could just hack them to ribbons and nobody would ask a single question. I'm Kermit with envy."

Xander looked at her. "Buff, they were slaying humans, y'know. It wasn't the same thing."

She shook her head. "That's even more unfair. I'm

always worried about getting in trouble, and I'm not even killing anyone who's still alive."

Cordelia appeared suddenly, spotted them, and came buzzing across the room.

"Okay," she said, "this is so completely disgusting. Did you know that married women in ancient Japan plucked their eyebrows, and I mean, all of them?"

Buffy and Xander stared at her.

"But wait," Cordelia said importantly. "There's more."

"Promise?" Xander asked.

Cordelia gave him a backhand to the shoulder and directed her attention at Buffy. "Okay, Summers, I know you're not exactly House of Style, but listen to this: they painted their faces white, and their teeth black!"

Buffy winced. "That really is disgusting."

Cordelia sniffed at Xander triumphantly.

"Y'know," he said, "I can see it now, Cordy. You on the runways of Paris, bringing back the fashions of ancient Japan. A whole new trend, and a devastating blow to toothpaste manufacturers everywhere."

She narrowed her eyes and drawled, "Why do I even bother with you?" As usual, Cordy left in a huff.

"What about you, Miss Summers?" Xander asked. "What's caught your particularly fanciful fancy?"

Buffy grinned shyly. "What do you think, Xander?

Xander stroked his chin, pretending to consider. "The weapons, but of course."

"But of course," she replied.

* * *

Willow had kind of hoped Oz would be on the field trip, but after she'd wandered around for a while, she gave up hope of seeing him. She didn't really want to talk about what had happened to her, but that was one of the coolest things about Oz. He always seemed to know when to just be quiet.

Her friends had done their best to cheer her up, and it had worked a little. But not much more than a little. Willow was still at a loss to understand what exactly had happened to her, and why. But she understood how it had happened all too well. She only wished the others could understand too.

Xander had been her best friend almost her whole life, and he might be sympathetic, but he'd never really get it. After all, he was a guy. Sure, he wasn't Schwarzenegger, but he wasn't scrawny Leo DiCaprio either. He just wasn't as vulnerable; guys weren't.

And then there was Buffy—who could kick Xander's ass and not even be able to call it exercise. How could she ever possibly understand what it felt like to feel powerless?

"Hey, Will."

Willow turned and saw Buffy standing next to her. She hadn't even noticed, and it occurred to her again how cool it was to be the Slayer. The bad guys wouldn't even know Buffy was coming until she took them down.

"Hey," Willow said, and sighed.

"See anything interesting?" Buffy asked, too cheery.

"Well," Willow said, and realized that she had, indeed, seen something interesting. Something that would take her mind off what a weakling she was for an entire minute.

"Actually, yeah," she replied. "I really liked the display on Kabuki theater and Noh plays."

"Color me purple, but I didn't even notice them," Buffy admitted. "And you know they'll be on any test, them being so historical and all. Where are they?"

"Let me show you," Willow said.

They walked into the next room together, and Willow told her what she'd learned about the ancient forms of entertainment, and pointed out the masks that she thought were especially cool or nasty-looking.

"What about you?" Willow asked. "Did you see anything cool?"

Buffy's eyes brightened, and she dragged Willow back through the labyrinth and into a huge room filled with ancient Japanese weaponry.

"Yeah," Willow said, nodding. "I figured you'd like it in here."

"Some of these weapons aren't like anything I've ever seen," Buffy admitted. "And the way the Japanese made their swords, folding the metal over and over, hundreds of times. The craftsmanship was incredible."

Willow's eyes were drawn to one sword in particular. Hung on the wall, it was a huge, crudely fashioned thing that looked like it would be more use beating someone to death than running them through. It didn't have the elegance of the traditional Japanese warrior's set of gently curving long and short swords.

"What's that?" she asked, pointing to the huge blade.

"Isn't that amazing?" Buffy asked. "Nothing like a *katana* or *wakizashi.*"

Willow smiled slightly and thought about how easy it was for Buffy to learn when she was interested in the subject. She stepped over to the huge sword and began to read aloud from the plaque affixed to the wall beneath it.

"'This form of sword, called a *ken,* is actually of Chinese origin, and was used in Japan in the eighth century, before the more familiar *daisho,* or sword pair, of the ancient Japanese warrior was developed. This example, recently discovered in the Chugoku mountain range, has proved to date back even further, and is one of a kind,'" Willow read, only half aloud. "Wow," she added.

"Read the rest," Buffy urged. "You'll love all the mythology stuff."

Willow did, but silently this time.

"'Upon the sword's discovery, locals began to claim it to be the *shin-ken,* or real sword, of the god Sanno, a Japanese mythological figure also known as the King of the Mountain, and usually considered to have made his home on Mount Hiei, near Kyoto and Kobe, Japan.

"'According to this legend, which some of the older farmers in the region believe to this day, the Mountain King was responsible for protecting Japan from invasion by foreign supernatural forces, an obvious reference to the tense relations between Japan and China at that time. This theory is supported by the myth surrounding Sanno's greatest battle, in which he apparently vanquished a Chinese vampire named Chirayoju, who had wanted to eat the Emperor of Japan, and thus destroy the nation.

According to legend, neither Sanno nor Chirayoju survived this battle.'"

Willow was stunned. "So, wait, you think this Sanno guy was the Slayer?" she asked.

Buffy blinked. "No. Big male-type person with a huge sword who lived on top of a mountain and let the spookables come to him? It's only a legend, Will. I just thought it was kind of cool."

"Yeah," Willow agreed. She looked at the sword again. "It's different from other vampire legends we've heard about. Or, y'know, met."

But Willow was thinking that it was also interesting because of Sanno. Not the Slayer. Just a big guy with a big sword. Taking care of business. For a moment, she thought about what she could do if she worked out a little. Worked out, and maybe had a big sword, too.

"Y'know," she said idly, not really paying attention to what she was saying, "with all the tutoring I've helped you out with, I was thinking maybe you could tutor me a little."

"Huh?" Buffy said, confused. "What subject could I possibly tutor you in, Willow? You're our Brainy Smurf."

Willow reached out with her uninjured hand toward the sword, touched the cool surface of the metal. Cool, yes, but with some weird heat to it as well. Like it was burning inside.

"Self-defense," she whispered.

Buffy sort of smiled and frowned at the same time.

"You do pretty well, Will," she said.

Willow held up her injured hand, wrapped in its small cast. Her smile was pained.

"No," she replied. "I don't. I've been lucky up to

now. I don't want to be a liability, Buffy. I don't want you to have to protect me all the time."

Buffy touched the cast on Willow's hand. "Will," she said, "it's not your fault those guys jumped you. And, trust me, there have been plenty of times when I would've been toast for sure if it hadn't been for you. So I'm better with pointy objects. So what?"

"I'd just feel better if I could defend myself," Willow said meekly, and turned to look at the huge blade on the wall again. "I'd love to be able to use something like this. Nobody would mess with me if I had a big sword in my hands."

"Especially if you were strong enough to lift it off the ground," Buffy said, trying gamely to lighten the moment, to cheer Willow up.

And failing.

Willow brushed her fingers over the blade and up to the cloth covering the hilt of the sword. Beneath the crisscross pattern was a trio of metal disks that looked like they were made of bronze or something similar. There was some kind of weird inscription on them, and Willow tried to get a better—

One of the disks fell out.

"Whoops," Willow said, trying to catch it.

A long drop to the floor, where it clanged like a fallen coin. Blushing, Willow bent to pick it up, and quickly tried to slide it back where it had come from. Her fingers found the blade instead.

"Will, I don't know if you should . . ." Buffy started.

Too late.

Willow hissed and pulled her hand back. There was blood on the index finger. She'd somehow slipped and cut her finger. The sword was so sharp it had only stung, but the cut looked kind of deep.

"That's gotta hurt!" Xander said as he stepped up behind them.

Willow spun on him in alarm, as if he were going to attack her.

"Back off!" she snapped.

"Whoa," Xander said, eyes blinking his surprise. "What'd I do?"

Willow shook her head as she sucked at her cut finger, hoping she wouldn't need stitches.

"Nothing," she said. "Sorry, just edgy after Saturday, I guess. Let's get out of here."

"Sounds good," Buffy said happily. "I guess we've stayed long enough for me to miss my math test."

"Goody for you," Willow said crankily.

Buffy looked taken aback, but suddenly, Willow didn't much care. She didn't feel well and she just wanted to get home and crawl under the covers. And Buffy's cheeriness, even if it was for her benefit, wasn't really cheering her up at all.

It wasn't until the bus pulled into the parking lot at Sunnydale High that Willow realized she'd stuck that weird metal disk into her pocket. And as soon as she realized it, she promptly forgot again.

Willow went home sick just before fifth period.

CHAPTER 3

By the time the bus pulled back into the school parking lot, Willow was feeling a bit nauseous.

"You look really pale," Xander told her.

She waited for the requisite crack about vampirism, or ghostliness, or her usual less-than-bronze pallor, but it didn't come. Xander wasn't teasing her, just concerned. That was when Willow realized that she'd better go home.

Even Mr. Morse was nice to her.

"Really, Willow, it's all right," the history teacher said, nodding too much as he almost pushed her toward Giles in the parking lot. "I'll tell Principal Snyder that you were ill. Go home and get some rest. You don't want to miss my pop quiz tomorrow, do you?"

A joke, Willow thought, beginning to feel disoriented. Mr. Morse had made a joke. To make her feel better.

And, of course, it only made her feel worse.

Willow felt like she was seeing everything in a weird, out-of-focus hyper-reality. Almost like a VR game, but with snippets of her real life. Xander looked at her, all brotherly, and told her to get some rest and that he'd call to check up on her when school was out. Buffy promised to tell Oz she'd gone home sick. Cordelia made a face and asked if Willow was going to throw up on her.

Giles drove her home. She didn't remember talking to him much. He made game attempts at small talk for a bit before giving up. In the end, he walked her to the door, where her mom made a big fuss as Willow had known she would, thanked Giles, and hustled her upstairs.

Willow fell into bed at one o'clock in the afternoon and didn't wake up until it was time for school Tuesday morning.

She slept like the dead.

"Hello, zombie alert!" Xander quipped as Willow walked through the library doors the next afternoon when classes had ended.

She smiled. Her first smile since the day before, and it felt good.

"I know I don't look my best," she said, "but I feel a lot better. Much. Much better."

"I'm glad," Xander replied, and smiled. "I was worried when you didn't call back last night. Your mom didn't want to wake you up, so I stayed up all night, tossing and turning with my concern for your well-being."

Willow raised an eyebrow. "You didn't even last until the news, did you?"

"Not even the ten o'clock," Xander admitted. "Which doesn't mean I wasn't worried! I'm just glad you're feeling better."

She was pleased. "Yeah. Feeling better is good. I don't know what was wrong with me yesterday. I just . . . I don't know, I totally lost it there for a bit. I've never felt like that before. I mean, I've talked to people who have had migraine headaches, and it sort of reminded me of some of the things they said. Except for the part where your head aches. Mine didn't."

"That's good," Xander said encouragingly.

"I'm just happy to be human again," she went on.

"Human is even better," Xander agreed.

"So where is everyone?" Willow asked, looking around. "I've barely seen Buffy all day."

"Oh, apparently she killed something else last night. Broke a centuries-old curse or something. Par for the course. The danger's over, but it seems that Giles is still excitedly interrogating her off somewhere. I'm actually just waiting for—"

"You ready?"

Willow and Xander turned to see Cordelia standing in the open library door looking as impatient as always. Willow still didn't get it, but she wasn't about to interfere.

"Hey, Cord," Willow said.

"Hi, Willow," Cordelia replied. "Feel better?"

"Kind of tired, actually," Willow said. "If I didn't know I'd been practically comatose for seventeen hours last night, I'd say I pulled an all-night study session." She glanced at Xander. "I'm much better, however."

"All-night study session?" Cordelia asked, frowning. "You're such a party animal, girl."

Then Xander was pushing Cordelia out the door. Cordy waved to her and Willow offered a half-hearted smile in return. After they were gone, she sat for a moment in silence, then walked over to the library computer that Giles always had her working on.

She spent a lot of time on her computer at home, and even more here at school, doing research, but also checking out chat rooms and news groups, meeting new people and surfing for information that might help Buffy and Giles. Too much time, she often thought. She had friends on-line, but she was never certain if they were *real* friends. If they were who and what they claimed. It was a lesson she'd learned painfully once before, and ever since, Willow had been less inclined to look into the Web world for a social life.

The real world was no picnic, but it was real. And she had friends who cared about her. Watched out for her. So, she wasn't a warrior princess, that much was clear. But she knew enough to know that there were things she was good at, things she could do that the others couldn't. For starters, of all the kids in school, she'd been asked to substitute teach Miss Calendar's computer course after the teacher had been . . . had been murdered.

Willow Rosenberg might not be able to do back-flips or roundhouse kicks, or even punch really hard. But she was a sorceress when it came to the Internet. On-line, she had power. She was confident. And when she'd woken up that morning, she'd known just what she was going to do: she was going to find her attackers. Or at least, she was going to try. It was what she knew how to do. Then, at least, she would feel as though she had fought back in some small way.

And that was what haunted her still. She hadn't fought back.

Once she had logged onto the Net, Willow began her search. The local papers, local and state police databases, crime reports from nearby towns. It was going to take a while, but Willow knew that if she was ever going to get over this feeling of helplessness, of horrible vulnerability, she had to do something.

Half an hour later, the library doors opened, but Willow didn't even look up as Buffy and Giles came in.

"Think carefully, Buffy," Giles was saying. "How many different demonic voices did you hear coming from inside the Monsignor?"

"Y'know, Giles, I wasn't really counting," Buffy replied, obviously tired of the subject. "I was just trying to stay alive. And I thought we'd already established that only one demon could ever exist inside a body at a time."

"Yes, well, the Monsignor is—or rather, was—the exception that proved the rule. It seems a sixteenth-century Italian noblewoman, a de' Medici, I believe, had her magician place a horrible enchantment on the Monsignor that acted as some sort of magnet for demons, attracting any of them within the city of Florence to occupy the poor man's body. Naturally, the strain killed him, and he became a vampire. But the—shall we say—overpopulation of his body also drove the Monsignor quite mad prior to his unfortunate demise, and transformed the demons inside him into gibbering idiots."

Willow looked up at last, intrigued by the conversation.

"This was the trouble you had last night?" she asked Buffy.

Buffy nodded. "Complete looney tunes. But Giles thinks he was a celebrity or something."

Willow watched as Giles's face went from surprise to wounded pride in milliseconds.

"Not at all," he sniffed. "I merely find it fascinating that the Hellmouth continues to attract creatures that have been widely considered little more than myths for centuries. I have read the Watcher's journal that stated outright that the Monsignor was nothing but a legend."

"He might as well be, now," Buffy said.

"Quite right," Giles said happily. "You freed him from his curse."

Willow had the impression that he couldn't wait to write down Buffy's latest exploit in his own journal. But the conversation was over, and the two of them moved on to more important things.

Sparring.

While Willow continued her search, Giles put Buffy through the hell she called "Slayer practice": weapons and martial arts training that more often than not left poor Giles with large welts and bruises he would be hard pressed to explain if he had a love life. That's why Jenny Calendar had made the perfect girlfriend for him. She knew. Of course, her knowing had also gotten her killed.

Willow kept thinking about Miss Calendar now.

Thinking that maybe if she had known what Buffy knew, if she had had that training, maybe she would still be alive. Maybe she would have been able to escape Angel, or hold him off until help arrived.

As she went through the motions of her search, this thought filled Willow's mind more and more, and she paid less and less attention to what she was doing. Finally, she gave up altogether and turned to watch as Buffy launched kick after kick at a heavily padded Giles. Her fists and feet flew, then landed hard, each blow connecting with a confidence that Willow didn't think she could ever feel.

Willow wasn't a fool. She knew that Buffy was capable of things that other girls simply were not. But she also knew that she would benefit from a bit more than the basic self-defense she already knew.

When Buffy and Giles started to fight with long wooden poles called bo-sticks, Willow watched with wide eyes.

Finally, Buffy noticed her.

"Giles, could we take a break for a bit?" Buffy asked sweetly.

For his part, Giles seemed more than relieved to have a few minutes to rest between getting his pride as bruised as his body. He slipped out of his pads and disappeared. Off to the men's room or the stacks—Willow wasn't sure which because she honestly wasn't paying all that much attention.

As soon as he was gone, Buffy strolled over, cocked her head slightly and raised her eyebrows, studying Willow.

"So, are you going to tell me what's on your mind, or are you going to force me to relive the nightmare game of charades that my mother made me play constantly as a child?"

Willow smiled. "I was just watching you," she said. "I wish I could fight like that."

Buffy chewed her lip a moment, then seemed to nod to herself, as though nobody else was watching or would notice.

"This is getting serious," she said. She pulled up a chair and sat down next to Willow at the computer. "This mugging is really haunting you, isn't it?"

Willow looked away, shrugged a little. She gestured toward the computer screen. "I've been kind of trying to track them down. See if there've been a bunch of attacks like this lately or if anyone has been arrested."

"So what did you find?" Buffy asked hopefully.

"Lots of attacks," Willow reported. "Unfortunately, most of them sound more like vampires than bullies robbing kids for milk money."

Willow heard the bitterness in her own voice, but she couldn't help it. And when Buffy reached out for her hand to comfort her, she couldn't help but draw back as if she'd been burned. She wanted help, not pity.

"Willow, there wasn't anything you could have done," Buffy said. "It wasn't your fault, and it has nothing to do with being strong. If you had tried to fight them, you might have been hurt worse."

Willow felt hot tears start to fill her eyes, and she gritted her teeth, determined not to let those tears fall.

"You're missing the point!" she snapped. "There was something I could have done! I could have fought them, but I didn't! Buffy, I just froze up—completely paralyzed with fear. I've been in situations with you where I knew for a fact my life was in danger. In this case, it wasn't even that. They didn't want to kill me, or I'd be dead."

"Will," Buffy began, but Willow shook her head.

"Angel wanted to kill me, once. He would have, too, if not for Miss Calendar. Yes, I know that wasn't really Angel, but that's not what I'm talking about. He wanted to kill me, but I can still look him in the face. I can talk to him and turn my back on him. I can give him my trust."

Buffy nodded seriously, and looked as if she wanted to say something, but Willow couldn't stop herself.

"Maybe that's because of who he is, but I think it's because of who I am too. Because when it comes to this life, to Slaying, it doesn't feel like just me, Willow Rosenberg, against all this horrible stuff. It's *us* against *them,* do you understand?

"But alone in the dark. On that street with nobody around? I froze, Buffy. I didn't even try to fight back. I haven't admitted that to anyone, never mind to myself. That's part of the reason I didn't report it to the police . . ."

"You didn't?" Buffy asked, staring at her.

"Of course not," Willow said. "How was I going to explain where I'd been, where I was coming from, and why I was out without my parents' permission?"

Buffy looked sort of embarrassed. "Will, I'm sorry."

"It isn't your fault, Buffy," Willow replied shakily. "It isn't even my fault, I know that. But I could have prevented it. If I'd been better prepared."

Buffy seemed to be at a total loss for words. For once, she didn't know what to say. *So she isn't perfect after all, is she?* a small voice in Willow's head asked.

"Y'know," Buffy said, "Giles and I are pretty much done now. If you really wanted, I could . . ."

She started to gesture toward the open area of the library, where she and Giles had been training. Willow flinched as if Buffy had slapped her. *Now she offers,* Willow thought bitterly. *Now that I've humiliated myself.*

Confusion spread through her in an instant. Where had all these bitter thoughts toward Buffy come from? She certainly hadn't done anything to deserve them. Nothing except trying to be a good friend.

But Willow could not get over the pity she saw on Buffy's face.

"Know what, I think we should try it another time," Willow said. "I'm actually still not feeling completely better from yesterday." She gestured to her arm. "I'm just going to work on this a while longer, and then I'm going to go home."

"You sure?" Buffy asked, looking a little hurt and confused herself.

"I'm sure," Willow replied, and offered a smile that she barely meant at all.

Later, when Buffy had left and Giles was toiling away in silence up in the stacks, Willow returned to her computer. But she abandoned her previous search efforts. This time, she began to search for information about weapons from around the world and their uses. She was a smart girl. She would figure them out for herself.

In fact, just looking at several of them—mostly the swords—she could almost feel their weight in her hands. Feel the heft and hear the whickering of steel through air as her blade whipped down toward its target. Feel it slice flesh and snap bone.

Willow's eyes rolled back in her head for a moment, and she nearly blacked out. Her lids flickered, and she heard a small voice—maybe the voice of her conscience, maybe another voice entirely—whispering in her head.

Yesssss, it hissed.

Her hands flexed around the hilt of an imaginary blade.

Willow's eyes snapped open.

"Whoa," she said to herself.

She stood shakily and gathered up her things. Maybe she wasn't all better after all, she thought. She certainly wasn't feeling normal.

Normal girls didn't have daydreams about swords. About . . . murder.

CHAPTER 4

"They are screaming."

The Great Empress Wu bowed low before her own dragon throne, its jade wings outstretched, its pearl eyes gleaming evilly in the glow of oil lamps. Her vast silk robes shimmered across the floor like the Yellow River in a summer sunset. But it was winter now, and near dawn, and deadly cold inside her palace.

On the throne sat Lord Chirayoju, her former Minister of the Interior, who smiled and folded its hands across its chest. Its fingernails were sharp claws. Its teeth were fangs tinged with blood.

It had recently fed.

She herself had brought it the victim, a good man completely undeserving of such a horrible death.

"Tell me, Great Empress, are they screaming in pain or in fear?" it asked, closing its eyes as it anticipated her reply.

"I—I know not."

Its eyes opened. They were completely black. Soulless. The fires that raged within them were all that was left of the ambitious court sorcerer that Chirayoju once had been. That man, who had toiled for years to wrest the secrets of the universe from the gods themselves, had also died a vile death. But his sacrifice had been the necessary price.

That which remained was immortal. It was a savage demon that flew like a falcon over the fields and paddies of China. It was a merciless spirit that compelled fire to scorch the lands of those who dared oppose it and to burn their sons and daughters alive. It was a force above nature, commanding even the wind.

And it was something worse.

Something magnificent.

It opened its mouth wide and showed the Empress Wu its fangs. She shrank back, and it knew she feared it utterly. After all, she had seen it feed. Beautiful maidens with tiny, bound feet, who meekly submitted to their fate like the dainty peonies they were. Fierce warlords in full armor, their swords and lances drawn and slashing as it advanced on them. The soldiers always fought hard to the end. Chirayoju vastly preferred the valiant tigers to the timorous rabbits.

"If you know not if it is pain or fear, let us go together and observe them," Lord Chirayoju said, rising.

The Empress could not suppress her shudder as it stepped down from the jade dragon throne and approached her with its hand outstretched. Together they glided from the throne room to the secret door in the lacquer panel behind the great chair. Before its great change, she had graciously taught it where the pressure plate was located and now it smiled at her as it pointed with one taloned finger at the plate and the door magically opened.

The cave entrance was narrow, and Chirayoju invited the Empress to walk ahead. It saw her terror in the stiffness of her back and the manner in which her shoulders rose as she passed in front of its cold, dead body.

It couldn't help its smile of delight—could barely resist whipping her around and tearing her heart from her chest. But it would be a fleeting joy, and for the moment—perhaps a long moment—it needed her.

She led the way to the first chamber.

With a flick of its hand, Chirayoju illuminated the chill, evil-smelling place. This was the Cavern of Vengeance. The smallest of the three caverns, it reached as high as a dragon's head. From floor to ceiling it was walled with human bones. These were the remains of Chirayoju's most illustrious enemies.

The second chamber was the Cavern of Divination. It was larger, and in it Lord Chirayoju kept the treasures that had once belonged to the piles of bones in the first room. It surveyed with pride the heaps of jade, pearls, and silver—the treasure with which it had bought the Empress's loyalty. Here, too, rested its favorite square cauldrons, where it had performed the human sacrifices that had gained it the knowledge of eternal life—the calling forth of the vampire that had taken the sorcerer's human life. There were also heaps of dragon bones, which it used to foretell the future.

And Chirayoju had foreseen a glorious future indeed.

The screaming echoed from the third chamber, which was so immense Chirayoju could not see the far wall as it and the Empress passed through the entrance carved to resemble a great fanged mouth. The walls and the ceiling were carved into images of sorcery: monstrous tigers, dragons, and human skulls. Vast columns of ornate pillars held up the ceiling.

This was the Chamber of Justice.

Chirayoju had killed over twenty thousand of its enemies in this place.

Including the sire who had turned Chirayoju, a sorcerer consort to demons and witches, into Chirayoju the vampire, the demon sorcerer.

Now Chirayoju cocked its head and listened. Agony, terror, despair, horror. The four elements of its being.

The Empress shrank back. It took her elbow and urged her onward.

Below them, in an enormous pit, five hundred men screamed as serpents and starved rats attacked them, biting and clawing, stinging, shredding. Around the perimeter, the Empress's quaking guards thrust their spears at anyone who attempted to scrabble out of the death trap. Not that they could escape. The walls were straight and high, and by now, very slick with blood.

Chirayoju looked at the bulging eyes of its enemies. These were scholars and scribes, men who had dared write about him. Their scrolls and books had already been burned, along with their families, friends, and anyone they might have told of the dread lord that lived in Empress Wu's mountain fortress.

"It is only pain," it said with disappointment. Then it brightened as it gestured with its right hand. "But now it shall be fear."

Chirayoju swept his hand over the pit. Invisible doors opened in the sides of the pit. With unholy shrieks, legions of vampires rushed from the doors into the whirling mass of human misery. Like the rats, they, too, had been starved for just this occasion.

The blood drove them mad.

As they slaughtered the human prisoners, Chirayoju watched in delight. And some envy.

It, too, was hungry.

But it was also suddenly very tired. That was the sign it had awaited.

With great anticipation, Chirayoju pointed to the ceiling.

"Let us depart, Your Majesty," Chirayoju shouted into the ear of Empress Wu. "It is time."

As they hurried from the Cavern of Justice, Chirayoju made a fist. The roof exploded. Chunks of rock crashed down on vampire and human alike.

The dawning sun poured into the hole.

The screaming vampires burned to dust.

Empress Wu and Chirayoju returned to the throne room. As the ceiling in the third chamber collapsed, the palace shook violently. The alarm was sounded. Earthquake! The Empress's household was in a panic. Gongs rang. Men shouted and ran to their Empress for protection.

"What if some of them survived?" Empress Wu

asked Chirayoju in a shaking, awe-filled voice as her
courtiers poured into the throne room.

"I shall deal with them," it promised her.

But it lied.

Another night fell. The enraged survivors raced
through the palace. The fanged, moldy-faced vampires spared no one in their fury.

As the Empress was thrown to the gold-plated
floor of her sleeping chamber, she shouted, "Chirayoju! Help me!"

But by then, Chirayoju had flown halfway across
the sea.

Let great China become a graveyard, for all it
cared.

Its dragon bones had spoken to it a single word.

Japan.

CHAPTER 5

"Willow, are you all right?" her mother asked softly as she pushed the door ajar.

Lying in bed with the covers drawn to her neck, Willow kept her back to the doorway and clenched her fists. *Yeah, I'm terrific,* she wanted to shout. *That's why I keep coming home sick.*

Sweat poured down her forehead. She was soaked. The room spun so fast she had to close her eyes or be sick, despite the oddly comforting sight of twilight darkness floating through the venetian blinds and edging across the carpet. With the night would come solace. With the darkness, she would be well again.

It was Thursday, and she'd come home sick from school again. She'd felt mostly all right on Tuesday and Wednesday, though each night she'd seemed to sleep heavily and without dreams, and still woke up in the morning feeling more tired than when she went to bed. And maybe that's all this was, exhaustion creeping up on her.

Maybe.

But Willow thought, when she allowed herself to really think, that maybe there was more to it than that. That maybe she was going a little bit crazy. There was that voice, after all. The one that didn't sound like her conscience at all, if she was honest with herself.

The one that wanted to hurt people.

And not just in that frustrated way you want to push people out of the way in a crowd. No, she'd thought about it. It wasn't that. And it wasn't the weird urges she knew people sometimes got—that she sometimes got—like wanting to slug Principal Snyder just to see the look of astonishment on his face. Yes, ladies and gentlemen, even meek little Willow had a streak of the rebel in her. It was just buried very deep.

But this wasn't that. This was much, much worse than that.

"Honey?" Mrs. Rosenberg persisted.

Stop bothering me! she almost screamed. Instead she counted to ten, flexing and balling her fists, taking deep breaths. With tremendous effort she controlled her fury enough to respond, "I'm just real tired, Mom. I think I'll go to sleep." Stupid woman. Wasn't it obvious she was tired? She was in bed, wasn't she?

"Okay. Let me know if you need anything."

"Mom?" Willow called out, suddenly afraid. Something was happening to her. Something very weird.

"Yes, Willow?"

Get out get out get out.

Willow swallowed hard. "Could you shut the door, please?"

"Sure, honey."

And lock it up tight. Because if you don't, I just might jump out of this bed and . . . and . . .

Willow panted as the rage built inside her. She heard the door shut. She clenched her teeth. She balled her fists.

She burst into tears.

And then she laughed.

He was going to die. Of that, Xander was convinced. But sometimes the fulfillment of lust was a higher priority than survival. Witness black widow spiders—and the entire male half of the human race.

"Cordelia? The cliff says stop," he said anxiously, hanging onto the armrest on the passenger side of her car with one hand and the gearshift housing with the other.

"Xander, don't be a backseat driver," Cordelia snapped as she shot toward the stupendous view of Makeout Point. The cars of other, ah, view-seekers were lined up in a row like at the Sunnydale Drive-In. Except that, unlike Cordelia, they had decided to simply admire the night sky and the lights of the town below rather than become one with them.

"Cordy," he pleaded. "I'm so young."

"Do you have any idea how many times I've been up he—" She seemed to realize what she was saying—for Cordy, a truly amazing feat—and switched gears, both in her car and in her brain. The car went faster. "I know what I'm doing."

Xander wondered how many years of his life would fly before his eyes before he flew through the windshield. "I know you're eager to get there and all, but gee, girl, show some self-control."

"Oh, Xander, I don't know why . . ." she gritted out. His eyes bulged as he realized that she was checking herself out in the rearview mirror instead of watching the bushes and trees that were bearing down on them in a blur. "Why I have sunk so low . . ."

He thought of all the times he had seen movie and TV stars dive out of cars, roll on their shoulders, and leap to their feet. Fire off a couple rounds, save the day. Good thing he wasn't on TV.

"Help!" he shouted, pounding on the window.

"Xander, what is your damage?"

She slammed her foot on the brake and the tires squealed, burning rubber to within inches of the dropoff. Xander closed his eyes and rubbed the back of his neck.

"Some call it whiplash, but others pay a chiropractor fifty bucks."

"Shut up." Cordelia set the emergency brake and turned off the car. "And it's seventy-five, at least where I go." As if they'd simply pulled out of the driveway, she checked her hair and snapped open her purse. As he took slow, deep breaths, she whipped out her lipstick and carefully reapplied it.

"What are you doing?" he asked in amazement.

She regarded him with utter disdain. "Providing you with a marked target," she shot back. "Since you're so blind and timid."

He blinked at her. "Timid? *Moi?*"

She raised her chin. "Show me otherwise, Harris."

She pointed to her mouth. "Anything to shut you up."

He smiled and said softly, "Geronimo."

The gray twilight was good.

The black would be better.

As the little body writhed in the bed, the spirit grew in strength and began filling her. Undulating like a serpent, it slithered into her lungs, her heart, her eyes, her brain. It cascaded into her hands. Ah, so soft and small!

It burrowed through the muscles and veins of her legs. Not strong. Not powerful.

Yet.

It moved into her face.

It smiled.

It sat up.

The moon shone on the face of the Chinese vampire sorcerer known as Chirayoju as, for but a moment, it knew itself. Its face stretched long and jade-green with mold. Its eyes shifted into the almond shape of its home country. Its fangs grew long, sharp, and deadly.

Its hunger was overwhelming.

And then it was the girl again, her arms around her legs, face buried against her knees, sobbing gently from the pain and the fear.

It spoke to her: *Why fight me? Power is what you desire. Strength. I have them both. I am not greedy. I will share.*

"Mom?" Willow called tremulously.

Call her again and she dies, the vampire spirit promised.

Willow touched her forehead. She was burning up.

She felt like she was on some kind of very bad drug . . . that she had never taken. Drugs. Ever. But she was incredibly disoriented. When she looked around her room, it was as if she had never seen any of it before.

Her fever dreams were nightmares.

Groaning, she groped for her phone. She would call Buffy. Or Xander.

Something in her registered the names. Invaded, as if it were tearing her mind apart in search of something. Memorized the pictures in her mind that were attached to the names.

It knew their secrets.

Frightened, she pulled her hand away from the portable phone and cradled it against her chest. It was the hand on which she had cut a finger, and it throbbed terribly. It felt as if fire were burning deep inside it.

The blackness seeped through the gray, twilight giving way to full dark, and it both calmed and terrified her.

Cordelia came up for air and said, "Whoops, time to go."

Xander's face was covered with Sequin from the Mac makeup collection. He caught his breath and rasped, "Time to go?"

"I have things to do," she said imperiously, shooing him over to the passenger side. She started the car. It purred submissively and then roared to life.

"That's okay. Ego crushed." He smiled to himself. "Lips crushed. Fair Trade Agreement."

She screeched backward. "I hate it when you mutter to yourself. No." She held up a hand. "Actually, I prefer it. When you speak in a tone that I can hear, you scare me." She took a breath. "Most of the time."

"Face it, Cordelia," Xander said, patting her shoulder. "You adore me."

She snorted and put the pedal to the metal.

Xander found many new gods to pray to.

It raised its arms as the moon washed across the girl's face. And then, it knew itself at last in the dark night.

"I am Chirayoju. I am free. I live again."

It walked jerkily across the room, testing the body of the girl called Willow—excellent Chinese name, little Weeping Willow!—and flexed its arms. It had pushed her deep into the thing that she would call her soul, but it could sense her there, sense both her terror and the thrill of the presence of so much power around her. It was her hunger for that power that had allowed it to use her so completely.

It arched its back and grunted. Now and then she fought, but her struggles were puny compared to its strength. Had it not threatened the entire Land of the Rising Sun?

And this land, this strange new land. Without Sanno to stop it, would Chirayoju not be a conqueror once more?

A strange box glowed on a table. Chirayoju walked to it and studied it. *Computer,* came the word, in the tongue of this land. Images flooded into the spirit's mind. *But spirit no longer,* it thought. *Vampire, in living flesh!*

Chirayoju looked at the computer and realized that it did not need to learn these new things; in a sense, it already knew them. Possessing this body and this girl, it was itself and yet something more. As if there could be anything more powerful, more terrifying and wonderful, than the vampire Chirayoju!

It was time to move into this world. Time to begin assuming its rightful place.

It stared down at the flimsy cast covering its newly acquired wrist, and then tore it off. No more pain. No more injury. And the cut on the other hand? The slice in the girl's flesh where she had touched the razor edge of the sword of Sanno? Where her blood had flowed and allowed Chirayoju to take a bit of her life force and free itself? It would heal that as well.

Its host would be perfect, healthy and strong.

It found the knob of the French door to little Weeping Willow's room and pushed it open. A sweet breeze wafted over its face. What joy it was to feel again. To smell the scented flowers—roses? It thought longingly of the jasmine in the gardens of Empress Wu's Chinese palace. Of the beautiful Chinese maidens and strong young warriors who had done its bidding, including baring their necks to its fangs so that it might live. It had abandoned all that to cross the sea to the Land of the Rising Sun, in order to devour their emperor and reign over his people. Flying across the water on the wings of night, Chirayoju had wept for the grandeur of its home land—mighty China!—but it had pronounced the sacrifice worthy.

But then, Sanno had appeared. King of the Mountain, warrior god.

Sanno had defeated it.

Chirayoju laughed to itself. Sanno was not here. This place was undefended.

Buffy, came the thought of the girl. And Chirayoju listened to the thought.

Nodded.

Smiled.

If this girl, this Buffy, was the only defender of this land of Sunnydale, then Chirayoju would be emperor very quickly. Perhaps the girl, this . . . Slayer? Perhaps she would be a handmaiden in his new court.

Or fresh entertainment for the new pit he would dig . . .

It stepped across the threshold and was about to shut the door when Mrs. Rosenberg called out anxiously, "Honey?"

"It's okay, Mom," Chirayoju answered. "I just need some air. It's stuffy in here."

"Stay bundled up. You've got a fever, you know."

"Yes, I know."

But the fever was coming down. The possession, which had weakened this body, was now strengthening it. Chirayoju could feel its power growing along with its hunger. It had taken all this time to fully exert control over Weeping Willow's body. Even now, it would have to give up that control at dawn. For now.

But not forever.

As for this night, it must feed, and soon.

It walked, more steadily this time, from the door to the front of the house, and from there to what was known as the street. A car flew by—remarkable creation!—and it knew it would have to have one.

It raised its face to the stars. Their light beamed down on it. A poem came to mind:

> *Night, absent of soul.*
> *Gardens wither, the earth shakes.*
> *Open, gate of death!*

Chirayoju walked down the street, reveling in its freedom. It would walk until sunrise if it wished. It would walk until the feet of this child bled, and it would make the night scream.

Xander gave Cordelia a "when-did-you-get-re-leased" look of amazement and scratched his head.

"Let me get this straight. You drove over a rock."

"Or something," she agreed.

"Or something. And your tire went flat. And now you want me to get out of the car and change your tire so you can go do these 'things to do,' which I assume have something to do with a guy who is not me."

She said nothing. She only stared at him. Xander stared back.

Finally Cordelia said, "And your point is?"

"Is the word 'tacky' even in your vocabulary?" he asked her. "Let me spell it for you. N. O. Way."

"Fine." She glared at him. "I'll just do it myself." She spread her fingers as if her nails were still wet and scanned the dashboard. "The jack-thing is in the trunk," she said to herself. "And all I have to do is, um, here!" She brightened and pushed a button. Her emergency flashers began to pulse.

Xander sighed the sigh of the truly victimized and opened his door.

"Thank you!" Cordelia called plaintively after him.

He bent back in to narrow his eyes at her.

"You know, it's nights like these psychos escape from the nuthouse on the hill," he said in a low, scary voice. "So if I don't come back . . . lock your doors and close your eyes. Because the drip, drip, drip you hear will be the blood running out of my neck. And the smack will be my severed head landing on your front end."

"Oh, Xander." She gave him a look. "I don't know how you can even joke about stuff like that, after all the weirdness you and your bizarro pals have put me through."

He batted his lashes at her. "Cordy, my sweet. Lest you forget, you are now one of my bizarro pals."

"As if." She leaned toward him and grabbed the passenger armrest to urge the door shut. "Just go do it, okay? I'll be nice to you or something."

"'Or something' will do just fine." He rubbed his hands together like a mad scientist. "Wa ha ha, just fine, my pretty."

She let go of the armrest and threw her head back against her seat. "Oooh."

Xander grinned and shut the door. Then he walked back toward where the jack-thing would be, muttering, "Harris, you are such a schmuck."

The dogs of Sunnydale bayed as Chirayoju glided past their houses. Cats arched their backs and hissed. The moon itself hid behind a veil of clouds. It moved quickly, smelling fresh young blood beating through vibrant hearts. Eagerly it inhaled the aroma. After centuries of imprisonment, it was starving. Not merely for blood, but for what truly sustained it—life. The life essence of living beings.

To begin its reign of terror, though, Chirayoju knew that it would need slaves and acolytes.

And suddenly it knew where to find them. The air sizzled with the presence of other vampires, and it was so delighted its eyes welled with scarlet tears.

It raised its head to gaze at a hill above the town, and small, unmoving shapes upon the hill. They were cars.

Other shapes moved toward them, darting over the landscape like a small band of locusts. They were vampires.

Eagerly, Chirayoju began to lope toward the hill. Up it climbed, now running, though the body was tired. It willed power into the limbs and pushed blood through the heart. This body was young, but at this rate it would wear out quickly.

When that happened, it would have to find another.

Once he had put Cordy's spare tire on, Xander sat glumly in the passenger's seat as she drove down the hill. Cordelia drove past a small blur of a figure on the side of the road and shook her head. "Honestly. Someone is hitching to Makeout Point, can you believe it? Don't they have any idea how dangerous that is?"

"Who? Where?" Xander asked, looking up from sifting through the CDs in Cordelia's glove compartment. He glanced back but saw no one.

Cordelia looked in the rearview mirror. "Am I smeared?"

He pointed desperately. "Cor, look at the road."

"Just tell me if I'm smeared," she demanded, turning toward him.

"No, no, you are a goddess," he begged. "You look perfect." He stared hard at her, doing his best to look entranced by her beauty instead of petrified by her driving. "Honest. Please, please don't kill me."

She rolled her eyes. "Xander, you are *so* superficial."

Her foot was lead.

His life was over.

The wind whipped around Chirayoju as it glided behind the vampire swarm. There were only three of them—apparently, the other dots had been dogs—and they were scattered and unfocused, little more than ravening beasts. So had it been in China, before Chirayoju had left for the Land of the Rising Sun. And then, so had it been in Japan. Few of its kind were truly intelligent. Few possessed the ability to truly lead. And none but Chirayoju had mastered the dark arts as a vampire. The demon within the spirit was flush with pride at its achievements.

No, the others were like children to Chirayoju.

Which was to the good. They were easier to control and dominate.

Chirayoju watched as the hunt progressed. Better to call it a massed attack, for a hunt implied direction and working in concert. They swooped down on the cars, yanking open the doors and pulling out the inhabitants. A young girl with short, dark hair shrieked in terror as a female vampire with long, blond hair dragged her out of the car while another vampire, darker and larger, lifted out a boy in a leather jacket and ripped out his throat.

The third vampire, tall and balding, attacked a car farther down, which allowed the couples in nearer vehicles to attempt escape. However, the other two vampires were too fast for them. For a few heartbeats, there was screaming.

And then there were no heartbeats.

At that instant, Chirayoju stood up and spread its arms. Lightning crackled. The wind shrieked.

It boomed, "Know me as your master!"

The other vampires stopped in their tracks.

"What?" the female cried, and began to rush him.

"Stop!" Chirayoju commanded.

At first his words had no effect. Then it was as if the female vampire were little more than a marionette. She was brought up short as if strings held her back, and Chirayoju reached out to her dead mind, to the demon spirit that lived within, and it was the demon that he controlled. The demon that he enslaved. The demon that he forced to its knees.

"Master," the girl whispered.

"Hey, man, what's your deal?" the darker vampire said contemptuously.

Chirayoju turned its gaze on him. Their eyes met, locked. It knew the creature saw a mere girl, and willed him to see the truth behind the mask that was Weeping Willow.

The other vampire's mouth opened as if in pain—or shock. He knew what it was he saw, now. The vampire remembered death, of course, the time between the loss of his human soul and his resurrec-

tion as a vampire. He did not want to face that
horrible void again, nor did he relish the even more
nightmarish horrors he was promised as he gazed
into Chirayoju's eyes.

Chirayoju stared at each one in turn, pushing its
will against theirs. It felt their struggle.

The sky cracked open and rain pelted them. The
blood of the victims on the ground mixed with the
earth; the mud ran crimson.

Chirayoju singled out the balding vampire and
willed him to approach. To kneel. To bare his neck.

"Speak my name," it commanded.

In a steady voice, the vampire answered, "Lord
Chirayoju."

The moon hung in the trees above the graveyard,
casting Angel in a glow of stark white that accentu-
ated his pale skin. His eyes were dark, and as he
looked down at Buffy, he touched her cheek with a
tentative gesture. His fingers were cold, but his
caress warmed her. Her lips were swollen from his
kisses.

"In this light, you look like me," he said softly.

"Like a vampire." Her voice was louder, bolder.
"You avoid saying it, like it was a dirty word."

His laugh was short and bitter. "You're the Slayer,
Buffy. To you, it is a dirty word."

Buffy cocked her head and gathered up his hand in
both of hers. "Angel, for us to move along, we need
to move . . . along." She stood on tiptoe, raising her
mouth toward his. "This 'hate me, I'm a vampire'
stuff is old territory for us. We've been over the
worst terrain we could possibly find. I have the map
memorized. It's time to blaze a new trail."

He looked down at her mouth, and she could tell

he was struggling not to kiss her again. Her heart pounded. She could tell he heard the faster rhythm.

He whispered, "You know there's more to me than we both realized at first."

"I'll say." She put her hand around his neck and urged him closer. "And if I'm not afraid, why should you be?"

"Maybe because I lo—" He turned his head.

She did, too. There was something in the air, something that floated across her and threatened to pull her down, or to put its hand over her mouth and smother her. Something that held hands with death.

"Did you feel that?" she asked. "It was almost like a . . ." She searched for the right words. "Like the air got heavy. Or like a scream in my head." She frowned. "Something's wrong."

Angel nodded slowly. "Something's very wrong."

As one, they looked up toward the night sky and all around. Beneath the gravestones and monuments, the dead stayed buried. Through a sheen of clouds, the moon glowed. An owl hooted directly above their heads. All was peaceful. Yet the presentiment of evil lingered like a fog.

"I think I'm getting better at this Slayer thing," Buffy murmured. "I think something's up. I think I need to go see Giles."

Almost unconsciously, Angel draped a protective arm across Buffy's shoulders. "I think I'll go with you."

Together they hurried toward the graveyard gates.

CHAPTER 6

As Friday morning began, Willow was elsewhere.

Some voice from the real world echoed down the long, twisted dream corridor to her elsewhere, and the first real spark of awareness hit her. Music, from a long way off.

Country music.

Computer geek she might be, but Willow Rosenberg did not listen to country music. Oh, sure, she thought Garth Brooks and Shania Twain were cool enough, but that wasn't *you-listen-to-country-music?* country music. No, having country music on your alarm clock was just inviting ridicule. And, truth be told, Willow had never needed to send invitations. Uh-uh. The Willow ridicule party was eternal, and everybody crashed.

Except Buffy, and Xander, and Oz, and other people who were the objects of vast amounts of ridicule.

Alarm clock. Usually meaning you're asleep. Or have been.

Only the warmth of the sun streaming through her bedroom window made Willow realize how cold she was. Cold and aching all over like she'd climbed to the top of Everest for a midnight snack.

Midnight . . . snack. Something weird there. Something she could almost remember.

Then she felt the drool on her chin. Realized she'd been sleeping with her mouth open, even snoring, which wasn't something she did often, as far as her waking self knew.

Willow's face crumpled into an expression of disgust as she wiped her chin, realizing at last that she was, indeed, awake. Awake and exhausted and her eyes were burning like she'd been up all night watching infomercials again. Insomnia could make a person do strange things. But no, she hadn't done anything like that. Couldn't really remember doing anything last night after coming home sick from school. Except that somehow, she had set her alarm for the dulcet twang of the Grand Ole Opry.

Weird. Weird and disgusting, she thought. How could she ever spend the night with a guy if there was even a chance that he'd see her sleeping with her mouth open with drool on her chin? Uh-uh.

She opened her dry, burning eyes, then gasped and closed them tight as the sun hit her retinas. Willow hissed as a spike of pain shot through her head. She lay a moment, waiting for the pain to pass, assuming it was like the frozen headaches she got when she ate ice cream too fast. But it didn't pass.

In fact, by the time she crawled out of bed and dragged herself to the shower, Willow's headache had only grown worse. It wasn't a pounding ache, the kind where you could feel the blood pumping through your head. It was more like someone had pounded a nail into her skull.

Even after her shower, Willow didn't feel much better. Her mother called to her from downstairs, but the words didn't even register. Nor did she pay any attention to what she was putting on except to note that the clothes were clean.

It was while she was sitting on the edge of her bed tying her shoes that she glanced up at the computer on her desk and saw the little green sprout sticking up from her mouse pad. Willow frowned, a decidedly ill-advised action for someone with a headache so bad that her face hurt.

She stood and walked to her desk. Next to her mouse was a small, crooked bonsai tree, the kind that trendy stores in trendy malls sold to people who couldn't handle the responsibility of a pet to take care of. Gigapets for Boomers, in other words. But this was nothing from a mall. It had long roots still covered with dirt from where it had been torn from the ground.

"Okay, thanks but it's not my birthday," Willow mumbled uneasily to her empty room.

How the plant had gotten there, of course, was the big question. With the pain in her head discouraging much contemplation—much thought of any kind, really—the only thing she could think of was: maybe Angel?

Running around at night, showing up unannounced at people's windows. That was kind of vampire-like behavior. At least, Angel-like behavior. But she didn't think he would do that, unless it was some big surprise for her or something. And, come to think of it, during that whole Angelus thing that nobody really wanted to talk about, she and Buffy had placed a kind of ward over her room to keep him out.

So not Angel. But when she started to consider other options, the nail in her skull turned into a knitting needle. She massaged her forehead, realized she was going to be late for school—as if anyone would notice after a hellish week like this, when Willow Rosenberg and tardiness seemed as inseparable as PB&J. Still, she'd better show up today. Who knew what she had missed this week? Even the days that she had been there, she couldn't quite remember.

Except for the fact that she'd somehow scored a perfect grade on the pop quiz Mr. Morse gave about their museum visit to the exhibit on the art and culture of ancient Japan. Somehow, through her fugue state, she'd obviously learned something. And if she ever wanted to learn anything again, it was back to school for Willow.

Just before she left, she noticed something beside the uprooted bonsai. It was the disk or coin that had fallen from the hilt of that big sword at the museum on Monday. She'd forgotten to put it back after cutting herself; she'd been too distracted. Then it had made its way into the pocket of her jeans, and later disappeared. Or not, considering that it now sat prominently displayed on top of her computer.

Willow felt a little guilty about it. Maybe she should try to take it back this afternoon? As she reached for it, noting its odd engravings, someone started pounding that knitting needle into her brain with a hammer. Willow forgot all about the coin, turned, and stumbled toward the hallway, feeling suddenly as though she was going to throw up.

Strangely, and with great relief, Willow began to feel better almost immediately. The headache never disappeared entirely, but it receded until it was more of a thumbtack than a nail. It still hurt, but she could live with it. She might even be able to pay attention in class.

As she hurried out the door, her eyes ached from the bright sunlight, and she slipped on a pair of sunglasses she hadn't worn in months. They weren't her style.

Before.

Buffy sat alone at a round table in the cafeteria, math text open in front of her. The Noxema-filled plastic tubes the school dared to call baked stuffed manicotti sat untouched on her tray.

She had told Giles about the weird sensation she had had in the graveyard. He was intrigued but could find no specific reason for it. Even now, she supposed he was researching to see if Curse of the Rat-People Night was looming—which it probably was.

She saw Oz and gave him a wave. He smiled and moved on like he was hunting—ah, make that searching—for something. Or someone. Buffy hoped that someone was someone she knew. Known as Willow.

"Two plus two equals?" a voice asked behind her.

It barely registered. Xander slid into the chair next to her and began ferociously tearing into his plate of tubes with a zeal that might have given one the impression that he thought it was real food. Buffy spared a glance and a bemused frown for his table manners, then looked back at her book.

"Oh, hi, Xander," Xander said. "Sorry I don't have time to be sociable, but I've done it again. Bad me. I put off studying in favor of more athletic nocturnal activities, and now I'm up crit peek without a shaddle. Again. Oh, woe is me, my tutor Willow has forsaken me."

Buffy still didn't look up.

"See, I can tell you're nervous about the test because instead of your usual choice of beverage, Mango Madness, you've gone with the sixteen-ounce chocolate Quik. Major Buffy comfort food. Y'know, if it was food and not drink. Liquid. Beverage thing."

Buffy still didn't look up, but she did respond. "Eat your lunch, Xander."

"Which means, I guess, that you want me to be quiet so you can study for the makeup math test you have in, oh, thirty-two minutes?" Xander inquired.

"Eat your lunch, Xander," Buffy said again.

"Hey, no problem. I'm shuttin' up. I'm good at shuttin' up. Nobody's better than the X-Man at shuttin' up."

"Shut up shuttin' up," Buffy drawled in her best Warner Brothers cartoon gangster voice.

Xander grinned broadly. "See. Now haven't you always wanted to say that?"

"Yes," Buffy replied, finally looking up and fixing him with an amused but frustrated glare. "Thank you so much. One of my life's great wishes, really. You're a prince."

Willow plopped her tray on the table and slid into

a chair. "A prince?" she asked. "Somebody kissed the toad and didn't tell me? I'm always the last to know."

Xander and Buffy stared at Willow as she started to dig into the most terrifying meal the school ever served—and they served it once a week—the perversely named vegetarian meatloaf. But it wasn't her meal choice that had drawn their attention.

"Good God, what happened to you?" Xander asked, bobbing his head toward Willow in that head-bobbing, inquisitive way that he had.

Buffy whacked him on the arm.

"Will, are you okay?" he pressed.

"After a week like this, why wouldn't I be okay?" she snapped. No smile. No sheepish Willowy self-effacing grin.

"Did you get mugged again?" Xander demanded, shifting into the rescuing-the-damsel-in-distress mode that he'd been trying so gamely to perfect. Which explained the tire-changing thing, he decided. He was not Cordelia's schmuck boy after all. He was her knight in shining armor.

Willow finally looked up at them. Or at least, looked up at them through the black lenses of her sunglasses. Which she had on. Inside the caf, like she thought she was Courtney Love or some other demented denizen of the rich and famous lifestyle universe.

"Huh?" she asked. "No. Not even. In fact, my wrist is totally fine. Healed up real fast."

"Not really the concern," Buffy admitted. "It's more, well, cosmetic. Look, I'm pretty sure you don't have a hangover, so what's up with you?"

Cordelia had walked over and pulled up a chair as

they were talking, and now she tsk-tsked and tilted her head in her best imitation of a sympathetic friend.

"Willow," she said kindly. "I think what Buffy is trying not to say is that you look like a two-dollar hooker who hasn't made it back to her corner of the alley yet."

Buffy wanted to defend Willow, but for a moment she couldn't. Because Willow really did look that bad. Her hair was a mess, clean but uncombed and wildly tangled. She had on a lime-green, very fashionable top and purple sweatpants, an offense that should have brought the Fashion SWAT team down on the school the second Willow walked in.

And just when had she walked in? She certainly hadn't made it in time for first bell. Or even her first class, as far as Buffy knew. And what was up with those sunglasses?

Willow glared at Cordelia, her gaze intense though her eyes were hidden behind the dark glasses.

"How sweet of you to say, Cordelia," Willow snarled. "Particularly coming from you."

"Well, excuse me," Cordy said, flicking her fingers into the air as if she were trying to dry her nail polish. "Aren't we testy. I was just trying to save you from postapocalyptic embarrassment. See, I always told my therapist that trying to be someone's friend was just a waste of precious time better spent on self-improvement."

"Well put," Xander teased. But of course teasing Cordelia was only fun when she noticed. Which at this moment—sigh, like so many others—she didn't. Or she didn't care, which, since it was Xander, was likely.

"You're right," Willow told her. "You could use some time on self-improvement, Cordelia. Maybe then people would stop mistaking you for Barbie's friend Skipper turned crack-ho."

Buffy smirked. She couldn't help it. She almost burst out laughing, in fact, and probably would have if not for the look on Willow's face. It wasn't the triumph she expected to see there—she had, after all, just trounced Cordy in the insult category—but a look of such contempt that for a moment, Buffy thought Willow was going to hiss up a cat fight.

Instead, Will stood up abruptly enough to knock over her chair, then turned and stormed from the cafeteria, leaving her food and her friends behind.

"Wow," Cordelia said. "What's gotten into her? Sharpen those claws. It's going to be a bumpy ride." She reached for Willow's tray. "Guess she's not going to eat her tofu."

Xander slapped her hand. "Now cut that out!"

Cordy shot him a wounded look, but Buffy barely registered their exchange. She was watching Willow go.

"What is your talk show topic?" Cordelia sneered at Xander.

"Did you look in the mirror and strike yourself blind or something?" Xander snapped at her. "I've known Willow my whole life. She's been my best friend since . . . just since. Something's obviously really bothering her. She was so un-Willowy. It'd be like you wearing the same outfit to school twice."

Cordelia blinked. "You think it's that bad?" she asked worriedly.

"It's that bad," Buffy said, and they gave each other "uh-oh" looks.

"What do we do?" Xander asked.

"Give her some space, I guess. Try to talk to her, no pressure, and not all together. Ask Giles to talk to her," Buffy said, rattling off the ideas as they came into her head. "I think maybe getting mugged had more of an impact on Willow than we thought."

"Like post-traumatic stress disorder or something?" Cordelia asked.

Buffy cast a sidelong glance at her, faced with the realization once again that Cordy wasn't nearly as thick as she usually seemed. Well, not entirely. Sometimes.

"I'll talk to her," Xander said.

"Yeah," Buffy agreed. "I'll try to get her to open up too."

Cordelia whistled, eyes searching the blank, white-washed walls for something to look at. Lips puckered, she stopped whistling mid-note and rolled her eyes.

"All right!" she said. "I'll try, too."

"That's my Cordy," Xander said with pride. "Always thinking about others."

But none of them saw Willow again that day, and Buffy was so caught up in the Math Test from Hell that she didn't even think about trying to talk to her until she was on the way home.

Sometimes Buffy had company when she was on patrol, scouring Sunnydale for something unnatural that she could return to nature. Giles might come along to lecture her on becoming a better Slayer, hang on to her big bag o' tricks, and hand her a stake when she needed one. Other times, when she didn't think it would be too much of a distraction—who was she kidding?—whenever he wanted to come along, Angel prowled the night with her.

Also, there would be big smoochies during Angel-prowling nights, as Xander so quaintly put it on occasion. Very big smoochies.

"I could use a little distraction, right about now," she muttered to herself.

It was quiet, and a little chilly, and Buffy thought it would have been nice to have Angel around, or Giles. For different reasons, of course. She wondered if she ought to bring homework with her sometimes. She could sit under a streetlight and study if it got slow, just sit and wait for something inhuman and vile to attack her. Kind of like sitting in front of Greg "the Octopus" Rucka in bio.

"Deep sigh," Buffy whispered.

She slung her bag over her shoulder and started for home. On the way, she got kind of sidetracked and wandered over to the Bronze. Once she got there, though, she only stood on the curb outside looking at the door. It was possible Angel was there, inside. But if she went in, and he was in there, she wouldn't be in any kind of rush to get home.

Home. That place they named homework after. Where that work intended for home was usually done. And Buffy was way behind.

Tomorrow night, she thought. She'd see Angel tomorrow night.

She spun on her heel, started for home, and then stopped short. A weird feeling very like the grave-yard sensation from the night before ran through her, and she turned to peer into the darkness of the alley next to the Bronze.

Three of them, two guys and one very innocent-looking girl with short, dark hair. Buffy was the wariest of her. It was like high school: sometimes the ones you expected the least of really surprised you. If only her teachers' expectations of her would sink a little more, she'd be the pride of Sunnydale High.

"See, that's what happens to my grades," she said aloud, letting her bag drop to her side. "I have the best of intentions about my homework, but something always comes up."

Their faces were hideous, feral, and they snorted like animals as they stepped out of the alley and began to spread out to surround her. Buffy slid a stake from the bag, then dropped the bag to the sidewalk.

"Hello, procrastination," she said, and smiled.

"And a good evening to you, Slayer," the girl growled. "I hope you've enjoyed it, 'cause it's going to be your last."

"Thanks for caring," Buffy retorted. "You're so sweet."

"Oh, not at all," said the second, a balding-type guy, moving around behind her.

Buffy turned, switching the stake from hand to hand, trying to keep them in her field of vision. They made a semicircle and they moved in unison, creeping right, then left. Very drill team. Very weird.

"We've been waiting for you for hours," said the third, dark-skinned and heavyset. "We'd almost given up hope of killing you tonight."

For a moment, Buffy felt that sensation again, and an additional chill at the realization that they'd been waiting for her. Not out hunting for fresh blood. Just hanging out behind the Bronze, waiting for the Slayer to come by.

Vampires weren't generally known for their patience.

Buffy shook it off, slapped the stake into her right hand, and smiled. "You'd almost given up hope," she said with mock sympathy. "Now here I am, what you've been waiting for, and all I'm going to do is break your hearts."

Her face changed, then. A sneer—almost cruel—twisted her mouth.

"Oops, my bad. I meant *stake* your hearts, of course."

Baldy leaped at her, and Buffy acted. She threw her leg out toward him, lifted her left hand to grab him by the shirt front and toss him at the heavyset one on her right.

That was her intention, anyway.

But she never got hold of him. Baldy stopped short, stood up, and simply smiled at her. Buffy knew instantly what had happened. They had set her up. Big Boy was rushing in from her right, and the girlish bloodsucker was already reaching for her hair. Buffy was extended in the wrong direction, off balance.

The girl snagged her hair, hissed, bared her fangs. Big Boy barreled in from the right.

Buffy fell backward and the girl came with her.

"Oh," Buffy said. "A wiseguy. Remind me to kill you later."

Big Boy thundered past the spot where she'd been standing and nearly flattened Baldy with his bulk. Buffy threw a foot up into the girl's stomach and tossed her over her head to land in the street. Cars passed by now and again on the cross street, but nothing turned down toward the Bronze.

Fine with her. Nobody reporting back to her mom or the school that they saw her fighting in front of the club on a school night.

The girl was quick, though. Even as Buffy was getting up, she was rushing at Buffy again.

"Well, if you insist," Buffy sighed, and side-stepped, kneed her in the stomach, pulled her up by the hair, and staked her.

She exploded in a blast of ashes. Buffy didn't have time to appreciate her demise, however. She sensed Big Boy and Baldy behind her, and took off into the darkness of the alley.

They gave chase.

Morons.

A battered Chevy was parked in the alley. Buffy jumped onto the hood, then the roof. The two vamps got on either side of the car, and their smiles told her they figured they had her trapped.

"Now we've got you," Big Boy snarled.

"Y'know, I can see where you might have a hard time getting an actual date, but this is taking things a little too far, don't you think?" she asked. "Of course, I've heard the Internet is fertile territory to meet that special someone if you want them to love you just for your brains."

"I'll love you for your heart, Slayer, while it's sliding down my throat in ragged pieces!" Big Boy screamed and swiped at her legs.

Buffy leaped again, did a somersault, and came down behind him.

"Isn't that an oh-so-lovely image," she said, and staked Big Boy through the back. Harder that way, but if a girl worked at it, the end result was the same.

Poof.

Baldy stared at her across the roof of the Chevy.

"You could run," she suggested.

"I would be killed for my cowardice if I ran," Baldy growled. "In any case, I'm not afraid of you, little girl."

He leaped up onto the roof of the car, where she'd stood only seconds before. Buffy grabbed the Chevy's door handle and pulled. It was unlocked. She opened the door and hopped in, slammed the door just as Baldy shoved a hand in after her. She heard the snap of his arm bone and the howl of pain as he withdrew the arm.

Buffy slammed the door again. But she didn't try getting out the other side. Just sat there behind the wheel. Well, just a little closer to the middle of the car. Baldy shattered the window with his working fist a second later and then his face appeared in the broken window.

"Boo!" Buffy said, and punched him in the face.

Baldy slid off the roof, scrambled to his feet and stared at her through the broken window.

"Scared of me now?" she asked.

"Get out of that car!" he roared at her.

Buffy smiled shyly. "No."

Baldy came at her, grabbed for the door handle, and Buffy shoved the stake through the broken window and into his chest.

"You didn't say please," she told him as he exploded into dust.

The adrenaline pumping through Buffy as she made her way home felt good. There was a certain

Rocky Balboa-ness about being the Slayer, though Buffy would never confess that exhilaration when she was bitching to Giles about her life.

But that feeling was overshadowed tonight. Completely eclipsed by the dread that was beginning to weigh heavily on her. It was racing around her mind and she had a feeling she wasn't going to be getting much sleep that night.

These vampires weren't that much harder to kill than most of the others she'd taken on. But they were more focused. They'd waited around for her. They'd set her up at the start of that fight, as if they could predict what her first move would be. Actually, they *had* predicted it.

And when she'd told that last one to run, what he'd said in return had creeped her out.

"I would be killed for my cowardice."

Which meant someone had *sent* them after Buffy. Someone organized. Someone she hadn't already killed.

On the night after the night of the graveyard weirdness-thing.

Not good.

CHAPTER 7

Some called it morning.

After a refreshingly uneventful weekend—relatively uneventful—Buffy let out a vast Monday-morning yawn as she walked into the library and said, "Many vampires. Much homework. Vampires slain. Homework somewhat less than attacked."

She sighed. "So sign me up for remedial you-name-it, call my mom, and explain to her why I'm flunking unflunkable classes, such as P.E."

"Hmm?" Giles asked, looking up from one of his oh-so-dusty books. Buffy reflected that so much of her life revolved around dust. Inhaling it during research sessions, and creating it . . . out of dead vampires.

Giles smiled, pushed up his glasses, and closed his book. "Good morning, Buffy. You were saying there was a lot of activity this weekend?"

"Vampy only," she answered, mentally ticking

down a list of things that had not happened: home-work, the Bronze, big smoochies from Angel.

"Well, yes," he said, as if that was the only kind that mattered. Easy for him to say. He was not flunking being a librarian. Which raised some questions: How did people know if you were doing a good job? Check to see if the books were shelved in correct alphabetical order?

" 'Well, yes,' " she repeated. "Only these vamps were different from the vamps of yore." She perched on the study table and swung her legs, half-admiring her heeled boots, which were new—a product of a Saturday afternoon mother-daughter bonding ritual called "hitting the mall."

"These were organized vamps, like there's another leader in town," she informed her Watcher. "Had some nasties on Friday night. Another pair last night. No trouble, but it was kind of freaky."

"Really?" His brow crinkled. With both hands, he set the book down on the table. Dust rose off the cover like fog off the ocean.

"Really." Buffy leaned backward and peered into the stacks, on the lookout for her best friend. "Speaking of demons, Willow was a big no-show all weekend. She didn't show up at the Bronze, and hasn't returned my phone calls. Plus, she isn't in school today. No one's seen her. That spooks me a trifle."

Giles raised an eyebrow. "Spooks you a trifle?"

"Trifle. A little less than *Poltergeist,* a little more than Casper. Trifle."

"Ah," Giles said, then quickly moved on. "What does Willow's tardiness have to do with demons? Did you and she have a quarrel or something?"

"Or nothing. Ever since she got mugged, Willow's been getting funkier by the day." She pursed her lips. "She's actually acting . . . witchier . . . than Cordelia. And you know how pointed *her* hat is." Buffy sat forward and crossed her arms.

"Well, we do all have our bad days," Giles offered, scrutinizing her. "But I should like to hear more about these—"

Buffy frowned impatiently. "She was wearing sunglasses, and they were Gargoyles."

He blinked, clearly not getting it.

"Giles, read the magazines, don't just subscribe. Even geeks have put their Gargoyles away. And as for wearing them indoors, well, that went the way of the sequined glove and Bubbles the Chimp. It's so over even the geeks think it's over."

She reddened. "Not that I'm lumping Willow in with the geeks. Because I would never do that. She's my friend. And that's the point of my babblesomeness. She is not acting like herself."

Giles sighed. "Buffy, please, I beg of you, slow down. For someone who insists she's not a morning person, you bring with you a certain manic exuberance to our pre-class chats that I, for one, occasionally find a bit, well, exhausting."

"Well, of course," she said cheerily. "You're old . . . er than me," she amended, at his crestfallen expression.

They both glanced up as Xander strolled in, already talking as he walked through the door.

"Subject: Willow. Not even Oz the new true love werewolf boyfriend has seen her today."

"Subject: Willow," Buffy agreed, rubbing her hands together.

"Buffy, I really think we ought to concentrate on these vampires who targeted you over the weekend," Giles insisted. Before Buffy could protest, he held up a finger. "First. After which we may discuss Willow's change of attitude and declining fashion sense to your heart's content."

"Oh, all right," Buffy said, pouting. "Xander, come." She patted the study table. "Sit."

"I pant like a dog and obey like a doormat." He sat beside her and gave her a friendly bump with his elbow.

"We were going back through some odd occurrences of late," Giles told Xander. "Over the weekend, Buffy met up with some vampires who were very focused, very organized."

Xander nodded knowingly. "All right. Teamster vamps. Filed away. Next item?"

"She was in the graveyard with Angel the night before and felt something weird."

"Buffy," Xander said, scandalized.

"We both had this weird feeling," Buffy said.

"Yeah, I'll just bet you did. It being that weird feeling popularly known as lust." Xander looked angry. "Do you know how dangerous it is to make out when you're on patrol?"

Buffy frowned indignantly, even though she figured her flush was giving her away. "Not making out. We were both hunting."

"Hunting what?" he asked. "For rabies? Cuz if you keep kissing Dead Boy, you'll probably get them. I warned Willow about the same thing with Oz."

"And I'm sure Willow appreciated it as much as I do," Buffy said, frowning at him.

Xander held up his hand. "Plus, what kind of message are you sending to all those impressionable young vampire girls who might be spying on you two? You know, as the Slayer, you are a role model, whether you like it or not."

"I'll keep that in mind," she drawled, giving him a knowing look. "Next time I find you all over Cordelia."

"We are not talking about *my* strange hobbies," Xander said without a hint of embarrassment. "We're talking about your taste in boyfriends."

Buffy slipped off the table and began to pace. "Meanwhile, Will. I think she was so shaken by the attack that she's putting up walls so she won't get hurt again." She trailed off, thinking of when she had been defeated by the vampire known as the Master. How angry she'd been once she'd been brought back to life. How bitter and mean to all her friends.

How Xander had brought her back to life with CPR.

"At first I thought it would pass, but it's been more than a week now since she was attacked and she's only getting moodier. Now she's dropped out of real life completely, or something. We have to help her," she finished softly, giving Xander a look as she recalled how many times he had been there for her and Willow both. For everyone.

Xander said quietly, "And we will, Buff."

They smiled at each other.

"Okay, let me figure this out," Cordelia said, as she drove Xander over to Willow's house. "Whenever I inform you that we must cut short our perverse and disgusting display of mutual passion or whatever, I am then on a date with another guy. But whenever you call it quits and ask me to drive you to Willow's house, we are checking up on a friend?"

Xander peered through the window on the passenger side and nodded. "I swear, babe, hanging with me has increased your brain power."

"I am not 'babe.' I have never been 'babe' and I will never be 'babe.' Babe is a pig." She stomped on the brake. "And no dumb whiplash cracks, either. And as for my brain power—"

"I have said nothing. I have nothing to say," Xander said, opening the door and rushing to Willow's front door. The porch light was on, but it looked like nobody was home.

He rang the bell. They waited.

"I'm hungry," Cordelia whined.

"I've got a half-eaten candy bar on the floor mat on my side," he said. "Formerly, it was in my hand, but I had to drop it when we careened on two wheels around that last curve. The chewed part is probably covered with carpet fuzz, but what the hey, we all need our fibre."

"That's disgusting," Cordelia said. She leaned past him and knocked hard on the door. "She's not home. Come on. I have two hours until cheerleading practice."

Xander was tempted. Two hours in Cordelia's arms were two hours well spent. He was certain she was dumping an extreme amount of money into lipstick these days, because she was wiping it all over his face with an extravagance matched only by his purchases of Altoids breath mints.

But his concern for Willow was stronger than his practically overwhelming desire for big smoochies, et cetera.

"What's the big?" Cordelia demanded, as he stubbornly stayed on the porch. "So she's out."

"You don't get it, do you?" Xander asked. "It's a school night."

"So she's Bronzing with Oz." Cordelia shrugged. "Maybe she's gone shopping with Buffy." She thought that through. "No," she said decisively. "Those two would never actually go shopping for fun. If they put the least amount of effort into it, they'd just have to have better wardrobes."

He stood his ground. "I'm going to wait for her a little while." He put his arm around her and urged her against his chest. "C'mon, Cor, we can make out in your car here just as easily as at the Point. Moon, stars, lips? What do you say?"

She sighed heavily, a martyr to ecstasy. "Come on," she said, and led the way to the car.

Buffy gasped and froze in her tracks. "What's the matter?" Giles asked. "Do you feel that . . . 'oddness' again?"

"Weirdness, Giles. It was a weirdness. And, no," she said slowly. "It was just that . . . well, I think I forgot to change the dryer setting to 'delicate' before I put my clothes in." She groaned. "My new shirt is going to shrink."

"I see. Alas," Giles mumbled dismissively.

"Okay, maybe *you* don't care what *you* look like," Buffy said angrily, "but you are not a seventeen-year-old high school female."

"Quite true, Buffy, quite true," Giles agreed.

Buffy didn't miss his whispered "thank the Lord," but she chose to ignore it.

"You were going to tell me about the research you've been doing, sans Willow?" Buffy prompted.

"Ah, yes," he said, happy to be back in familiar territory. Giles hefted her Slayer's bag and used the stake he was carrying to push up his glasses. "There has been a veritable surplus of recent disappearances."

She nodded, all business now.

"Many of them are teenagers," he said pointedly. "They were known to frequent a well-known area where young people congregated for the purposes of—"

"Makeout Point," Buffy said, nodding. "Get on with it, Giles. I may not have a social life, but I know what one is. So, what, did someone go up there and vampirize a bunch of kids who were swallowing each other's tonsils?"

"It would appear, so, yes," Giles said, clearing his throat. "If you are correct about there being a new leader of sorts in the Hellmouth, it may be that he is gathering a group of vampires loyal to him to do his bidding."

"Much joy there," Buffy said. "If I can just get him on my good side, maybe he can force them to do my homework." She waved a hand to stave off the inevitable request from Giles to be more serious. "Or I can ask him to—"

She stirred, alert, gesturing to her Watcher.

A vampire lurked nearby.

Giles raised the stake.

"Wait," Buffy said, smiling.

A vampire, yes. Tall, dark, and not fangy at the moment. But handsome. Very, very handsome.

"Hi, Buffy," Angel said. He bobbed his head at Giles. "Good evening."

"What's the haps?" Buffy asked, trying to sound casual.

"I was out." He shrugged. "I was hoping we could—"

Just then, a ring of vampires fell from above, shrieking as they landed in a circle and surrounded Buffy, Giles, and Angel. At least a dozen of them in full fang face, crouched and waiting. Not rushing. Not crowding.

Not acting like your typical demon-infested, ravening corpses.

Buffy glanced around at the odd mix of vampires. Young and old, of varied races and sexes, they also differed in another way. Some were in funereal clothes, indicating that they had been taken to funeral homes and buried in the ground before reviving to undeath. But others were in street clothes or work clothes. One man wore only a bathrobe and boxers. Those were people who were killed and dragged away and never given a proper burial. Whoever had turned them had simply sat around waiting for them to come back to life.

Whoever had made them was making an army.

"This is not good," she whispered, glancing at a man in black who wore a white collar.

Giles said quietly, "This morning, a priest was reported missing. And an elderly lady wearing a jogging suit."

The priest was going after Angel. The old lady jogger growled menacingly at Giles himself.

The chubby guy in the bathrobe leered at Buffy. "Prepare yourself, Slayer," the vampire growled. "The Master has plans for you. You will make a most powerful slave."

Buffy spun, launched a high kick that took bathrobe boy in the chin and rocked his head back hard . . . but not hard enough to snap his neck, she thought with disappointment.

"Okay, people. *Former* people," Buffy corrected. "Maybe if you tell me what's going on, I'll let you live. Who's this master you're all so hot on? 'Cause I knew one guy who called himself that, but what's left of him is in some kid's sandbox somewhere."

The priest vamp laughed. "Soon you will know. When you bow down at his feet and beg for your life!"

As one, the vampires attacked. The priest, bathrobe boy, and a young girl with multiple nose rings and a stud through her lip all went after Angel. But behind them, things got worse. The next three hulking vamps were dressed in their Sunday best—the suits they were buried in. Young guys, not much older than Buffy when they died, and they looked vaguely familiar. She pushed the almost-recognition away. Maybe they'd played football for Sunnydale High or the parochial school two towns over. Buffy didn't want to know.

Giles was attacked by the lady in the jogging suit and a younger boy who looked no older than fourteen. Even as she fought off the vampire offensive line, Buffy kept an eye on Giles, concerned for his safety as always. But, as always, his skill surprised her. The old jogging lady was dispatched instantly. The boy proved to be a different matter indeed, making passes in the air with his hands and shooting out his legs as he twirled in huge, distracting circles.

Some kind of weird martial art, Buffy figured. Not something she'd seen before, though.

Whump! A fist connected with the side of her face. Not a solid hit, but even a graze of knuckles when the punch had vampiric strength behind it was enough to send her reeling.

"That'll teach me to pay attention," she mumbled to herself, and returned to the battle.

Pierced girl shot a kick up toward Angel's head, but he blocked her attack, parried, and sent her tumbling across the ground. The priest was right in front of him, and Angel kneed him in the gut, then he brought both fists down on the vampire's back, forcing him to the earth as well. The overweight guy in the bathrobe came at him then.

"Throw me a stake!" he shouted to Buffy.

But it was Giles who answered.

The Watcher ducked away from the youthful male vampire trying to gut him and hurried to the Slayer's bag. Half-turning, he was about to throw Angel a nicely carved stake when the boy vampire hurled himself at Giles. Giles's reaction was all instinct— the stake came up just in time, the boy shrieked and exploded into dust. Though the smallest bit taken aback, Giles didn't miss a beat as he tossed the stake to Angel.

As Angelus, he had been called "the Scourge of Europe." That was a different creature entirely, as far as he was concerned. But still, Angel was fierce in battle. With the stake in his hands, the other vampires didn't stand a chance. In moments, the priest was gone. Next, he took out the bathrobed man by flinging him onto his back and landing on top of him. Straddling him, Angel brought the stake down hard.

Of Angel's assailants, only the pierced girl remained. She sneered at Angel, "When we are gone, there will be more. My honorable lord has returned and he will conquer this land and grind your bones to dust."

"Returned? From where?" Buffy called out, anxious for information.

"If we all die, you'll never know," the girl said to Angel.

Angel looked at her for a beat, part of him unwilling to stake one so young. Then, as she bared her fangs and rushed him, he reflexively thrust the stake hard into her chest.

"Guess we'll have to take that chance," he said, as she exploded into dust.

Buffy saw Angel rush to help her, but she was faring just fine on her own. Already, one of the dead jocks had been dusted. The other two were persistent, and she'd fought them off several times without getting the opening she needed for a staking.

They moved around to trap her between them, and Buffy smiled. That trick hadn't worked the last time she'd been ambushed. It wasn't going to work now, either. They started in toward her. Buffy dropped to her hands, swept her legs around under her body in a move the gymnastics coach would have kissed her for, and took one of the dead jocks down at the knees. The other one was looming over her, but Buffy did a backwards handspring and brought both of her boots up into his face.

He grabbed his nose and eyes, staggered backwards, and didn't even look at her as the stake slid into his heart. While his buddy exploded in a cloud of ash, the last dead jock had started to get to his feet.

He never made it.

"Who's next?" Buffy shouted through the dust cloud, but the handful of remaining vampires broke into a run, fleeing like a pack in the same direction.

Buffy watched them a moment, thinking how odd it was that they should stay together. They were so much more . . . disciplined than vamps she'd seen before.

Panting, Buffy slid into Angel's now-empty arms and snagged a quick kiss. Giles approached, stake in hand. The three looked down at the piles of dust their conflict had left on the ground.

Then a chill wind kicked up, lifting the piles and scattering them. It whipped at Buffy's hair and clothes, stinging like buckshot.

"We should get out of here," Giles said, gathering up her Slayage equipment and stuffing it into her bag.

Angel took off his jacket and put it around her shoulders. "This is the second jacket of mine you've gotten," he teased her, having to yell over the wind. "Pretty soon I won't have anything to wear."

"That's a nice thought," she shouted back.

A bolt of lightning flashed across Angel's face and landed not five feet from them. Buffy shouted and jumped in surprise.

She turned, stared hard at something odd that had

been illuminated by the lightning. The departing vamps were running behind a figure who laughed and capered. Even now, Buffy could see her silhouetted in the moonlight.

"Oh, my God," Buffy whispered.

It looked like Willow.

CHAPTER 8

As was his custom, Sanno, the god whom men called King of the Mountain, rose from the dawn clouds surrounding Mount Hiei and walked the earth like a man. Each of his footsteps was like a small earthquake, summoning the faithful to greet him like the sun. For Sanno was a gracious god, benevolent and generous. He gave his people clear mountain springs to drink from, hares and other animals to devour, and wood for their villages and the castle of the local branch of the Fujiwara clan, nestled in the foothills of Mount Hiei. He anticipated their every need, and he provided for them.

So he walked, anticipating a fine morning with those who loved and revered him in the beauty of his shrine, on the far side of Mount Hiei.

But on this snowy winter morning, no one came.

Frowning in displeasure, he ascended Mount Hiei once more and with his mighty breath blew away the clouds. Then he looked down upon his lands and observed his people, gathered on the opposite side of Mount Hiei, cowering before the entrance to a newly erected temple with a strange, curved roof. Some of the women wept and tore their clothes. Their farmer husbands lay prostrate on the ground, their faces buried in the mud.

To the left of the wailing multitude, the local noble family sat on white tatami mats clothed in their formal kimonos adorned with the Fujiwara clan crest. They sat unmoving, like statues, mute and pale with grief. Sanno knew them well. Husband, wife, and son he saw, but not their beautiful daughter, Gemmyo, named after the Empress who had reigned some seventy years before.

Of late Sanno had thought of marrying Gemmyo, for should not gods possess all the happiness that mortals do? She was the loveliest maiden in the environs of his mountain, and the most gentle as well. Additionally, she was skilled in music and song. Many nights, he had made the earth tremble violently while dancing to the lively melodies of her koto.

He descended to earth again and walked into the midst of his worshipers, searching both for signs of Gemmyo and for the cause of all this distress.

At the sight of him, the villagers and nobles exchanged glances among themselves. Eyes red, chins quivering, they parted to make him a path as he advanced toward the entrance of the new, oddly fashioned temple.

Within the structure, beneath a canopy decorated with stars and on a bier of red satin lay his beloved. Gemmyo's eyes were shut as if in repose. She was dressed in a beautiful white kimono decorated with herons. At first glance, one might think that she was asleep, even though her body was stark white. For on occasion, it was not unheard of for women to paint themselves with an ivory sheen.

But at her neck gaped two large wounds, and from these wounds blood had run onto the folds of her gown.

Sanno caught his breath, realizing that she had been foully murdered and by the vilest of demons: a vampire.

His eyes filled with ungovernable rage. The pulse at his neck throbbed with fury. Thunder and lightning crackled and roared across the sky and the clouds quickly gathered. The earth rolled like the back of a dragon disturbed from its slumber.

Sanno whirled on the hapless villagers, who stood in stark terror, and bellowed at them, "Who did this?"

No one spoke.

Sanno stomped his foot against the earth and it cracked.

"Who did this?" he bellowed again.

The villagers remained silent.

Then, as Sanno prepared to shake the earth to pieces beneath their feet, a wizened old man staggered forward. Though it was cold, he wore no shoes and his coat was made of straw. Sanno recognized him as Genji, a poor farmer whose wife was dead and who had no children to serve him in his old age. He had come often to pray at Sanno's shrine.

The old man feebly raised a hand and said, "Sanno-no-kami, these cowardly villagers are silent because the murderer of Gemmyo has threatened them with death if they name him. But I am very old, and I have prayed often for happiness in my declining years. Now I see that my prayers are answered, for I, and I alone, dare to challenge your enemy. If it means my death to reveal his identity to you, then I shall die happy."

In the clutches of his anger, Sanno reached for his great, ancient sword and said, "Speak then, Genji, and know that if your courage deserts you, I shall kill you myself."

The old man shook his head and bowed low several times. "Please, my gracious lord, do not trouble yourself. I'm glad to speak his name aloud. He is Chirayoju."

At the mention of the name, the other villagers drew back in horror. A few began to weep, others to wail.

"Chirayoju?" Sanno repeated. "I know no *tengu* by that name."

Genji said, "He is a vampire who has flown over the sea from the great land of China. And he is a sorcerer who can set fire to our houses with the merest flick of his wrist. He can fan the flames with the smallest exhalation of his breath. And he has promised to do all this if we tell you who he is. For this reason, all fear his wrath. But I shall burn myself to death willingly before I displease you, great Sanno-sama."

"You foolish old man!" shouted another villager, a young man named Akio. He ran to Genji and struck him down with his fist. "You've doomed our whole village!"

"No. *You* have done so," Sanno replied to the youth.

The Mountain God stomped violently on the earth, forcing Akio to his knees. Then he raised his sword and brought it down on Akio's neck, beheading him.

Sanno stomped until no one could stand. He took the heads of those nearest. Then he whirled around and from his hands shot flames of purification onto the body of Gemmyo, so that she might enter Paradise.

The flames traveled from her body to the canopy of stars, to the rest of the temple in which she lay, to the trees, and to the huts of the villagers. And over the trees and bushes to the garrisoned keep of Gemmyo's Fujiwara clan.

That day, a thousand people died because of Sanno's fury.

No longer was he seen as benevolent or kind. No longer was he worshiped.

He was only feared.

CHAPTER 9

Panting in the backseat of her car, Cordelia pushed Xander away. "Stop moaning," she ordered, sitting up. She leaned into view of the rearview mirror and fluffed her bangs. "I hate it when you moan."

"Wh—wh—" he panted back.

"Because when you moan," she continued, answering the question he had been unable to ask, "it reminds me that it's you, okay?"

"Reminds you . . . *oh.*" Xander scowled at her. "Isn't that lovely? So what you're saying is that when you're with me, you pretend you're with someone else."

When she said nothing, only turned and blinked at him in that blank, yeah-so? expression of hers, he looked at her in complete disgust.

"Okay, fine. I am outta here," he said. He flailed for the door handle. Cordelia reached around his head, obligingly flicked the handle, pushed open the door, and let him fall half out of the car.

"I am so outta here that I am . . . really outta here." He scooted backward the rest of the way and tumbled to the sidewalk. Standing, he regained his footing, if not his dignity, and slammed the car door shut.

"Fine!" Cordelia scrambled back into the driver's seat and started the car. She peeled out and shot down the street.

"Buckle your seat belt!" Xander bellowed. "You nympho!"

She roared down the street, tires squealing.

Xander stomped to the porch and sat down, pulling his knees beneath his chin. He sighed. Wished he'd brought something to do. Even his homework. Now there was a novel notion.

He was just about to doze off when he heard light footsteps on the walk. He opened his eyes and sat up.

"Will," he said happily. "I was worried about you."

Willow stood with her legs wide apart and her hands on her hips. "Little boy," she sneered, "you worry for me?"

"Well, sure, Will," he said slowly. "Um, have you been forgetting to eat again? Because I know the computer can be all fun and everything, but you're kind of grouchy and perhaps the blood sugar has plummeted? So—"

"Silence!" Willow ordered.

"Willow?" He gave her the Nicholson eyebrow. "Are you trying out for a play or something? Because otherwise, I think this is an act you should drop. You are not exactly making friends and influencing people. We want to help you, if you'll just let us."

Willow's face seemed to change. For a moment she looked very sad and little-girl-lost. He went to her with open arms, fully expecting her to slide into them and finish that cry she'd begun last Monday morning.

"Xander," she said miserably, coming toward him. She was limping. Her hands went up to her head as if she had a monster hangover. Which she would not, she being Willow.

"Xander, something's very wro—"

And then she shouted, "No!"

She flew at him, kicking him in the face before he had time to react. Then she landed on top of him and pushed him back, grabbing his hair and slamming his skull against the porch. She made a fist and rammed it into his face. Hit him again. And again. She pummeled him with both fists as he fought to throw her off.

"Wi . . . Wi . . ." Blood streamed down into his throat. He began to choke on it, until the only sound he could make was a desperate gurgle.

"Ah, the scent of life is upon you," Willow said. She threw back her head and laughed. Then, just as he thought she was going to let him up, she hit him again, very hard.

Fade to black.

Very black.

The familiar squeal of tires. Chirayoju looked up from the boy and listened. The mother of Weeping Willow was about to drive down the street. She would see the form of her daughter crouched over her young friend and she would ask far too many questions.

Chirayoju stood and picked up the body. Hoisting the boy over its head, Chirayoju walked to the side of the porch and unceremoniously dumped him in the bushes. Chirayoju was furious at having been interrupted: the youth was not yet dead. His spirit would be delicious. With its sorcery, Chirayoju fed not on mere blood, but on the essence of life itself.

But not this night.

The car pulled up.

"Honey?" Mrs. Rosenberg said as she got out of the car. "What are you doing here? I thought you had a tutoring session with Buffy."

"It ended early," Chirayoju answered. "I wasn't feeling all that hot and Buffy said she was coming down with something, too. Xander gave me a ride," it assured Willow's mother, who was looking concerned.

"I've been kind of nervous ever since you were attacked," the woman admitted.

Yes, ever since your daughter was attacked, you have allowed me to take her over and use her. You will allow me to kill her. You Western mothers and fathers, with your blindness and self-interest, allowing your children to wander the streets like orphans. Is it a wonder that they are all so weak and foolish? That I have pickings here the like of which I never saw in ancient China and Japan, where the parents were more careful?

It took every ounce of Chirayoju's strength not to burst into laughter and crack the woman's spine in two, then drink the life, the spirit, from her paralyzed and dying body. But it needed shelter from the coming dawn, and the sanctuary it had found elsewhere was a distance away. More importantly, it had become apparent that all the girl's friends were vampire hunters—and the lovely blond maiden was their leader—and it saw no point in revealing itself to them at this moment. Or perhaps at any moment.

So when the woman came up to it, put her hand on the forehead of its host, and said, "You feel hot. Come on inside, sweetie," it meekly obeyed.

As soon as the door is shut, it promised itself, *she dies.*

Such a puny body could be easily hidden.

"Okay. One more time," Buffy said to Giles. Angel, glancing through a book that featured various incantations against "vampyres and other creatures most abhorrent," set it down and listened.

She held out her hand. "Vampires." Held out her other hand. "Demons." Juggled. "Demonic possession."

"Yes. Quite right," Giles said. He looked proud of Buffy. Angel knew the feeling. Buffy was the one thing in his life he could point to with unmitigated pride.

Then Buffy made a face and juggled again. "But vampiric possession? Oh, Giles, I don't know."

"How else can one explain what you saw?" Giles asked. He looked to Angel as if for backup. Angel shrugged. He was just about as perplexed as Buffy.

"None of this sounds at all familiar to me," he had to admit, flicking the pages of the book as if the answers lay there. "I've never come across anything like it. As far as I know, vampires can't possess the living."

"However," Giles mused, "one could argue that vampirism is a form of demonic possession. Vampires are basically soulless human corpses with demons residing within." He had the grace to clear his throat and say, "Present company excepted."

"I'll go along with that," Angel conceded. "But the demons who inhabit vampires can't jump from body to body, or influence another person the way other demons can. There was that vessel thing with the Master, but that was just a vicarious way for him to feed."

"Well, I'm very sorry I didn't pay closer attention to your concerns about Willow," Giles said to Buffy. "Clearly, something quite serious is happening to her and—"

Buffy shifted uneasily. "I don't know what I saw. I thought it looked like Willow, but maybe it wasn't. I only saw it for an instant. Maybe I thought I saw her because I'm so worried about her." She gazed at the phone. "I'd like to call and check on her, but her mother would kill her. And then mine would kill me."

"It's been a very long day . . . and night, for all of us. Perhaps it's best that we wait until the morning," Giles agreed. "I'm certain Willow will be at school, and all will come clear." His half-smile was only half-reassuring.

"Come on, I'll walk you home," Angel said, taking Buffy's hand.

"Okay," she said, with her quick, eager smile that sometimes cut him to the quick.

Once outside the school, Angel took Buffy in his arms and kissed her long and hard. He couldn't believe that of all the mortal girls there were in this world, he had fallen in love with the Slayer. And knowing that she loved him too made his strange and lonely existence more bearable. He was an outcast among vampires, yet still one of them, and sometimes her love was all that sustained him. That, and his vow to rid the earth of his brother and sister abhorrent creatures of the night.

He smiled down at her as she peered up at him with her huge blue eyes. She had no idea what dark thoughts were running through his mind.

She murmured, "Angel, I'm so confused."

"Why?" He trailed his fingers through her hair.

"It's just that . . ." She shrugged and laid her head against his chest. "Well, like with Willow. She's been acting like such a b . . . bad person, bad, and so cranky and all. So then we get attacked by vampires and I decide I see her with them."

"You might have."

"No. In my heart, I know Willow's not possessed. She's just scared. I can't believe I would even think such a thing. But then, it's like my mom and me."

"She thinks you're possessed?" Angel said, amused. He suspected he knew what was coming.

Buffy did not disappoint.

"It seems like half my life, my mom is saying, 'Buffy, this just isn't like you.' Whenever I've done something to disappoint her. But if it wasn't like me, I wouldn't have done it. I couldn't have done it." She tilted her head back and gazed up at him. "Do you know what I mean?"

He let his smile fade so that she wouldn't think he

was laughing at her, but his heart went out to her. There was nothing he could do to spare her from growing up.

"I think so," he replied.

"Look at Xander and Cordelia," she went on. "Talk about possessed. They can't even explain why they do what they do." She shuddered. "I mean, it's just so weird."

Chuckling, he nodded. Xander and Cordelia had surprised him, too. But when he thought about it, the spark had always been there. The way they bantered, throwing barbs at each other. Hotheaded and passionate, both of them.

Yes, it made sense.

"It was a lot easier when I was your age," he told her. "When people did the unexpected, we said they were possessed and left it at that." He moved his shoulders. "Actually, we didn't leave it at that. We usually burned them at the stake or hanged them. Or, on a good day, we committed them to asylums."

He cupped her chin. "A strong-willed girl like you would have been labeled a witch. We'd definitely have burned you."

"'C'mon, baby, light my fire,'" she quipped, but he could tell he had unnerved her.

He knew that sometimes she forgot how old he was—242 to her 17. It was easy to forget because when he had been turned into a creature of the night, he had been near her age. The decades had not aged his physical appearance at all.

Some of the mortal women he had known through the years had considered that a blessing . . . and begged him to change them at the height of their beauty. That he had not done, once his soul was restored to him. Not one could have fathomed the curse he would have laid upon their shoulders had he done so.

"Your mother sees all that's best in you," Angel told Buffy as he traced the hollow of her cheek. She, too, was a beauty, but like many truly astonishing women, she didn't see it. "Your face is the mirror of her love for you. When she looks at you and sees a flaw, a part of her blames herself for failing you in some way."

He cupped her chin and raised her face toward his. "That's why she's so hard on you, Buffy. Because she loves you so much."

"I'm her mirror?" Buffy asked tentatively. She thought that over. "Her cracked mirror," she snorted.

"No. Clear as glass," he said. "Pure."

She shook her head. "Not me."

"Yes. You."

"But what about you, Angel?" She was changing the subject. He let her. "You don't have a reflection."

"When I look at you, I do."

He kissed her, tentatively at first, then with more passion. She answered back, and he held her tightly. With all his heart, he wanted to be what Buffy wanted him to be. He wanted to be exactly what she needed. But he was a vampire, a half-demon, with a human soul warring against the darkness within every moment of every day.

And he blamed himself fully for the many times he had failed her in the past. If there was any way he could undo what he had done . . .

"Angel," Buffy whispered, "I love you."

"I love you, too, Buffy."

"I want—" she began, but he stilled her voice with a finger across her lips.

"Let me walk you home now," he said gently.

They strolled arm in arm, like a girl and a guy going home from a date.

In Willow's room, Chirayoju got ready for bed and listened to the boy's slowing heartbeat in the bushes outside the house. The youth would very likely be dead before dawn. If not, Chirayoju knew it would have another chance at the boy. Xander. He cared for Weeping Willow, and it would be the death of him.

The vampire sorcerer glided to the high windows and looked out. In the darkness, it could see the silhouettes of its minions, the many vampires it had pressed into its service, as well as those it had caused to be created. Those that had already hunted and were sated for the night had gathered near the home of Weeping Willow, where their master resided, to pay homage to him until the dawn forced them to seek shelter.

Chirayoju had begun to build its army. A small force, true. But growing with each passing night. Or it would have been, if not for the damnable vampire Slayer. As Chirayoju continued to gain strength, it would need more time to assemble its troops, not as in the days of old when it could command entire villages to rise up as one. But once it had reached its full strength, not even the Slayer would stop it from building a regiment of the dead large enough to enslave all the lands touched by the light of the moon.

A cold breeze whistled through the open window.

It thought of the cherry blossoms on the mountains of Japan, and the beautiful trees that had once bloomed in the garden in Sunnydale. Even now, it saw their quivering phantoms, recalling its peace as it had sat among them, plucking from the earth a withered bonsai tree to begin its shrine in the girl's room.

Willow's mother knocked on the door. Chirayoju said, "Yes?"

"Honey, I'm . . . are you all right?"

"I'm fine," Chirayoju snapped. "Just tired."

There was a pause. "You don't seem yourself."

Chirayoju crossed to the mirror on the wall and stared into it. Through sheer force of will, the girl's features blurred and its own floated over them like a shimmering green diaphanous mask. It grinned at the fury it saw there. The unconquerable spirit. The vitality and strength of purpose.

"I am myself, Mom," Chirayoju answered. "Who else would I be?"

Willow's mother gave a short, awkward laugh. "I guess that's the question most parents of teenagers ask themselves."

She pushed the door open, came in, and sat on Willow's bed.

"You were so cute and little when you were born," she said wistfully. "I held you for hours, just staring down at you. I couldn't believe how perfect you were. Your hands and feet. Each finger, each toe."

The woman picked up a pillow and held it against her chest. "The first time you had a temper tantrum, I was so shocked. My perfect little baby! But I was proud of you, too. You were becoming independent."

She plucked at the corner of the pillow. "As soon as a baby is born, she spends her days learning how to leave her parents' care. First she rolls away, and then she crawls away, and then she walks away."

She sighed. "But I have hope that in the end, when she's all grown up, she'll come back. Not as my little baby, of course." She smiled. "But maybe as my friend."

Chirayoju stared at her. It couldn't believe her utter weakness. Nor that she honestly believed that the parent, who should be idolized and worshiped as a god, could be looked upon with such lack of respect that he—or she—would be treated as a friend.

When it conquered this land, it would ensure that all such thinking was banished.

Even by the dead.

It smiled. "I hope that, too, Mom," it said.

She was alive only because as they had entered the house, it had realized that if it murdered her, there would be an investigation. Because she was an adult, there would be too many questions. Already, the authorities were looking into some of the deaths it had caused—the holy man, the old lady killed by his minions. But the boy in the bushes was only a boy, and children died in all kinds of tragic and unexplained ways, even in these modern times.

In fact, especially in these modern times of drive-by shootings and incredible violence. And especially in this place, the Hellmouth, where evil flourished and grew.

So it was safe to kill the boy. He was disposable. And unnecessary to the furthering of its ambition.

Willow's mother crossed to it and kissed it softly

on her daughter's cheek. It was very sorry that it could not kill her. Every time Weeping Willow heard her voice, she fought to regain possession of her being. Chirayoju found her struggles distracting and slightly tiring.

With time, it would obliterate her, and she would struggle no longer.

Outside, the boy's heartbeat slowed even further. Soon, very soon, his struggles would also end.

CHAPTER 10

"Mirror, mirror, on the wall," Buffy said to herself as she checked her visual presentation in the girls' bathroom. Around her, girls milled and talked about guys and clothes. The pleasant aspects of teenage-hood. And the not so pleasant: homework and fights with their parents.

The pleasant stuff she couldn't really relate to. The other stuff, sadly, she knew all too well: last night her mom had gotten a gander at her latest catch of "below averages." And when she said, "Buffy, is this the way it's always going to be?" Buffy tried to remember Angel's lovely speech about how she was a mirror and her mom loved that mirror, but all it felt like was that she was in for seven years of really hard labor.

A few girls said hi to Buffy but no one really rushed over to get her autograph or hear what she had to say about *Dawson's Creek*. She had no other real girl buds except for Willow. She missed Willow—her version of Willow, not the update, Will version 6.66—more than ever.

In fact, she sort of missed the way things had been when she'd first come to Sunnydale—the basic threesome of her, Willow, and Xander: the Three Musketeers, one for all and all for one. Now Willow and Oz were getting together, and Xander and Cordy were doing whatever it was they called it. Their friendships had changed, and that had changed their lives.

On the other hand, she had Angel. As if that wasn't weird enough.

But since she was the Slayer, relationships had to take a back seat. Top priority was figuring out who the new top vamp in town was. So far, she'd had no luck beyond being haunted by the idea that the lithe figure she'd seen in the cemetery the night before had been Willow.

She meandered out of the bathroom and was about to have a post-Starbucks, pre-first-period chat with Giles when Cordelia rushed toward her with her cell phone in hand. Buffy raised her brows and waited for whatever bombshell Cordy was about to detonate. Probably about a run in Buffy's pantyhose, or the fact that her hair was "askew," as Willow would put it. It was true: bad hair day was upon the Slayer. Cordelia's revelation would not be news.

Cordelia stopped short, looked left, right, must have decided none of the Cordettes could possibly witness her speaking to one of the untouchables, and rushed over to Buffy.

"Buffy," she said, taking a breath, "Xander isn't in school today. And neither is Willow."

"Ah ha," Buffy said slowly. "And you're thinking what? Xander and Willow have eloped to Las Vegas?"

"I'm thinking, Miss Slayer, that I left Xander at Willow's last night because he was all so worried about her, and now they're missing."

Buffy considered. "Given the fact that we live on the Hellmouth, and that Willow has been acting more like you than herself—"

"And that Xander and I have been, ah, meeting for breakfast every morning and he would have called if he had to skip . . . breakfast," Cordelia insisted.

"Have you considered that maybe he's mad at you and just blew you off?" Buffy suggested.

Cordelia rolled her eyes. "Trust me. Xander would not miss one of our . . . breakfast . . . meetings if he had a choice in the matter." She huffed. "C'mon, Buffy, this is *me* we're talking about. I mean, I know I feel like I must have done something horrible in a past life to be so completely unable to control my attractions, but Xander . . . Xander must feel like he's won the lottery. He wouldn't just not show."

Hard as it was for Buffy to admit it, she did see Cordelia's point. Xander was, after all, a guy.

"What did he say when you called him?" Buffy asked, looking down at Cordelia's cell phone.

Cordelia looked as if Buffy had shot her. "When *I* called *him?* Buffy, excuse me, I do not call boys. They call me."

"Except if they're dead," Buffy said, letting her irritation show.

"Ooh." Cordelia whipped open her cell phone and demon-dialed Xander's number.

"I was changing my nail appointment, you know," she said to Buffy, then blinked and nodded at Buffy. "Hello, Mrs. Harris?" she asked sweetly. "This is Cordelia. What? Cordelia *Chase!* Xander must have told you about . . . May I *speak* to Xander? *What?*" She looked stricken. "The police?"

"Oh, my God," Buffy whispered. "What? What?"

"Okay. Yes, of course. Yes, of course I do. I will. Good-bye."

Cordelia whipped the phone shut and grabbed Buffy's forearm. She had a surprisingly firm grip.

"Buffy, Xander never came home last night." Her eyes were actually welling with tears. "His family thinks he might have been abducted or murdered or whatever, you know, with all these missing persons lately." She pressed her fingertips against her eyelids and choked back a sob. "And if he's dead, the last thing I told him was to stop moaning."

Buffy took that in but moved on. "What about Willow? Call her house, too." Now Buffy was sorry she hadn't gone ahead and phoned last night, no matter how late it had been.

Cordelia handed her the phone. "You. I don't know her number."

Buffy punched it in. Waited. There was no answer. She hit redial, in case someone in the Rosenberg household was using call waiting. There was still nothing, not even the phone machine. She traded stricken glances with Cordelia.

"Giles," they said in one voice.

They raced to the library. "We'll get him to cover for us," Buffy said. "We can spend all day off campus without getting busted for anything. He's got all these amazing hall passes they never tell us students about, Cordelia. Work furlough thingies or something."

"I always knew this place was just a well-disguised prison," Cordelia muttered. She skidded on the tiled floor. "Of course I had to wear heels today."

Shoulder to shoulder, Buffy and Cordelia pushed open the double doors to find Giles speaking very seriously to Oz and handing him a large canvas sack that clanked as Oz took it. The two guys looked startled, then both relaxed.

"Hi, girls," Oz said. "Just picking up the new and improved Oz-wolf restraint system." He pointed moonward. "It's that time of the month."

"Oh." Buffy nodded. "Werewolf time. Understood. Um." Oz had recently learned that due to a little finger nip from his cousin Jordy, he turned into a werewolf three nights of every month. Willow understood, which was very nice. In fact, all the Scooby Gang understood. It wasn't his fault, and he never hurt anyone.

Oz peered at her. "Are you okay? Is everything all right?"

"Sure." She smiled and elbowed Cordelia, who lit up like a Christmas tree.

"Everything is super-duper," Cordelia assured him.

"I hope Willow gets over that stomach virus soon," he said, and started to leave.

"Wait," Buffy said urgently, grabbing his arm, then let go of him and cleared her throat. "You spoke to her?"

"Got an e-mail. See ya."

Clank, clank, clank, he was out the door.

"If she's sending e-mail, maybe she's okay," Cordelia said, at the same time that Buffy ran up to Giles and said, "You've got to cover for us. Xander and Willow are missing."

"Yes, yes, of course," he began, a worried expression on his face, "but what—"

"I'll drive," Cordelia said. "I'm the obvious choice."

"Since you have the car, and a license, and y'know, know how . . . I'll go along with that," Buffy said. "Pit stop at my locker for my Slayage stuff."

They whirled and left. Behind them Giles called, "Yes, all right. But what's going on?"

"Please don't kill me," Buffy murmured as they shot around the corner and headed down the straightaway toward Willow's house.

"You sound just like Xander," Cordelia said. "Only, I can understand it from him. He's lived in Sunnydale all his life. Home of the five, count them, five, major traffic intersections. But you've lived in L.A."

"Just jumpy, I guess," Buffy said. "And more aware that it's possible to die at an early age."

"Here we are."

Cordelia slammed on the brakes just as Buffy, having been warned, rolled herself forward like you do when your 747's going down. Cordelia sighed, irritated, but flew out of the car and chittered toward the walk in her very high heels.

Buffy, in knee boots, met her there, then stopped Cordelia from leaping onto the porch.

"We don't know who or what is in there," she whispered. "No one answered the phone."

"Oh, right." Cordelia was wide-eyed, excited and scared at the same time.

"Let's look around first," Buffy said quietly. "I'll go left and you—"

"I'll go left, too," Cordelia said firmly.

"All right. Stay behind me."

Buffy hefted her Slayer's bag, making sure she had both a stake and a cross within easy reach. It was the middle of the day, of course, but you never knew what you were going to run into in Sunnydale. She scrutinized the lawn as they tiptoed silently over it, seeing nothing that would cause any alarm.

They came to a cluster of bushes. Buffy parted the nearest one. Nothing. She moved to the next one and crept around it.

On the other side Xander lay, his face mottled and bruised, as still and white as death.

"Oh, my God!" Cordelia shrieked.

The front door burst open and Buffy whipped around, stake in hand, ready for a fight.

Instead, she saw Willow's mom in her chenille bathrobe, her eyes ringed as if she hadn't had any sleep.

"Buffy, what's wrong?" she cried.

"Mrs. Rosenberg, go call 911. It's Xander."

"He's dead," Cordelia wailed, throwing herself across Xander's still form. "Oh, my God!"

Mrs. Rosenberg started to go toward Xander, but Buffy took her firmly by the arm and led her into the kitchen. She took the portable out of its charger and punched in 911. "Where's Willow?" she asked.

"She took off," Mrs. Rosenberg said anxiously. "I've been hoping and praying for a call, but . . ."

"I called here about half an hour ago," Buffy said.

"Emergency services," the operator said.

"There's been an accident," Buffy announced. "Please send an ambulance." She handed the phone to Willow's mom to give out the particulars of her address. Buffy was so freaked out that she couldn't remember Willow's house number.

Then she flew down the hall and into Willow's room while Mrs. Rosenberg dashed outside to check on Xander.

As Mrs. Rosenberg had said, the room was empty. The bed was unmade, and Willow's stuffed animals lay in clumps on the floor. In twisted, headless clumps, Buffy noticed, as she bent and examined one of them, a tiny white unicorn. A pencil had been driven through its chest.

Her hair stood on end. Her face was hot. *Willow, what's happened to you?* she asked silently.

Then the computer announced, "You have mail." Buffy stood and walked to it. She clicked on Willow's mailbox. It was from Oz.

Hope you feel better. Drink lots of liquids and take a lot of vitamin C, he had written. *P.S. Luv ya.*

So they were still in the puppy phase, not having progressed to the more committed conjugation of the verb, which was, *I love you.*

Next to the computer was a little dried-up bush. Buffy picked it up and examined it. It looked vaguely familiar, but she couldn't place where she'd seen something like it before.

Beside it lay a foreign coin. No. It was the disk Willow had accidentally knocked off the big Japanese sword on the wall. And beside that, a little green flower made of folded paper. Buffy stared at it a moment. Her heart pounding, she unfolded it.

A siren blared outside. Red and blue lights strobed through the venetian blinds. The ambulance had arrived.

Buffy put the disk and the tree in her Slayer's bag. As she moved from the room, she unfolded the note. It read, *I'm sorry.*

"The paramedics are here," Mrs. Rosenberg called. "They'd like to speak to you, Buffy."

Without speaking she nodded and dropped the note into her bag as well. She would show them to Giles.

Walking back down the hall, she stumbled and fell against the wall. She was trembling from head to toe, terrified for her friends. Tears streamed down her face. If she lost them, if she lost any of them because of who and what she was, she would never forgive herself. Ever.

Which is the burden Angel carries, she realized sharply. He had not only lost loved ones, he had killed them himself, and done it with a song in his heart, as he had once told her.

She shivered, pitying him beyond words.

Then she ran to the ambulance, following Xander's gurney. He was strapped to the cot. Blood and liquids dripped into his right arm, and there was an oxygen mask covering his face.

"I'm going with," Cordelia insisted, scrambling into the ambulance.

"Me, too," Buffy said.

Cordy sighed. "All right, I'm not leaving my car here, so we'll drive."

This ride in Cordelia's car was significantly different. Not that Cordelia was any more cautious or skilled than before. But this time, Buffy said nothing. She was preoccupied with her fear. Fear that Xander could die, though it now seemed he would be all right with a transfusion and a few days' bed rest. Fear that Willow might already be dead. All of it because she had not focused on finding the vampire that was organizing a new wave of horrors that swept across Sunnydale.

And now seemed to be focused on Buffy and her friends.

But there was another fear building inside Buffy. One that she wanted very much to push away, to ignore. Instead, it started to overwhelm her with its logic. Fear that she *had* seen Willow the night before, in the cemetery, silhouetted in moonlight. And now Willow was gone, and the note she had left behind was an apology. For what? Buffy thought she knew, and her suspicions made her sick and afraid.

Vampiric possession. It had seemed just a theory last night. Now it seemed one of the most horrifying possibilities she had ever encountered.

Despite technological advances that would have made futurists such as H. G. Wells and George Orwell faint with amazement, the world's scientific community hadn't been able to make an international phone line which didn't have that hollow, tinny quality that Giles found so annoying. It had taken him several phone calls to finally track down the phone number he was looking for, and when he finally did, he hesitated to use it.

In Sunnydale, it was just about noontime. But in

Tokyo, Japan, it was already five o'clock the following morning. He didn't relish the idea of waking a seventy-three-year-old man at the crack of dawn. But, then, he didn't have much choice, and even less time to quibble over social courtesies.

After he'd dialed the number, Giles was pleased to hear it ringing clear on the other end. Hollow and tinny, yes, but at least without that horrible echo that sometimes accompanies international long distance and makes real conversation almost impossible.

There was a click, the sound of the phone being picked up on the other end. *"Mushimushi?"*

"Ohayo gozaimasu," Giles said, in the little Japanese he had learned for this call. *"America kara, Giles desu . . ."*

"Ah, the esteemed Professor Giles," the man replied in perfect English. "This is Kobo. It is an honor to speak with you. Your Japanese is excellent, but if you would be so kind, I would enjoy taking this opportunity to practice my English."

Giles smiled to himself, despite the gravity of the situation. He had never spoken to Kobo before, but he knew the man by reputation. And his response fulfilled Giles's expectations completely. For Giles's Japanese, what little of the language he knew, was horrible. Kobo had offered to speak English not because he wanted practice—he was obviously fluent—but because he wanted to save Giles the embarrassment of speaking Japanese so very badly.

The Japanese culture was so completely different from American culture—or any Western culture for that matter, including his own—that at times it was difficult for Giles to remember just how different.

The Japanese would never address a subject directly when it could be gotten to by a more circuitous route. And certainly, they would never embarrass someone else, or even allow them to embarrass themselves, for fear of humiliating themselves, or losing face, as they called it.

Kobo was a traditionalist. Giles would have to tread carefully in this conversation in order not to offend the old man. However, he did feel that he possessed a certain advantage in that he was British, more reserved than an American, and, one hoped, less brash and impatient. At least, that was how he had been when he'd arrived in Sunnydale.

But when one spent the majority of one's time in the company not only of Americans, but Southern Californians, and to add to that, Southern Californian adolescents, one could no longer assume that one's cultural reflexes remained intact. After all, even the sarcastic young Xander had referred to him recently as "one happ'nin' dude." And only with a certain amount of irony . . .

"Thank you, *sensei,*" he said, using the Japanese word for "teacher," the highest title of honor there was in that language beyond prostrating oneself before the gods and the Emperor. Besides, it was an accurate title: Kobo was a professor at Tokyo University.

"Please forgive me for waking you at this unconscionable hour, but I am in the midst of a rather urgent matter and I had hoped you might be able to illuminate certain areas where my own records and research are lacking."

There was silence for several moments at the other end. If it hadn't been for the crackle and hiss of the open line, Giles would have thought he'd lost the connection. When the Great Teacher spoke at last, his words came as a great surprise.

"I knew your grandmother," the old Japanese man said.

"My . . ."

"She was the greatest Watcher I ever knew," Kobo-*sensei* continued.

"That's very kind of you," Giles said, slightly taken aback. "She spoke very highly of you as well, *sensei*. In fact, she often said that everything that she knew she learned from you."

"Ah, no, it was she who was the teacher, Professor Giles. Your grandmother was already a Watcher when I knew her," Kobo replied. "I would be honored to be of whatever humble assistance I can."

Giles pushed up his glasses and leaned on his elbow as he gestured to the piles of books on his desk, despite knowing the man couldn't see him.

"Well, to be honest, I have had little time to even begin my own research on the matter at hand. At the moment, I'm still attempting to put together a hypothesis from which to begin."

Giles told the retired Watcher all that had happened in Sunnydale thus far, including the behavior of the vampires that had been stalking Buffy, as well as the events at the museum, and Willow's, and now Xander's, disappearance. As he hadn't heard from Buffy since she and Cordelia had left, he had to assume something was going on. Given Buffy's position as Slayer, and their geographic location in the Hellmouth, it was a safe assumption.

"If you know anything about this Sanno deity, it might be helpful," Giles mentioned. "I am a bit confused, however, because I've found no references to vampires at all in Japanese legend."

"Excuse me, please, Giles-*sensei*. Though I am certain your research was exhaustive, I can only suggest that the texts you consulted were unfortunately incomplete. The truth is that there are few, if any, *Japanese* vampires in Japanese legend," the old man said, his voice crackling over the line. "In our stories, vampires are usually portrayed as Chinese, due to the historical rivalry between our two nations."

"I see," Giles said carefully, not wishing to force the professor to rehash any painful past history of his nation.

"In fact, most of them probably *were* Chinese in antiquity. China was a more advanced nation, where the undead were more likely to be discovered and effectively hunted. Japan must have seemed fertile territory at the time."

"An excellent point," Giles allowed.

"You honor me." The old man cleared his throat. "As for Sanno, if he is the Mountain King from the legends I am familiar with, I know him as *Oyamagui no kami*. I'm sure he has other names. It's an old legend, and not one that is often repeated. Though I do seem to recall . . ."

The old man paused a moment before continuing. "Excuse me, please, but are the collected Watchers' Journals available to you, Professor Giles?"

"Yes, of course." He would be horribly remiss as Buffy's Watcher if he did not have a full set.

"How fortunate. Do you recall Claire Silver?"

Giles searched his memory for several seconds before recognition hit him. "I have examined her journals," he said, "but the last time I did so in depth was years ago."

Silence again on the other end of the line. Giles thought again of the Japanese traditions of honor and face, and wondered if, despite his required compliments, Kobo might be quietly disapproving of Giles's lack of knowledge on this subject. Of the Watchers left alive, Kobo-*sensei* was one of the most respected. The idea that the man might look down on Giles's performance as a Watcher had not actually occurred to him until now, pressed as he was to help Buffy, and now that it had, the tone in the older man's voice was unmistakable, no matter how hard he tried to hide it behind politeness.

"I respectfully suggest, Giles-*sensei,* that a man of your scholarly achievements might find Claire Silver's journals instructive," the old man said. "I seem to recall discussion of the King of the Mountain in them. But the last time I read them was a very long time ago, when I still had a Slayer to watch over. Thus I have allowed the story to slip from memory."

There! Giles thought. That was a barb, for certain. An implication that Giles himself had been lax in his duties by not committing more of the Watchers' Journals to memory. He ignored it. The information he required was more important than saving face for himself.

"But Claire Silver was a Watcher in Britain in the nineteenth century," Giles countered. "What has that got to do with ancient Japan?"

"Sadly, I have told you all I can remember, Mr. Giles," Kobo said simply. "I fear that I have wasted your valuable time."

Giles paused before replying. The old Watcher

had admitted he didn't know everything. But for Giles not to defend the man, even to himself, would be a direct insult. Kobo might have insulted him, but he had done it indirectly. Even if it was just for appearance' sake, or for the memory of his grandmother, Giles would do what was expected of him.

"Oh, no, *sensei*," Giles insisted, "you have been a great deal of help. Your wisdom and experience are unparalleled and you honor me with your assistance. I thank you. I am certain that this conversation will be of great help. It might even save the life of the current Chosen One, as well as several of her friends."

This time, Giles actually heard Kobo sigh. "Giles-*sensei*," the old Watcher said slowly, as if reluctant to speak. His amiable tone was obviously forced now. "I must applaud your dedication to the Chosen One, for of course I have heard of it. Ah, yet it is most unusual for a Watcher to place the satisfaction of the Slayer, even her well-being, and particularly the well-being of her *friends*, above the mission of the Chosen One. Few Slayers have ever *had* friends. You honor her by your loyalty to her many needs, even those that may seem frivolous to an old Japanese man."

Giles froze, stared at the phone as if it were the offending object, as if it had insulted him.

"I apologize if such concerns do not meet with your standards for the appropriate behavior of a Watcher," Giles snapped. "And, with all due respect, sir, and as you pointed out, at least the Slayer I am responsible for is still alive."

He hung up, angrier and more confused than ever. For several minutes, he searched the volumes of

Journals for those of Claire Silver, but he had been in the midst of reorganizing them when this crisis arose.

The phone rang. He glanced at it before picking it up, wondering if it was Kobo, ready for another volley.

"Yes?" he demanded sharply.

"Giles, it's Buffy. We're at the hospital. Xander's been . . . um, he's . . ." she whispered into the phone. "*Attacked,* if you know what I mean."

"I'm on my way," he said, rising from his chair.

"I'm going to look for Willow."

"No. Wait for me, Buffy," he said sternly.

"But—"

"Wait." He hung up and ran out the door, nearly crashing into Principal Snyder.

"So sorry," Giles said in a rush. "Must dash. Sorry."

"Mr. Giles?" Principal Snyder called after him.

"Sorry!" Giles called back.

At the hospital, the nurse was trying to reach Xander's mother on one phone, even as Buffy hung up with Giles on the other. Their conversation was brief and hushed, and when Buffy was through, she felt even worse about things than on her ride over with Cordy. More than anything, she wanted to run out and find Willow, as quickly as possible. But Giles had ordered her to stay put.

Buffy was a strong-willed girl—you had to be when you were the Slayer—and she didn't like taking orders from anyone. But if Giles felt strongly enough about it to try giving an order, the least she could do was follow it.

So she paced in Xander's hospital room with Cordelia, who was sunk tiredly into a chair pulled up to his bedside. She'd cried a little when the doctors were fussing over him, and her makeup was a mess, but not once did she ask Buffy if she looked okay. She only held Xander's hand, half-holding and half-massaging it, as if she could warm him again and take the ghostly pallor from his cheeks.

He had lost a lot of blood, and there were holes in his neck.

Could Willow have actually put them there? Willow, a vampire? Buffy wondered if she would have to . . .

. . . would have to . . .

"No," she said, clenching her teeth. She couldn't be certain what she would do when she found Willow.

But one thing was certain: it would be very much better to find her friend before the sun went down. For the moment, however, she could only pace.

By the time Giles got there, she was frantic. Though stunned by the sight of Xander, he briefed her on his conversation with the Japanese Watcher and she practically pushed him back out the door.

"Library, Giles," she begged. "We've got questions. You get answers."

"I'm not so certain I should go," Giles argued.

Buffy looked at him, then glanced quickly at the others in the room. Cordelia, who sat next to Xander with a worried look on her face. Xander himself, who was still unconscious, although recovering, according to the doctors. He wouldn't be running the hundred for a couple of weeks, but he'd be home sucking down chocolate milk shakes and making his mom do Blockbuster runs within a few days.

Buffy glanced around to make sure Xander's mother—who had stepped out into the hall to speak with the doctor—hadn't returned, and then she looked up at Giles again.

"We need to know what happened to him," Buffy said, staring down at Xander. It was obvious Giles's protective streak was overpowering his sense of logic. Buffy was touched. Her Englishman was the best Watcher a girl could ask for.

"Your job is not to stare at Xander and fret," Buffy insisted. "That Kobo guy told you where to look for the knowledge stuff and a librarian's gotta do what a librarian's gotta do."

Giles was obviously about to protest when Cordelia said Giles's name. Her voice was so low that at first Giles didn't hear her.

"Giles," Cordelia said again, emphatically. "I'll be here. I'm not going anywhere, not right now. Whatever happened, I'll call you as soon as Xander's able to talk about it."

Giles pursed his lips. "You don't think it would be better if . . ."

"I can handle it," Cordelia said, only half-looking at him. "I'll find out what happened to Xander. You go back to the library and read Claire What's-her-name's Journals." She looked at Buffy with satisfied self-importance. "We all have jobs to do, right, Buffy?"

"And that's my cue to start the hunt for Willow," Buffy said.

"Take my car," Cordelia said generously.

"I don't have a license," Buffy said quickly.

"Yeah, but you can drive it if you have to, right?" Cordelia asked.

"I'm not sure that's the wisest course," Giles began, but Buffy cut him off. Cordelia was right.

"I think I can manage," Buffy said. "Okay, I'm gone."

Then she turned and almost ran from the hospital. It was nearly one o'clock already. Dusk already seemed too close.

Of course, in Sunnydale, the night always came too soon.

CHAPTER 11

Ah, this undefended land! These foolish, weak people!

And, best of all, these demons!

They flocked to Chirayoju, desperate for a leader. *Oni,* who had traveled from China with the Buddhist faithful. The vampiric *kappa,* strange, scaled creatures whose bowl-like heads were filled with magic water. When the water spilled, the *kappa* lost their powers, but not their yen for blood.

Blood that Chirayoju found for them in plentiful supply.

Itself, it had not dined on anything as exquisite as the maiden Gemmyo—although it had sampled at least a hundred humans since it had left Mount Hiei, but its new army of followers had assured it that the Emperor, being holy, would taste the best of all.

And so, with its minions who now numbered in the thousands, Chirayoju descended like a nightmare upon the capital of this Land of the Rising Sun, called by some Heijo and by others, Nara.

In the forest its army camped and measured the defenses of the Emperor's palace. Fierce warriors guarded the walls, but within, the court of the Emperor Kammu languished like fat cattle. They were obsessed with the airy cultivation of art and culture and the monotonous veneration of the Lord Buddha. Nunneries and monasteries littered the wooded hills. A statue of Buddha as tall as eight men greeted the sun daily. Chirayoju was contemptuous, considering the Buddha himself a weak, unambitious being who preached the obliteration of ambition as the key to happiness.

While the nobles within the palace walls wrote poems and discussed philosophy, the people outside the walls starved. Taxes were high and crops failed despite the fertile land. They were ripe for unrest and rebellion.

Chirayoju saw much to please it.

So it left behind its fearful minions and walked the nights among the starving peasants, whispering to them of all the things it could give them—treasures, weapons, and warriors—if only they would call it master. They began to listen. They began to believe. Soon, they looked forward to its nightly visits and its tales of how their lives would be, if only they would deliver the Emperor to it.

It began to seem natural for them to hate their supreme lord, who was a god on Earth, and to practice the hacking and slashing of mortal combat with their fishing poles and pitchforks. They began to anticipate the battle with the heavily fortified palace, forgetting that they possessed neither armor nor weapons, and unaware that their general, Chirayoju the Liberator, had promised its second wave of attackers their own blood in exchange for *their* loyalty and aid.

This second wave were the *oni* and the *kappa*.

Who likewise did not know that it had promised its third wave of attackers the delicious and magical blood of the *oni* and the *kappa* in exchange for *their* loyalty and aid.

This third wave consisted of the vampires it made from the ranks of the *eta*. In the dark of night, alone and in secret, it would fly to the hovels in the filthy quarter of these, the Untouchables of Japan, who butchered animals and tanned their hides into leather and prepared the human dead for burial. Shunned by all except other *eta,* reviled and cursed, they fully embraced the new life Chirayoju offered them. They would willingly die any death Chirayoju ordered in exchange for the power and freedom it gave them.

So, with its three ranks of soldiers ripe for battle, Chirayoju shut itself deep within a cave and on the longest night of winter, cast its dragon bones. It sought the most auspicious moment to strike at the Emperor and devour him.

Not knowing, at the time, that Sanno, the Mountain King, had gathered thousands of followers of his own and stood poised in the foothills for battle. In his left hand he held fire and lightning. In his right, water and wind.

He vowed he would destroy Nara before he allowed Chirayoju to escape him. He would destroy all of Japan, if need be.

His only thought was of vengeance.

But his actions spoke otherwise: he went with a

small company of retainers to the gates of the palace and demanded an audience with Kammu. From the guards' behavior, he deduced that word of his deadly temper had not spread as far as Nara, and that he was believed to be the benevolent deity he once had been. For the guards, astonished to see the god in their midst, quickly ran and informed the Emperor of his esteemed guest.

Hasty and elaborate preparations were made, and Sanno was welcomed with pleas by Kammu himself that he excuse the poor banquet and clumsy entertainment laid on in his honor. In fact, of course, the entire evening was most sumptuous. Sanno and his retinue enjoyed the meal and drink, and when he rose to dance after many toasts and protestations of loyalty and friendship, the palace shook to its foundations under the tread of the Mountain King.

Thus was Chirayoju alerted that Sanno had arrived.

The vampire sorcerer called its armies together, and the siege began.

CHAPTER 12

Buffy had no license, but Buffy drove. If you could call it that. Shrubbery suffered. So did curbs. But she managed to avoid getting pulled over.

She was halfway down the block—actually, down the center of the block—when she realized she'd forgotten to tell Giles about the little shrub and the disk and the note. Maybe there was something to that whole take-a-deep-breath-and-think-things-through thing he had going. She'd decided to kill two birds with one stone and meet up with him back at school. It could be that Willow had her wits about her, and it was possible she would go there looking for help from Giles.

It was worth a shot.

Way too short a time later—at least as far as Sunnydale's speed limits were concerned—she pulled into the school's faculty parking lot, tires kicking up sand as she put on the brakes. She was in a rush, or she might have cared a bit more about positioning the car between the lines. Details, details.

Before she ran into the school, she slipped the disk onto the chain she wore around her neck with a large cross dangling from it, then jumped when a jolt shot through her. It could easily have been static electricity, she reasoned, but she took note of it nonetheless.

She made sure she had the little tree and the note from Willow's bedroom, and then she was off.

It was already fifth period, and the halls were empty as she hurried toward the library. She banged open the door, a naive little part of her mind hoping she'd see Willow there, at the computer, doing that hacking thing that she did.

Uh-uh.

"Willow!" she called. "Please, come out, come out wherever you are!"

"Yes, I'd like to know where Miss Rosenberg is as well," an insinuating voice sneered from behind her. "And the school librarian as well."

Buffy whirled, ready to fight off whatever horrible monster had followed her into the library. But it was worse than that.

It was Principal Snyder.

"Oh, um, good afternoon, Principal Snyder . . ." she began to stammer, glancing around, before remembering that Giles would arrive in time to rescue the Slayer in distress.

No joy.

"Don't give me that, Miss Summers," Snyder said, cynical as ever.

She knew Snyder had never liked her, and the

feeling was mutual. The guy looked only slightly more human than one of the Ferengi on *Star Trek*. But he was the principal, and after all, he knew Buffy's mom's phone number. By heart.

"Um, give you what, sir?"

"I'm on to you, Summers. On to you and all your delinquent friends. Bad enough you run roughshod over the rules of this school, over the fundamental respect for authority that we all need in order to get along in this world. But then you come in here and holler for your friend as if you were at one of those drug-addled rock-and-roll clubs all of you hoodlums frequent."

"Speaking of which, have you seen Willow? Or, um, Mr. Giles?" Buffy asked, wincing in anticipation of the principal's response.

"Don't interrupt me! There is a thing called decorum, Summers."

Buffy didn't have time for this.

"Y'know, Principal Snyder," she flared, "maybe if you'd asked what I was in such a hurry for . . ."

"I was just getting to that, Summers. Don't think I haven't noticed that you were off campus. I saw you running up the walk. You know I could suspend you for that alone."

Buffy thought fast.

"Well, actually, sir, Mr. Giles had sent Cordelia Chase and me over to the Sunnydale library to get a book we needed for a research project he's helping us with."

He looked less sure of his self-righteousness. "That's no excuse . . ."

"I'm sure he'll show you our permission slip to leave campus whenever he gets back from . . .

wherever he is," she added earnestly, keeping her eyes wide and innocent and terror-free. "And when we left, we both had study hall, so you see, we didn't miss any classes or informational content or, um, knowledge acquiring."

"Don't think I won't check on your story," Snyder grumbled. "And it's fifth period now. You're definitely missing class." He narrowed his eyes at her. "You know, that knowledge-acquiring thing you find so foreign and new? I'd say you're both in for detention all next week, even if your story checks out."

Buffy *really* didn't have time for this.

"Listen, you . . . sir . . . Xander Harris is in the hospital and Willow Rosenberg is missing. Her mother thinks she might have been abducted or something. That's why Cordelia and I were gone so long. Cordelia's at the hospital with Xander right now."

"Why would Cordelia Chase have anything to do with any of you, particularly That Harris Boy?" Snyder remarked, crossing his arms and looking very stern. "You're going to have to do better than that, Miss Summers."

Buffy sighed. Though it was hard for her to call Cordelia a friend, she supposed that it was true. But as much as she brushed it off, it hurt to know that Snyder couldn't even conceive of such a thing. Sure, Cordy tried to maintain her rep as the most popular girl in school by not letting anyone know she hung out with Buffy and company. Which would have really hurt if she thought Cordelia had any idea how insulting that was. But when a child-hating geek like Snyder was dishing on her, Buffy had had enough.

"Y'know what?" she said huffily, "I'm completely powerless to stop you from doing whatever it is you want to do."

She realized it was useless to try to wait for Giles. Useless, too, to even hope to write him a note about Willow's strange little collection. And no way was she leaving Willow's stuff where Snyder could scoop it up and throw it in the trash.

She raised her chin. "So I'm going to go to the bathroom, and then I'm going to my sixth period bio class."

Buffy spun on her heel, ignoring Snyder's vows to suspend her the next time she pulled a stunt like this. Next time. Those were the operative words. Detention was even okay, since that didn't necessarily mean a call home.

Of course, next time could be awfully soon. Especially since, once inside the bathroom, all she did was pop open the window and slip out. Then she was sprinting across the lawn for Cordelia's car.

There was a ticket stuck under one wiper.

Buffy grimaced and tossed it into the car.

Miraculously, the ticket was still there when Buffy pulled up in front of the main branch—in fact, the only branch—of the Sunnydale public library in Cordelia's car, gears grinding. She parked illegally there, too, but she hoped the ticket would keep her from getting another. On the other hand, the only thing that really mattered at the moment was not getting towed. Getting towed would be bad.

No Willow at the library.

Xander had once pointed out, with his usual loving sarcasm, that before Willow started to spend so much time hanging out at the school library because of the whole Slaying thing, she had spent almost as much time at the public library. Quiet. Surrounded by lots of books and computers. It was just Willow's kind of place.

Not anymore, apparently. Which sent Buffy scrambling madly across town in Cordy's car, burning gas as the afternoon wore on and she checked small specialty bookstores, the place Willow had gone to have her hair tinted, and the weird video store Xander had dragged them to when he'd gotten on his Hong Kong action movie kick.

She phoned the school library to talk to Giles. The phone was busy.

It was busy the next time she tried.

And the next.

By the time she stopped for a breather and fed the Cordymobile, it was nearly six. There was one message for her on the message machine at home, but it was only to say that he was back in the library. Yet the phone was still busy. She began to worry that the phone was off the hook. Then she got through, but there was no answer.

Dusk wasn't that far off, so she left off trying to reach Giles and called Willow's mother to find out if there'd been any word. None. Mrs. Rosenberg had been crying.

After Buffy hung up, she had to take a few deep breaths. A sinking feeling was setting in with the sinking sun: this was going to end badly.

Buffy slapped the roof of Cordy's car as she finished pumping the self-serve.

"C'mon, Willow, where are you?" she said aloud.

Her only answer was the weird stare she got from a heavyset man gassing up his Lincoln.

The dim light of encroaching dusk filtered into the hospital room where Xander Harris lay, still unconscious from a few nasty raps to the noggin and the fact that his best friend had turned him into a Slurpee. Or at least, that's what somebody was saying about him as Xander started to come around. He thought he remembered the phone ringing, but there wasn't much else in his head except cotton and some kind of liquid that sloshed around in there when he tried to move.

"Not so loud," he croaked.

"Oh God, Aphrodesia, I've gotta go," the voice beside his bed said. "I think he's waking up."

Click. That was the phone going back in its cradle. Really loud. Really, really loud, and Xander didn't like it at all. He winced again. Carefully, he opened his eyes just slightly. Not too bright in there, which was nice. With the way his head hurt, the light might just crack it open.

"Xander?" that same voice said in an excited hush. "Are you . . . okay?"

A face floated into view above him. He knew that face.

"Daphne?"

With a snarl that was nearly a roar, the face dropped down so that he was eye to eye with it, with the girl . . . with Cordelia.

"And just who is Daphne?" Cordelia demanded.

Xander blinked. "Huh?"

"Daphne!" she snapped. "You just called me

Daphne. I've been parked here for hours waiting for you to wake up, completely ruined my makeup crying because I thought something horrible had happened to you, and here you're talking about some girl named Daphne!"

Xander exhaled, frowned, though it hurt his head even worse. "Um, Daphne from Scooby Doo?" he suggested, though he had no idea if that was the truth. He already couldn't remember ever having called her that, at least to her face.

"Uh-huh," Cordelia replied.

With another sigh, Xander slumped back against the bed and stared at the ceiling. He was in a hospital, that much he knew. But he couldn't quite recall how he'd gotten here. When it came to him, it struck hard, like a blow to the gut, and he struggled to sit up, staring at Cordelia.

"Where's Willow?" he asked urgently. "Or Buffy?"

Cordelia rolled her eyes. She opened her mouth to complain but was interrupted by the arrival of a rather frazzled-looking Giles. In his right hand he clutched a pair of thin, faded books that looked like old diaries.

"Yes, that's what I'd like to know," Giles said, rubbing his eyes beneath his glasses. Xander thought he looked haunted, but as far as he was concerned, Giles always had that kind of distracted thing going on. Sort of a cross between Obi-wan Kenobi and the Absent-Minded Professor.

"It seems my timing is propitious," Giles said. "Xander, what did happen? Willow is missing, and there have been enough clues and coincidences to lead us to some horrible conclusions. I hope that you can dispel them as erroneous."

Xander blinked. "Whatever you said. But if one of your horrible conclusions is that Willow fanged me . . . yeah, that's the way it looks."

Xander felt sick. Just saying the words gave him a chill. Willow was closer to him than a sister, and the idea that she was now . . . one of *them,* was more than he could bear.

"Actually, we have reason to believe that Willow is not, technically, a vampire. At least, not yet. She was seen in daylight as recently as Monday by her mother, and though she is still among the missing, if we can find her, we might be able to save her from further harm."

"Let's go," Xander said, and sat up painfully.

"Xander, what are you doing?" Cordelia cried.

He winced with pain from the bruises on his head, from the tightening in his chest that told him he probably had a few ribs that were at least cracked, and he reeled from the disorientation that made him feel like he was on a fishing boat instead of dry land. But Xander got up. He put a hand against the wall to steady himself. Felt a draft. Hung his head and smiled at his own abject humiliation.

"And, of course, Xander Harris is wearing a hospital gown, isn't he? The kind that covers about as much as an apron? Yes, of course he is!"

He spun around quickly and slumped against the closet door, frantically searching for the knob.

"Ah, nothing. Nothing to see here," he said. "Or, well, nothing that should be seen . . . that very nothing anyone needs to see at this particular moment."

"When he starts talking about himself in the third person that's usually a sign that he's embarrassed," Cordelia observed. She looked very proud of herself. "Third person being an English grammar, um, thing, where it's *him, her,* and *it.*"

Giles began to study his shoes as if they were completely fascinating, and was still doing that when Xander stepped unsteadily from the closet wearing the greatest invention in the history of mankind.

Which would be pants. Pants were very, very good.

Xander started for the door to the room. Whoa. The tide was coming in. He staggered awkwardly and lurched forward.

"Xander, what do you think you're doing?" Giles demanded.

"Wearing pants is what I'm doing. What a man does. Wear pants." Xander stuck out one hand to stop the room from spinning on its axis, reached out the other one, and found himself being steered by Giles back toward the bed. He sat quickly and squinted at the sudden jolt of pain in his head.

Giles cocked his head. "Xander, get back in bed. You're in no shape to be up."

"We've got to find Willow," Xander insisted. "And Buffy. Before she . . . before they end up hurting each other. We've got to do something."

"Xander," Giles said gently. "We've got to do what we're good at."

Suddenly Xander shivered as fresh memories rushed in to fill the blanks.

"When she . . . she bit me, she laughed," Xander said, and fought off the burning sensation in his eyes, the urge he felt to cry at the thought of it. She was his best friend, and now this horrible thing had happened to her, and in a way, to him as well. "Willow laughed while she drank my blood."

"Did . . . did you drink her blood as well?" Giles ventured.

Xander frowned. "What am I, pervo boy? I don't think so."

"Okay, I missed something," Cordelia said. "Willow was out during the day, yesterday, right? We've established that. So now, what are we thinking? She's somehow *possessed* by a vampire? Can that be done?"

"It certainly seems that way," Giles replied.

"One thing's for sure," Xander added. "The person who attacked me last night? Maybe it had Willow's face, but it wasn't Willow. It wasn't even her voice. And it referred to itself as something else. Some weird Japanese name or something."

Giles softly said, "Perhaps it was Chinese."

"Perhaps," Xander said. He went on alert. "So this makes some kind of sense to you?"

Giles sighed. "It's beginning to."

"Look, I read the last panel of the Sunday comics first to save myself the suspense. Could you spill, already?" Cordelia said, her hands flapping the way they always did when she was frustrated.

Giles walked to the window and looked out at the darkening sky.

"I suspect the name you heard was Chirayoju," Giles said. "Do you recall our visit to the museum the other day? Willow cut her finger on an ancient sword that belonged to a Japanese warrior-god called Sanno, the King of the Mountain."

"Riiiight," Xander said, tentatively. Nervously. Less than joyfully.

"Which has exactly what to do with this Cheerios guy?" Cordy asked.

Giles faced them, looking as troubled as Xander had ever seen him. Maybe even more so, if that was possible. They'd all seen some pretty troubling things in the company of the Slayer.

"The text that accompanied that sword told of a legendary battle between Sanno and a Chinese vampire named Chirayoju, which ended with both of their deaths. I had a conversation earlier with a retired Watcher, who directed me to this."

He held up the pair of slim journals he'd had when he came in.

"The Journal of Claire Silver, Watcher," Giles explained. "During the first half of the nineteenth century, Miss Silver was instrumental in cataloguing the Journals of all the Watchers down through the ages. She was quite a scholar."

"Yeah, great, we can read it later," Xander said. "C'mon, we've got to go!"

Giles held up a hand. "We need to arm ourselves, Xander. We can't just run out into the night. Much as we would want to," he added under his breath.

"Actually, much as we have before, and it turned out okay," Xander insisted incredulously.

Giles opened his book. "I'll read to you."

"Just put me to sleep," Xander said. But he started to sway, and much as he wanted to stay upright, he lay back in his hospital bed.

"If it starts with 'once upon a time,' I'm outta here," he grumbled.

"Ssh." Cordelia was all ears and she sat up straight. "*I'm* listening."

"Very well."

Giles opened one of the books.

Journal of the Watcher, Claire Silver
January 6, 1817

The doctor has just left, taking with him all my hopes for Justine. The poor girl lies senseless upon her pillow, her wounds grievous and many, and there seems nought that I can do.

I must face it, but I cannot: she is dying.

As I look up from my pen to stare at her pale form, I know that somewhere on this vast planet, another Watcher has been alerted, and readies his young lady for her debut (if I may be so macabre) into the terrible world that shall be her secret domain: the world of the Vampire Slayer. As my young miss escapes at last this most unholy and unwholesome life, another soon shall find her existence irrevocably transformed— shall I say what I am thinking, that this new Slayer's life will be ruined?!

All that shall then remain of my dear Justine and her many battles, victories, and this ultimate defeat, will be these words that I write, and her monument in the churchyard.

I cannot bear it. I cannot face the notion that the forces of darkness have beaten us at last, not after all that Justine has suffered and endured.

And I—if I can bear to think for one moment of myself—I shall become what Justine and I have so often scoffed at: a genteel English lady, gowned and ribboned like a useless bisque figurine. I shall fill my days with teas and dances and gossip. I shall pretend I know nothing of weaponry and fighting and beheadings and the proper way to stake a vampire through the heart. All that I have learned in order to serve as Justine's Watcher I shall lay aside. I shall be as useless as a retired governess.

But who comes? For upon the window clinks a pebble. Does someone come to pay his respects? Someone who knows that Justine, the Slayer, lies dying after a vicious attack?

In our society, it has not been possible for Justine to accept suitors, knowing as she does what her life is, and what society requires of young ladies. Imagine explaining to a young man that you must of a night cudgel demons to death, or that the lady posing as your aunt last Tuesday sent a warlock to a fiery death in another dimension!

And yet, of what use have all our efforts been, and to what benefit our sacrifices?

Will this visitor be someone to whom I can utter these thoughts?

The maid knocks now, and waits for my permission to enter. I lay my pen aside, and shall return . . .

I do not know whether to cry in triumph or in fear, but my hands tremble so that I can scarcely put pen to paper. Our visitor was none other than Lord Byron, that infamous poet and ladies' man. He was impeccably, if eccentrically, dressed, wearing a brocade vest of Italian design and affecting some sort of large, floppy hat.

I was much amazed, for he has not been seen in England in five years. I was also much frightened, I must admit, for as I have written before, Justine and I have often wondered if Byron himself is a vampire. So much points to it—his pale complexion, his strange hold over numerous persons, and his extreme passions.

In any case, Justine has never met Byron before, and I only once, at a party Midsummer last, yet here he arrives on what may well be the last night of her life, giving to me certain books as well as fragments of ancient Oriental scrolls! With a strange smile, he told me of his high regard for "our work" and made several veiled references to Justine's "special talents." Thus I may conclude that he knows All, though I cannot swear to it.

But hush! Justine awakes, and requests some water. My girl, my Slayer!

I would give my life would it save her own.

January 7, 1817
Justine has survived the night, and though I am weary, I rejoice to tell her of the marvelous tale I am unfolding! It appears that the legend we have often wondered at may be indeed true. This, namely, being the Legend of the Lost Slayer. As opposed to the tragically usual way of it—a Watcher outliving his Slayer—I have upon occasion come across references to a Slayer who lost her Watcher quite early in her career. We have no idea who the Slayer was, nor what happened to the Watcher, but we have both often wondered at it.

Nearly all the writings contained within this box have been translated into the tongues of Europe, but the whole of it is a jumble, with scattered notes on fragments of paper, passages referring back to various scrolls translated into English by one hand, and others discussed in Italian by another. Additionally, a few are in Latin. Fortunately, these are two languages in which I possess facility. I have had a time putting things to rights, and much of it I have not been able to decipher at all. Some of it is in German, and to translate those items I will have to appeal to a third party. This appears to be a life's work.

The irony of those words is not lost on me. For most marvelous indeed is Justine's weak promise to me to remain on this earth until we solve the mystery. If searching among these writings for the key to the legend keeps her beside me but a single moment, I shall go to my own grave praising Lord Byron's name.

And so, to work . . .

February 1, 1817
What we had not counted on was that Justine, though in a weakened state, is still alive, and therefore remains the only Slayer of her generation. Though she can not rise from her bed, she alone wears the mantle of the Chosen One against whom the forces of darkness are arrayed.

This has depressed her greatly, for she feels that she is failing in her duty, and at one point today cried out to me, "Oh, Claire, if only I could simply stand aside! Better that I die than leave the world unprotected!"

I encourage her to believe that she shall recover, but the doctor has taken me aside several times and reminded me that on occasion, those who soon will leave us rally briefly so that they may bid farewell. He still holds little hope for her recovery. I find this astonishing, for she does seem much improved.

Tonight I shall go out hunting. Someone must, and she is in no condition for it. In truth, I undertake it only so that she will not fret so. I am for myself, selfishly, much afrighted. I am only a Watcher, though at this moment I would I were more.

February 13, 1817
I feel that we are in a race. As the doctor predicted, Justine has taken a turn for the worse. Her face is ashen and her chest rises and falls as if she is perpetually gasping for breath. And yet, an hour ago she opened her eyes, smiled like an excited little girl, and asked, through her pitifully cracked lips, "What have you discovered now? Are we still on the trail?"

Either she is being brave for me, or else she remains as captivated by the search for the legend of the Lost Slayer as I. Through a lengthy volume of Chinese lore called Emperor Taizu's Book, *we have found this:*

> It is true that in the first place, demons owned this world. They lost it in a grand battle with the Emperor, and fight to this day to take it back again.

This is precisely what Watchers and Slayers are taught to believe! Although, of course, we believe that it was not a battle with a Chinese Emperor which caused the forces of darkness to lose their control over the world. But what is significant is that according to our unnamed translator, these words were written in A.D. 971!

February 28
My girl is dead. In the moment that I saw the light go from her eyes, I clutched the bedpost and cried aloud, "Truly, I knew not it would be this difficult!" For

though I have steeled myself for this moment, I was—
and remain—unprepared.

They are coming to help me wash and dress her
poor body. To the churchyard we shall go on the
morrow. I cannot bear this. I am in a state of agony.
Whatever shall I do with my days and nights?

The answer lies in the scrolls and parchments. For
her last words to me were, "Promise me you'll solve
the mystery."

And so I shall.

Oh, Justine!

January 6, 1818
It is a year since Justine's defeat in battle. I am glad
to say that her successor found her murderers and
dispatched them as a personal favor to me. I went to
the churchyard to tell Justine of our side's victory.

At the least, I am not as useless as I had believed I
would become. I am someone honored among the
Watchers, for I was Justine's Watcher, and she was
much admired. And as I continue unraveling the
legend of the Lost Slayer, others have begun sending
me pieces of information they have unearthed. In
some cases, this includes entire volumes!

To wit, I have just opened a packet from a colleague
at the new University in Ghent. It concerns a certain
Japanese legend about a god, or goddess, named
Sanno. This Sanno was also called the Mountain
King, and he or she was the patron deity of Mount
Hiei in Japan. Part of the legend concerns a Chinese
vampire who vowed to devour the Japanese emperor.
Sanno saved the emperor by dispatching the vampire
with a magickal sword through the heart.

My colleague writes, "Could this Sanno be your

Lost Slayer?" I have no idea. If Sanno was female, perhaps she is!

March 18, 1819
How delightful! I have just received a copy of my book, Oriental Magick Spells as Collected by Claire Silver, a Watcher.

Privately printed by one of our own, there are five copies now circulating among my fellow Watchers. It is a comfort to me to be of use to my fellows, for though it has been over a year since my Justine left me, I feel the loss of her as deeply as though it were yesterday. I visit her grave daily, telling her of the progress I have made.

Though I have now discerned that Sanno was not the Slayer, as he was male, yet pursuit of that knowledge led me to investigate and record many fascinating and useful Oriental spells, contained now in my very own published work! I will take it to show Justine this afternoon.

Giles looked up from the book. "Damn," he said.
Cordelia blinked. "What?"
"I have the feeling that's the volume we're really after. Her book of spells." He checked the other book he had with him, flipping through the pages. He shook his head. "This is quite useless. It appears she married and had children. This is about their travels in Switzerland."
"How thrilling," Cordelia said ironically.
As if he seconded that emotion, Xander snored loudly in his hospital bed. Cordelia rolled her eyes.
"He doesn't usually snore," she offered, then blushed and stammered, "or so his, um, sister says."

Giles had never heard of a sister of Xander's before, but whether or not Cordelia was an expert on his, ah, nocturnal habits was quite beyond the scope of the matter at hand. Anxiously, he glanced at the phone.

"If only Buffy would check in," he said.

Cordelia waved her hands at him. "You go back to the library and get the book, and I'll wait here in case she calls."

"Mmm. All right." He rose and spared an extra moment to gaze at Xander. "Youth is remarkably resilient," he murmured. Then he read Cordelia's blank stare and said, "The color's already returning to his cheeks."

"It's blood," she said bluntly, indicating an empty blood bag hooked into an IV in Xander's arm. "The nurse told me that was the last bag just when you were getting to the part about Lord Brian."

"Byron," Giles corrected automatically, then sighed. "Yes, Lord Brian indeed. Quite right."

"Go get the book," she urged.

He sighed. "I suppose I must. But do take care."

He left his books there and hurried out of the room.

Cordelia was a little shaken. All that talk about the Slayer dying . . . eeuu. It creeped her out. It must really creep out Giles. And Buffy, too, of course.

She rubbed her arms, suddenly cold. Xander might have died, if Buffy hadn't insisted they go look for him. That creeped her out worst of all.

About five minutes later, the phone rang. Cordelia picked it up.

"Oh, hi, Harmony," she said. "No, I'm still stuck

here, can you believe it? His mother had to go pick up someone somewhere or something. Well, yes, he had a pretty nasty, ah, fall. A *sale?* I'm missing a *sale?* You're on your cell? Go to the petites right now. Go! If that leather jacket is marked down, you *have* to buy it for me. Of course I'll pay you back!"

CHAPTER 13

The hospital phone was still busy. Xander must have a lot of worried relatives, or else maybe someone had knocked it off the hook.

Buffy sighed and got back in Cordelia's car.

The golden glow of the sinking sun glared against the windshield as Buffy braked the car in front of the building where Angel lived. She grabbed her Slayer's bag, hopped out, and scrambled down the stairs to pound on the door. It was the last place she could think of where Willow might be hiding out. Angel would have taken her in if she really needed a place—if he didn't know what else had happened.

Or maybe even if he did. Angel was a surprising person . . . make that vampire . . . make that person . . .

But when the heavy door scraped the floor as it opened, and she saw the bleary-eyed face of the dead man she loved, she knew she was out of luck again.

Whatever Willow was going through, Buffy somehow knew that her chances of helping Willow were draining away with the last rays of the sun. She had maybe twenty minutes, and they might as well be twenty seconds. Or two.

"Sorry to wake you," she mumbled as she pushed past Angel into his dimly lit apartment and dropped her bag to the floor. She had long since grown used to the eclectic furnishings there, but it seemed as though each time she visited, she saw something new. Well, something old, but new to her.

Not this time. This time, everything seemed all too familiar.

"Buffy, what's wrong?" he asked.

"Willow," she whispered. Then she filled him in on everything that had happened up until that moment.

Buffy's eyes welled up as he came to her and tilted her head so she could lay it against his chest, a chest where she would never hear a heart beating. They'd been through so much together, suffered so much, and yet still she loved him. What else could she do? Love was like that.

"What's this shrine you found at her house?" Angel asked.

"I don't know," she admitted. "I was in such a rush that Giles and I didn't even have a chance to go over it. And I can't seem to locate him or even talk to him. I guess I should've hung around the hospital, for all the good I'm doing Willow."

She sighed. "I guess I'll go back there."

"Can I see the things you took?" he asked.

Buffy reached for her bag, unzipped it, and pulled out the note first.

"Origami," Angel said. "An Asian art form."

She nodded. "I knew it was a word like that. All I could think of was rigatoni."

She showed him the disk on the chain around her neck.

He shook his head. "No idea what that is."

The withered little plant.

"Hmm," Angel murmured, and Buffy glanced up sharply to see if he realized how much he sounded like Giles. Apparently not.

"Looks like a bonsai tree," he said finally. "But it's been dead a while."

"How do you know all this stuff?" Buffy asked.

"I've traveled a lot," Angel replied.

"I never get to go anywhere," Buffy said, half-mocking herself.

Angel kissed her, then, deeply and with a kind of gentle sympathy. "I'm sorry all this is happening," he whispered. "I wish I could be more help, but I've never heard of anything like it before. If Willow is a vampire—we don't know that, but if she is—she shouldn't be up and around during the day." He half-smiled. "Vampires don't go to school, Buffy."

Buffy stared at him.

"What did you say?" she demanded.

"I said . . ."

"Vampires don't go to school!" Buffy shouted. "Angel, that's it!"

He stared at her, stupefied.

"The things on Willow's desk aren't exactly the kind of souvenirs she would keep," Buffy said quickly. "Whatever, whoever she is now . . . that's who put those things there. I've been wasting my time looking in all the places *Willow* might go. She's changed now . . ."

The thought threw Buffy for a moment, stealing some of the joy of her realization. Her face became grim and her mind determined. "Origami. That dead bonsai tree was ripped from the ground." She slapped her forehead. "The Chia Pet garden! That's what it reminded me of."

Hastily, she explained about the Japanese friendship garden exhibit. "The real garden is still in Sunnydale," she said. "It may have some kind of weird connection to the one in Kobe. So maybe there's some extra vortex thingie there or something. And Willow as vampire is drawn there."

"Well, there aren't many other places in Sunnydale where you can get a bonsai tree," Angel said, nodding.

"In L.A. you can buy them at the mall," Buffy said, almost sadly. Suddenly she missed her old, normal life more than she ever had before. She was tired of all the weirdness. It seemed that the moment she thought she'd adjusted to her role as the Slayer, something came along to change it. Up the stakes.

So to speak.

Angel glanced at the window.

Buffy said, "There are about eighteen more minutes of daylight left." She took a breath. "When you're the Slayer, eighteen minutes can be a lifetime."

Angel nodded. "Go. I'll come after you the second the sun goes down."

She kissed him lightly on the lips and looked away quickly so he wouldn't see her fear and worry. "See you soon."

"I'll hurry," he promised, but Buffy was already out the door and bounding up the steps.

A tiny slice of the sun was still visible on the horizon as she got into Cordelia's car. The sky was a garish pink on one end, and a deep, almost ghostly blue on the other.

Buffy put the car in gear, praying she wouldn't get stopped.

The disk clanked against the metal chain as if it were a time bomb sequenced for countdown.

Giles returned huffing and puffing with a leather book in his arms just as Xander closed the bathroom door and walked all by himself back to his bed.

The Watcher actually stumbled over his own feet and said, "Xander, what are you doing up?" Then, before Xander could answer, he glanced at Cordelia and said, "Has Buffy called?"

"Oops," Cordelia said, looking guilty. "I mean, no."

Xander looked curiously at his little lustbuddy and wondered what that oops was about, but concentrated instead on Giles.

"Cor says you went off to get another book," he said, bobbing his head at that thing called *libro* by some—the ones who took Spanish—in Giles's arms.

"Um? Oh, yes. Yes." Giles was actually smiling. "It's just that I'm so delighted to see you up and about. Although I'm sure you're supposed to remain in bed."

"Yeah, well."

"He didn't like the bedpan," Cordelia offered helpfully.

"Thank you, Nurse Chase," Xander huffed, rolling his eyes. She did the same, and it looked like another fine evening with the Dueling Banjos except that they had more important things to talk about.

"The book," he urged Giles.

"The book," Giles concurred, and his smile grew. "As one might say, bingo."

Xander sat down and rubbed his hands. "Then bingo it is. And please read-o."

"Yes."

Giles read.

"In early Japan, executions were carried out by means of either strangulation or immolation, that is to say, burning. The spilling of blood revolted the fastidious Japanese mind. However, with the arrival of Buddhism, seppuku became the favored method, the victim voluntarily inserting a sword blade into his abdomen and slicing his bowels, thus causing a copious amount of bleeding (and, one must add, however indelicately, pain of a truly unimaginable sort). If at all possible, the head of the condemned was summarily cut off with another sword in order to spare him further agony. However, to be decapitated without first freeing one's soul from the body (for the Japanese believed that the soul resides within the abdomen) was truly a dishonor."

"And we couldn't have that," Xander quipped.

"Be quiet," Cordelia snapped. "Giles, keep reading. Please," she added sweetly.

"Further regarding the ritual Magic of Ancient Japan, it is considered possible to imprison a Spirit

inside an inanimate object. One then says of the Spirit that it is 'bound' and that the Object is 'alive.' Thus, one says of a Bell into which a Spirit has been bound, Suzu ga imasu, *rather than* Suzu ga arimasu. Imasu *being the verb for things that are alive, while* arimasu *is used for the things which are not.*

"In various versions of the legend of Sanno the Mountain King, we read that his Sword is a living thing, which leads one to assume a Spirit had been bound into it. Blood is prominently mentioned, specifically, the blooding of his enemy. The story regarding Sanno's victorious battle with the evil Vampire Chirayoju generally includes the line, and Chirayoju was blooded, and thus vanquished.*"*

"So it got out when Willow cut herself?" Xander said, staring hard at Giles.

Giles returned his gaze. "It would appear so."

Xander ran his hands through his hair. "Listen, Giles, whatever happens, I'm not letting anyone put a stake through Willow. No way."

"Well, what I've been pondering is the uniqueness of this case," Giles began, and Xander wondered how many trails they were scheduled to meander down before they reached Giles's point. Because he had already reached his own conclusion: he'd lock Willow up like Oz—only, just for the rest of her natural life, instead of three nights a week—before he would ever allow her to be harmed.

"Yes, the pondering thing," Xander said, weary, pain-ridden, and very anxious.

Giles completely missed his impatience, or else was being very British and very polite about pretending not to notice it. "It seems to me that if the demon was extracted from one form, perhaps it can be done again."

"Okay, trap the vampire ghost. Got it," Xander said. "And we do that by . . . ?"

Giles smiled grimly. It was times like these he wished he was back in the land of tea, crumpets, and baked beans for breakfast. "I suppose we'll find that out after Cordelia and I have broken into the museum and had another look at that sword."

Fighting vertigo, Xander sat up. "Cordy, I never thought I'd say these words to you, but help me finish getting dressed."

"And I never thought *I'd* say this," Cordelia shot back, "but no way." She held her hand out to Giles. "Let's go."

"Hey, wait a minute," Xander protested.

Giles shook his head. "I'm terribly sorry, Xander, but you've got to stay here and get well." He gestured to the phone. "Besides, Buffy may call."

"Oh. Okay," Xander said, to Giles's surprise. "You're right. You two run along." He folded his hands and made a show of climbing back into bed. "I'm sitting here obediently, healing away. That's what I'm doing."

"Well, good," Giles said uncertainly.

As soon as they were out of range, Xander threw back his wafer-thin hospital blanket and climbed awkwardly out of bed. The room spun for a shorter period of time than the last time, and he figured that meant he was ready to put on his Robin cape.

He shuffled once more toward the little closet

containing his clothes—his admittedly disgusting, blood-caked duds—and opted for his jeans and a scrub top he found hanging in his bathroom. Used? Covered with ebola virus?

Then it occurred to him to look for some scrub pants.

In a few minutes, he looked like Dr. Greene on *ER* after he'd been mugged. He strolled out of the hospital and followed behind two hotties in outfits similar to his own. As they neared the parking lot, he made a show of groaning and turning back around.

One of them said, "Hey. Hi. What's the matter?" She stared at his face and he remembered he was kind of gross-looking.

He made a face. "I forgot that my roommate, Doctor, ah, Summers, has my car. Porsche. His is in the shop. His Beemer. I told him I had a double shift but we, ah, ran out of emergencies so I'm going home early because I'm still healing from my skiing accident." Inwardly, he winced at his unconvincing story.

The redhead looked impressed and said, "Oh, you're a doctor?"

"Yeah. I numb 'em." He shrugged casually. "I'll have to go call him. I just called the museum and told them I'd drop by to work on some lecture slides. On ebola. And numbing."

The hotties gave each other a "let's-go-for-it" look. The redhead said, "We can give you a lift, Doctor."

"We'd be happy to," added her little blond pal.

Xander said, "Thanks, ladies," and followed them to a Camry with a bumper sticker that read LOVE A NURSE.

But the ironic thing was, Xander was too sore and too exhausted to even consider it.

"Oh, God, this thing is such a clunker," Cordelia wailed from the passenger side as she kept scanning Claire Silver's book of spells. "Giles, when are you going to get a real car?"

"Cordelia, I realize that as a young Southern Californian caught in the clutches of the obsession with—"

"Wait," Cordelia said, waving her hand. "There's a loose page stuck in the back of the book." She glanced at it. "Oh, my God, Giles, listen!"

June 17, 1820
I have just learned something absolutely fascinating! A scroll has made its way to me from the actual Buddhist monastery on Mount Hiei, recording a number of events within the chronology of the Sword of Sanno. For indeed, such a sword exists, and resides there now!

The Emperor Kammu kept this sacred and dangerous object with him, housing it in the pavilion wherein dwelled the embodiment of his ancestor, Amaterasu-no-kami, the Sun Goddess.

But after widespread unrest (due to an unfair system of taxation and other social problems), the Emperor Kammu ordered the nation's capital moved from Nara to Kyoto. (Interestingly, this is when the current system of Japanese writing began to become codified, and there are many more documents preserved about magick spells from here on than in the previous centuries.) At any rate, during this enormous undertaking, an earthquake occurred, and Emperor

Kammu became concerned that this violent shifting of the earth had aught to with the sword.

The Emperor sent the Sword of Sanno, with great pomp and ceremony, to the monastery, bidding them to protect it for all time. But to the head monk he wrote a remarkable and mystifying thing:

"I charge thee to do all thou canst to maintain the peace between thy patron kami, *Lord Sanno, and the most dishonorable demon, Chirayoju, both housed within the weapon. For thou alone keepest the secret, and as we have agreed, I shall tell no one else. For Lord Sanno's wrath would be terrible indeed, and no amount of atonement could ever satisfy the betrayal he must certainly feel by the actions of this most desperate Emperor."*

From this I conclude that the Emperor bound Sanno within his own Sword.

"So there's someone else in the sword?" Cordelia asked. "Or is he the guy who's possessing Willow, or what?"

"I don't know," Giles confessed. "But we're there now, so . . ."

He slammed on the brakes.

"Good heavens, is that Xander?" he asked, pointing at a car pulled to the curb just ahead of them.

As if on cue, Xander straightened and waved at them.

CHAPTER 14

As Tsukuyomi, the Moon God, glittered over the wintry landscape, Lord Chirayoju's hellish army marched swiftly and silently toward Emperor Kammu's palace. Once they had been sighted, runners burst into the Emperor's exquisite banquet hall with news of the invasion.

As the cold, exhausted men tumbled into the exalted company, the music stopped and all eyes looked to them. They lay prostrate until the Emperor gave them leave to speak. For daring to burst in as they had, it would have lain within his provenance to command them to take their own lives. One waited on the Emperor's invitation; one did not dare to thrust oneself into his presence. But it was clear there was a crisis, or they would not have been so bold, and the Emperor quickly learned what was transpiring beyond his palace walls.

Sanno listened with glee as one of the runners answered the Emperor's calm and careful questions, the words tumbling out of the frightened soldier's mouth: "They are legions of demons, oh Great One, and vampires, and an angry mob of peasants. Their leader is a hideous being who floats on the lightest breeze. Its face glows green and slick, and it is nothing of Japan."

The court drew back in horror. Exquisite ladies turned to their warrior husbands and begged fate not to make them widows. Poetry-loving dandies clenched their fists inside their sleeves, fretting that they might be ordered to actually fight against such creatures.

After Emperor Kammu had finished with the runners' interviews, Sanno turned to him and said, "This is the evil Chinese *tengu* Chirayoju. It has sworn to drink your blood, but rest assured, most mighty sovereign, I shall protect you."

With his hand on the hilt of the sword in his belt, Kammu inclined his head in great thanks and said to Sanno, "My debt for your assistance will never be repaid. I will give your retinue weapons, soldiers, and horses."

"I have my own army, camping in the foothills," Sanno replied haughtily, "but I will accept your generous offer, for no army should ever turn down provisions."

Then Sanno clapped his hands and an icy winter wind whistled into the banquet hall. The assembled courtiers shook with cold, the oldest and youngest nearly turning blue, but Sanno did not seem to notice their discomfort.

He bellowed a fearsome battle cry, which was

taken up by the wind, then shouted in ringing tones, "Come to me. It is time."

Carrying his words, the wind streamed in the opposite direction. Finding there a door of rice paper, it blasted through, leaving a gaping hole in its wake. In another instant, it burst through the very wall of the palace itself.

The Emperor noted the damage and was silent for a moment. Then he dared to say to the Mountain God, "It would be well if you would meet him outside my castle gates. Within, my people are defenseless."

Sanno glared at the Emperor. He thundered, "Am I not here to protect you, oh living god on this earth? Would you have my army expose itself to unnecessary harm and possibly fail in their mission? My troops will occupy this palace, and your courtiers must look to themselves."

Then Sanno bowed low, perhaps mockingly so, and added, "For your life must be preserved at all costs, Great Kammu."

"Then I shall share the danger," Kammu answered, rising and descending the dais where he sat with his Empress. "I go now to don my battle armor."

Sanno nodded, satisfied. For it was well that the Emperor joined the battle. In truth, the Mountain God's hatred for Chirayoju raged so fiercely that he did not care if Kammu's life was saved or lost. He did not care about the dishonor Kammu's death would cast on him. He only wanted the demon vampire dead. And the sight of Kammu at the head of his own army would inspire Sanno's warriors to fight more courageously.

As he left the banquet hall with every face lowered to the ground save Sanno's, the Emperor went not to the armory but to the pavilion wherein dwelled the form of Amaterasu, the Sun Goddess, who was the Emperor's ancestor. She stood on a pedestal in a beautiful, flowing gown of rose and scarlet, her mirror—part of the royal regalia—in her grasp.

Humbling himself on his knees, Kammu said to her, "Divine One, I fear that Lord Sanno has come not to protect our familiy, but with the sole purpose of vanquishing the Chinese demon that marches on us. I fear that in the heat of battle, the Mountain God will sacrifice whatever he must in order to kill this Chirayoju."

The room blazed with light as Amaterasu moved from her pedestal and stepped down from the platform, until she stood only one step higher than her descendant. She was so beautiful that it was difficult for Kammu to look upon her, so he kept his gaze lowered and stared at the floor.

"You are a wise man, Kammu," the Goddess said. "For indeed, Lord Sanno will take no care to curb his violent hatred of Lord Chirayoju. If one of our family stands between him and the demon, he would cut through that one as easily as his winds tear rice paper."

Troubled, Kammu listened, and became more troubled still as Amaterasu continued.

"My brother, Tsukuyomi, has told me that Lord Sanno's heart has changed for all time. His rage will remain after Lord Chirayoju's death, should he prevail in this war. He will never rest because Gemmyo, the Fujiwara daughter, has been taken from him. He will destroy the palace and all the land of Japan."

Kammu's blood ran cold. Summoning all the resolve in his warrior's heart, he said, "Divine Ancestor, I pray you to tell me how to stop both Lord Chirayoju and Lord Sanno."

Amaterasu's fiery presence cooled as she said gravely, "There is a way, but the rituals I reveal to you in my mirror must be precisely executed. In the chaos that will crash down upon this place, it will be most difficult."

"I will prevail," Kammu assured her.

"Does he carry an object of personal significance?" she asked.

"Hai," he said eagerly, " a great sword."

"A sword. That is the best answer that you could have given me." She lowered her head, and a golden sunbeam tear slid down her cheek.

"However, it may be that you will fail, Emperor Kammu. In that case, you will die an excruciating, humiliating death. You will never see Heaven. And the world as you know it will end."

Kammu sighed, his heart heavy with dread. "But if I do not attempt it, all will surely be lost."

Amaterasu slowly nodded in agreement. More tears slid to the floor, catching the mats aflame. For truly do the Divine Ancestors love the Emperors and their families.

At midnight, Chirayoju's army of peasants, devils, and vampires attacked the castle with savage ferocity.

Emperor Kammu's men, fierce warriors all, had

never battled such terrifying opponents, but they bravely fought with swords and lances as from the battlements, the archers let fly their flaming arrows.

Beside them, Sanno's army flung themselves head-long into the fray, as if they had no fear of death.

Fires blazed around the castle as the terrible invaders drew near, and the situation looked bleak indeed as rank after rank of Sanno and Kammu's combined armies fell beneath the onslaught.

Still, there was hope. Instructed by Sanno to string measures of rope low to the ground before the castle gates, the bloodthirsty *kappa* tripped and spilled the magic water in the bowl-like indentations in their heads. The human peasants of Chirayoju's army, sent ahead to absorb the arrows and lances of the Emperor's troops, were cut down like straw. Many of the *eta* vampires turned to dust as they were staked through the heart. And the *oni* were just as likely to turn on each other in the violent frenzy as on their nominal enemies.

Yet their leader, Chirayoju, seemed unconquerable. With its green, moldy face and taloned hands, it was a terrifying sight as it rose into the air and hurled volleys of fireballs into the castle courtyard.

Sanno answered in kind, and the two pummeled each other with fire and blazing whirlwinds. Sanno stamped the earth in fury. The ground shook so hard that trees were uprooted, waterfalls sprayed upward, and dragons threatened to escape from the cracks and fissures. The castle itself began to disintegrate. Timbers crashed to the castle floors. Kammu's fa-vorite daughter was crushed to death, as were many others.

In desperation, realizing that the powerful demon

and the equally powerful *kami* would soon lay waste to all of Nara, Kammu prayed to his Divine Ancestors and all the Heaven People, and suddenly the sky lightened a few degrees as Amaterasu showed her face far earlier than expected.

"Chirayoju!" Sanno called to his enemy. He pointed at the mountain range. "The sun will rise soon, and she will bring your death. Let us finish this. Surrender, and I will kill only you. Your vile followers may continue their miserable existence."

Sanno's challenge confirmed the Emperor's greatest fear about the Mountain God's real intentions. The thought that the remaining *oni* and *kappa* and vampire *eta* would be free to prey on his subjects was insupportable.

"Never!" Chirayoju shouted, as it pounded the castle with more fire. More than two-thirds of the beautiful palace blazed, and Kammu's second oldest daughter was burned to death in her chambers.

Emperor Kammu sat straight on his warhorse and lifted his hands. "Lord Chirayoju," he said, "it is as Lord Sanno has said. The sky lightens. Soon you and your vampire warlords will burst into flame, even as my palace and my child have burst into flame. I propose combat between the two of you. And I swear that I will offer my blood to you if you are the victor."

"What are you doing?" Sanno thundered at Kammu.

The Emperor lowered his voice and said, "My Divine Ancestor has revealed to me how you may kill it. I will arm you with the knowledge."

As reassurance, he spoke of some of the rituals and incantations that Amaterasu-*no-kami* had shown him in her mirror. But the Emperor did not reveal that he knew how to defeat the Mountain God as well.

Satisfied that he now held the upper hand, Sanno waved his banners and shouted to Chirayoju, "Demon lord, though you are a foul pestilence, yet are you powerful. I have pledged to the Emperor Kammu that I would protect his household. Yet with our combat, you and I are destroying his palace and killing his children. I, too, swear that if you defeat me, I will allow you to destroy me."

Chirayoju looked intrigued. As the monster hung in the air high above its followers, it looked toward the horizon. The mountain tops were dusted with the first purple washes of day. Perhaps it realized that if it did not defeat Sanno very soon, it would have to retreat, leaving its back vulnerable to every blow the Emperor and Sanno could deal.

At length it said, "I accept your challenge. I will come alone."

They met in the courtyard, the great Mountain God at one end, the fearsome vampire sorcerer at the other. The sky was still dark, but the divine light of the sun would soon lift the veils of night.

The Emperor had chanted over Sanno's sword, which was already an enchanted weapon, being the sword of a *kami*. But now it was even more powerful. If Sanno pierced Chirayoju straight through the heart, it would surely die.

Chirayoju faced the Mountain God without fear. This was but one minor deity; he was capable of devouring all of heaven itself!

Mockingly, Chirayoju made an elaborate bow and

thought to himself, *Soon, this fool will die. And then not only shall I drink the blood of the weak-minded Emperor, but I shall devour Kammu completely.*

Also armed with a sword, Chirayoju assumed a battle stance.

Above them, in the parapets, the Emperor had donned clothes all of white. Around his head he wore a cloth inscribed with a character from the incantation the Goddess had taught him, the single word for the Life Force, which is *ki*.

He stood on sacred tatami mats blessed by the priests, and he poured ritual sake—rice wine—on the woven straw.

Below him, the two supernatural beings rushed at each other, brandishing their swords above their heads. The blades clanged, and sparks shot into the heavens like the lament-laden death songs of ancient dragons.

On the tatami before the Emperor lay his own sword. If he failed to stop them both, he planned to offer his own life to the gods, in the hope that they would protect his poor nation. As the Goddess had foretold, he would die an excruciating death, for he would slice open his own abdomen as atonement for his incompetence. The blood that gushed from his mortal wound would be the only blood of his that Chirayoju would enjoy.

But he prayed that this would not be his fate. He prayed that, instead, he would see Sanno victorious, and thus betrayed. He could not allow Sanno to walk the earth, for the Mountain God had become an evil thing, much like the demon he fought. Kammu's Divine Ancestor had assured him of this. And so she had revealed to him the sacred incantation, which would bind not only Chirayoju into the sword, but Lord Sanno as well.

"Chirayoju!" Sanno shouted. "I offer you an honorable death. Commit suicide with your blade, and I shall write a death poem for you."

Chirayoju sneered at Sanno and flew high into the air. "If your poetry sings like your sword, I would writhe in the spirit world to hear its discordant verses."

And so, as they charged each other in the courtyard below, Emperor Kammu prepared his tatami mat with salt and sake, and ran through his mind the phrases he must utter to bind them both into the steel.

As their swords clashed, the wind rose violently. The earth shook, rolled, and trembled. Around Kammu, his castle blazed. Though he would surely burn with it, he would not move from this place until all was accomplished.

Softly, he whispered a poem of his own:

> *"Weep now, earth, air, fire,*
> *Tears for Kammu's dead children,*
> *Water, Earth's fourth soul."*

The Emperor Kammu would not falter.
He would bind them—or die.

CHAPTER 15

There was no way anyone was sending Xander home, and that was that.

Now, that settled, he asked in a whisper, "Has it occurred to anyone that part of hanging out with the Slayer means getting a whole new education in petty crime?"

They watched as Cordelia approached the front door, nervously glancing back at them. Giles and Xander both urged her on. Finally, she began to pound on the door, screeching for help as loudly as she dared. They wanted the night watchman to come running, but they would rather not draw the attention of anyone working security at any nearby buildings. Not that there were many that could be deemed "nearby."

"Help me!" Cordelia cried. "Oh, please help!"

"For someone whose life has been in jeopardy

several times, she's truly horrible at maintaining any kind of pretense," Giles whispered.

"Which is, y'know, a really, really bad thing," Xander replied with very little conviction.

They heard the locks ratcheting back. The door swung open and the night watchman appeared, a rather rotund individual in an ill-fitting dark-blue uniform, holding a long nightstick in one hand.

"Miss, what is it?" he asked with genuine concern.

"Oh, my God, help me, they're after me!" Cordelia said desperately, throwing herself at him more as if she were the first customer in line at the Macy's after-Thanksgiving sale than if her life were in danger. "Please! Two men were chasing me, I think they wanted . . . I don't know what they wanted, but you've got to help me! Really!"

"We're dead," Xander whispered. "This is never going to work. I've seen better acting on canceled daytime soaps."

Giles turned to regard him with one eyebrow raised.

"Which I never watch, and only ever saw while I was channel surfing, searching for the college squash . . . um, no, basketball games," Xander quickly corrected.

"Whatever we may think of her skills as a thespian, Cordelia's performance seems to be having the desired effect," Giles replied quietly.

Xander watched in awe as the night watchman patted Cordelia's shoulder. She poured on the boo-hoo a little too thick, particularly since she had insisted she not be required to actually cry, as tears would ruin her newly applied mascara. Still, the guard seemed to be falling for it.

"Where'd these lowlifes come after you, darlin'?" the watchman asked.

"Over . . ." *Sniff*. ". . . over there," Cordelia said, and pointed off in the other direction, where a stand of trees separated the museum gate from the lawn.

Xander rolled his eyes. It was a sure bet the guy would wonder what she'd been doing over in a far dark corner of the grounds to begin with.

"All right, missy, don't you worry 'bout a thing," the middle-aged, potbellied watchman comforted her. "You go on inside now and call the police. I'm gonna have a look around. You lock her up and wait by the door here for me to come back. Don't let anyone in but ol' Eddie, you hear?"

Cordelia whimpered in agreement and allowed Eddie to usher her into the museum, where she promptly slammed and locked the door. Xander stared in disbelief as the watchman started across the lawn as if the *Mission: Impossible* theme were playing in his head.

After a moment, he and Giles moved around the corner—Xander very gingerly—and tapped lightly on the door. Cordelia opened up quickly, they ducked in, and then she was twisting and sliding all the locks shut behind her.

"Well, that buys us about three minutes," Cordelia said archly. "Now what?"

"Hmm?" Giles asked, and glanced up innocently, with that I'm-sorry-was-planning-this-caper-supposed-to-be-my-idea? face.

"Oh, no," Xander said, wagging his finger at the Watcher. "Uh-uh. There'll be no *hmms,* do you understand, Giles? No *hmms!* Now. What do we do when he comes back?"

"Oh, well." Giles nodded, glanced away distractedly. "I suppose Cordelia should merely pretend to be too frightened to open the door. Cordelia, you might tell him he'll have to wait outside until the police arrive, just so that you can be sure of your safety."

"That's your plan?" Cordy asked. "For me to act like a stupid ditz?"

"What there is of it, yes." Giles lifted his chin as if daring them to call it a bad plan.

"That's a bad plan," Xander said. Cordelia looked pleased. "Not that you can't act like a stupid ditz, Cor. In fact, I've seen you do it."

Giles blinked, apparently surprised that the old lifting-the-chin-trick hadn't intimidated them.

"Yes, well, when you've developed a better plan, please do inform me," he said tartly, and turned to walk deeper into the museum toward the Japanese exhibits.

"See," Xander began, as he followed Giles, "my plan would have included making sure we didn't go to jail, which, in case you didn't know, is not some kind of modern slang for 'tropical paradise.'" He paused and caught his breath. "Are you getting this, Giles? Jail, bad!"

"Xander."

"Coming!"

A short time later, they stood staring at the Sword of Sanno.

"Fascinating."

"What is it, Mr. Spock?"

Giles sighed and glanced at Xander. He was not without a sense of humor himself, of course, but the boy did choose the oddest times to exercise his peculiar brand of levity.

"Take a look at this." Giles pointed at the large sword on the wall. "This is the sword that Willow cut herself on. The Sword of Sanno. There appear to be Oriental characters engraved in the guard."

With a pen, he indicated the metal plate that separated the blade from the hilt of the sword. "I wish I knew what these meant."

Then he looked a bit closer. The hilt itself was wound with braids of silk in a crisscross pattern that seemed to hold in place several small disks on either side.

"Look here," he said, more to himself than to Xander. Absently he listened for Cordelia's high-pitched cries, which would signal the return of Eddie the large watchman, but she was silent. In the silence, he fervently prayed that she had not forgotten her job.

"What am I looking at?" Xander asked.

"Well," Giles said, pointing at the hilt, "notice the silk braiding here, which seems designed to both hold and expose these round plates."

"Yeah," Xander said. "And I notice the same thing on just about all the other swords in here."

"Indeed," Giles admitted. "But those swords are *katana* or other, similar swords, all from a later period. Something this ancient would never have been treated in this way. It is a style that wasn't developed until much later. Also, the plates have markings similar to those on the guard."

Xander was silent. Giles turned to look at him.

"I thought you said you didn't know anything

about Japanese history or culture or whatever," Xander said.

"Well, I recall very little from my schooling, but I did come to the exhibit. As did you." Xander just shrugged. "I've just finished reading Claire Silver's journals. In fact, we learned the most fascinating thing on the way over here. It seems that Sanno the Mountain God was also bound inside the sword."

"No kidding." Xander look askance at the weapon. "He's in there *now?*"

"I'm not certain." Giles looked at him. "But I think so."

"Maybe those little disk things were added when he was, um, bound in. Maybe it happened later, so that's why all that extra stuff is from a later period."

"Perhaps," Giles said. "But if the enchantments were that powerful, Willow's simply cutting herself should not have been enough to allow Chirayoju to be set free. Though certainly, her blood would have been a partial catalyst, and Buffy did say that her state of mind was rather vulnerable. Still, if there was a binding spell, in fact, more than one, I don't understand how . . ."

"Hey, check this out," Xander said, and moved past Giles to point to the hilt. "It looks like one of the disks is missing. Here."

Giles stared at the spot where a disk had been. "Thank you, Xander, I believe you've just answered my question."

Xander blinked. "I have?"

"Now I've got to figure out how to remove that spirit from Willow and bind it again. We'll have to lure her here somehow," he said absently, deep in contemplation.

"Or we could just take the sword."

"No, wait!" Giles cried.

But it was too late. Xander had already reached for the sword on the wall, grabbed it by the hilt, and lifted it down.

"We're—" Xander began to say, but the sentence ended there, and the smile disappeared from his face. His eyes narrowed, his nostrils flared, he thrust his chest out as though he were trying to impress the girls. He lifted his chin with an arrogant flair, and for a moment Giles thought Xander was mocking him again.

Then he spoke.

"Free," he said.

But it wasn't Xander's voice. Not at all. It was deep and resonant, as though it came from all around the room. It was filled with a power and a pride that made Giles want to drop his eyes to the floor in deference. He fought that urge, and instead stared right at Xander's face.

Xander's face. But Xander Harris was gone.

"Ahem," Giles cleared his throat nervously. "Sanno, I presume?"

Eyes that once were Xander's locked on Giles's face, and the Watcher felt his spine melt. If it wasn't for his memory of Xander's particularly foolish sense of humor, he might have shrunk from those eyes.

"I am Sanno, King of the Mountain," the spirit wearing Xander's flesh spoke to him. "Where is the vampire?"

"Well, I'm not quite sure, but you should know that . . ."

"No matter. I can smell it. Once and for all time, I

will destroy it," Sanno thundered, and began to walk toward the back of the museum, toward a pair of French doors and away from the front, where Cordelia was now trying to hold off Eddie the watchman with her damsel-in-distress routine. In the shock of Xander's transformation, Giles had missed the watchman's return.

"Cordelia, a small change of plans. We've got to go!" Giles cried urgently. "Quickly!"

Giles heard her running down the hall, and turned to see her appear in the doorway. "Well it's about ti—" she began, but didn't finish the sentence. Instead, she stood next to Giles and watched Xander, bearing in his right hand a sword Giles could barely have wielded with two, striding toward the French doors.

"The eternal war ends tonight!" Sanno declared, and crashed through the French doors, setting off numerous ear-shattering alarms.

Giles thought of Willow. "Yes," he whispered to himself. "That's precisely what I'm afraid of."

"We must hurry," Giles said at a trot. Cordelia fought to keep up. "We don't know where Willow is, and if we lose sight of Xander, we may never know. We'll be too late to do anything."

"Okay, yeah, but you aren't wearing heels!" Cordelia snapped, as she watched the distant figure stride across the museum lawn. In the background, the security alarm had fallen silent. Eddie the watchman must have decided she was a psycho and told the police to go home.

The figure seemed to shimmer as it walked. It seemed bigger and taller than Xander, and yet, if she squinted, Xander was the only thing there. It was Xander they were following, but it wasn't.

She caught up to Giles and glommed on to him, trying like anything to step out of her shoes. With each step they took, her too-high heels sank about two inches into the lawn.

"Cordelia, please, take those wretched things off!" Giles pleaded.

"I'm sorry. I just need to stop for one second so I can get them off." She watched Xander up ahead and felt as if she might cry. "These are Ferragamos! Do you know how much they cost?"

Giles shook his head impatiently.

"A lot!" She added, "What's happened to Xander?"

"It appears he's been possessed by the Sword of Sanno, well, actually, by Sanno himself," Giles said anxiously as he watched the figure thunder away from them.

"Well, then why is he speaking English?" she asked, confused.

"I suppose Sanno has accessed all of Xander's knowledge, including the language center. Xander wouldn't be used to actually having to form the sounds required for ancient Japanese. Also, it must realize we wouldn't understand it otherwise. Fascinating, really," Giles replied.

"Oh, yeah, that'd be my response too," she said sarcastically as she yanked off her shoes, "but it's not. I mean, I know he's possessed, but how?"

"Cordelia, I'll try to explain later. We must hurry!"

"That's all I am to you guys," she said sadly. "The one you're going to explain everything to later—!"

"Cordelia, come!" Giles ordered, urging her along.

"—The one you talk to like she's a collie!"

She hurried after him, her precious shoes slung over her shoulder.

A cold wind kicked up around Giles and Cordelia, gathering in strength and pushing them forward. About twenty feet ahead, Xander turned and smiled at them.

"I thought to hurry you along," the booming voice told them. "So that you may witness the destruction of the vampire. It does not yet realize I have freed myself, but when it does—"

"You freed yourself?" Cordelia shouted at it. "Excuse me, but my boyfr— . . . the guy I . . . Xander Harris freed you, Mr. Santo."

"I am *Sanno!*" the voice thundered. The figure lifted its arms and the wind blew so hard it almost lifted Giles from the earth. "The Mountain King." It lowered its arms and strutted. "I am the protector of the Land of the Rising Sun!"

Though she was losing her balance in the bitter gale, Cordelia was not about to capitulate. Giles found her scrappy behavior remarkably refreshing, as opposed to her penchant for superficiality

"Well, well, um, you aren't in the Land of the Rising Sun, you're in the land of Sunnydale," Cordelia said. "And things are different here. We have our own person who destroys vampires." She waved him away. "So you can go home now."

"Silence!" Sanno bellowed. "Silence, mortal girl! *Baka no onna!"*

With a point of his fire, Cordelia was slammed to

the ground and pinned there. She began to shriek and struggle, near tears.

Giles knelt on one knee and bowed. "Oh, great and magical warlord, *gomenasai*. Forgive the female," he said carefully. "She is very young and ignorant. She acts out of fear for the boy whose body you inhabit, knowing what is to come."

He hissed at Cordelia, "Apologize!"

"I'm sorry," she said meekly.

Sanno said, "Very well."

Immediately the wind stopped blowing. Blinking, Cordelia brushed her bangs from her eyes, waited a beat, then clumsily got to her feet. She looked drained.

"Thank you," she said.

Sanno turned and strutted away.

Cordelia raced over to Giles. "'What is to come'? I don't know what is to come. Do you?"

Giles gestured to the retreating figure. "Oh, my dear girl." He sighed. "I'm afraid he's going to fight Chirayoju."

Cordelia stared at Xander, and then at Giles. She said, "What? But that's Willow."

Giles sighed harder. "Precisely."

She cocked her head. "Willow and Xander are going to duke it out?"

"And other things. I imagine some magic will be involved." Gently he took her wrist. "Come along now. We must keep up."

"Magic?" she repeated, stumbling after him. "Why will there be magic?"

"Isn't there always?" he asked, trying to make a joke. But it wasn't at all funny.

"How do we know when one of them wins?"

He didn't want to answer her, but she shook him hard. "Giles!"

"Oh, well." He halted and looked at her sadly. "I suppose when one of them . . . loses." He swallowed, hating to say the words. "That is to say, when one of them dies."

CHAPTER 16

The ruined Sunnydale Friendship Garden was not the weirdest thing Buffy had ever seen, but it was close. It was enormous, which both surprised and worried her: why hadn't she ever seen it before? She'd lived in Sunnydale an entire year and she'd been sure she'd seen all its seven wonders—but this beat all of them by a mile.

The garden was sunk into the ground. She stood on the ridge above it and looked down on the skeletal trees and rotted hump-backed bridges as she scanned the area in the gray twilight. She flicked on her flashlight. The yellow beam flickered over stone lanterns and little red temple-things—*pagodas,* came the word, although she had no idea how she knew a thing like that when she couldn't even remember *origami*—and in the distance a large, darkened building made of wood with a gently curved tile roof. Wow. When this place was built, it had represented a lot of high hopes. And money.

Buffy looked up. The sun was peeking just above the horizon, dimming the landscape. Buffy heard no sounds, not even the chirping of crickets. That in itself was enough to give her the creeps.

But what she saw coming out of the building made her knees turn to water.

Willow was dressed in an elaborate Chinese robe and, over that, some kind of upper-body metal armor. She carried a spear, maybe a long sword, and she glanced up, apparently not noticing Buffy, then strode back into the building.

A light flickered in one of the open windows, as if from a candle.

Buffy swallowed hard and began to walk down a set of stone steps toward the building. Every sense was on alert; her gaze darted left, right, as she tried very hard to look casual and unafraid.

To her right was a deep indentation that looked as though it might have been a pond or pool at one time. A wooden bridge rose over it, the center portion smashed, probably by vandals.

Buffy walked through the silent garden.

Then she thought she heard weeping.

She quickened her pace as she approached the building. The weeping came from inside. It could only be Willow. Or so Buffy hoped.

There was a small wooden porch attached to the building. Carefully, aware that the wood could give way at any moment, Buffy stepped onto it and peered inside.

In the center of the bare, wood-floored room, Willow wept all alone, the tears splashing down her face. With a large, jade-green candle set in an ornate red candle holder before her, she was seated on a scarlet pillow, staring at the spear she had been carrying. On the floor nearby was a sword, a traditional Japanese *katana,* and Buffy didn't even want to know where or how Willow had come by all of these things.

Not that she had time to think about it. Not while Willow was pointing the sharp tip of a spear directly at her own heart.

"Willow, no!" Buffy screamed, running toward her.

The floor beneath Buffy made a strange singing sound as she ran across it. It startled her, making her falter.

Willow's head jerked up. With a whiplike motion, she turned the spear around and pointed it at Buffy. Then she said, "Oh. It's only you." She wiped her face and stared with brutal hostility at the person who was supposed to be her best friend. The spear remained pointed at Buffy.

"Oh? It's only me?" Buffy echoed in astonishment.

"I thought you might be someone else." Her tears were gone. She was a different person.

Oh, yes, a very different person.

"Who were you expecting?" Buffy demanded, sliding her hand into her Slayer's bag as discreetly as she could. "Pizza delivery? Cable guy?"

Willow pursed her lips. Then she smiled a cruel, knowing smile and patted a cushion across from her own. "I have within me a memory that in the past your childish humor amused me. Sit while I await the setting of the sun."

Buffy didn't move. Now that she had found Willow, with the sun at its last gasp, she didn't know what to do. Eerily, Willow continued to pat the cushion. Her smile broadened.

She gestured to the floor. "This is a 'Nightingale Floor.' A very ancient tradition, which I learned in Japan," she said. "The emperors installed them so that no one could sneak up on them. But of course I knew you were coming." She chuckled. "I could smell your blood. I cannot wait to taste of it."

"Willow," Buffy tried again. "Something very bad has happened to you. Let me take you to Giles so he can fix you."

"No one can 'fix' me." Willow raised her chin. "It is too late."

And then, for one awful moment, Willow's chin quivered and she reached toward Buffy with both her hands. She was trembling. "Stop it," she begged. "Buffy, stop *me*." Then she fell forward as if someone had shot her.

The sun had gone down. The night had fallen upon them all.

Buffy acted. She darted toward Willow over the strangely singing floor and grabbed away her spear. In one motion she cracked it over her knee and tossed the two pieces across the room.

"And what has that accomplished?" Willow asked, in a lower, deeper voice. "That was not the weapon you should fear."

"Okay," Buffy said slowly, glancing at the sword on the ground not far away, trying to buy time. Angel should be catching up to her any second. "And the weapon to be feared would be?"

"I am that weapon," Willow said.

Slowly she sat back up. The floor clinged and clanged. Buffy blinked. She could almost see another set of features superimposed over Willow's. A luminous green face with blood-red lips. Almond-shaped black eyes that bored into her. The face seemed covered with some kind of glowing growth, like mold or rotted wood. It was horrible.

Laughter boomed across the room even though Willow did not laugh.

The floor sang, though Buffy stood frozen.

"I am," Willow repeated.

She clapped her hands. Like arrows, vampires leaped into the room from every window and rushed Buffy. She realized they must have buried themselves in the garden the night before, to be so close so fast.

Instantly Buffy jumped to her feet and assumed a fighting stance. She kicked the first vamp to reach her in the face and scrambled to get a stake out of her bag, cursing herself for being caught off guard as another vampire grabbed her from behind. She thrust her body forward and down, flipping the vamp to the floor with a satisfying crack. She grabbed a stake and dispatched them both quickly, in twin clouds of dust.

The floor's song became a long screech of fury. The vampires descended upon her, a small army, and she punched and kicked, fully realizing for the first time that the other night at the Bronze, the vampires who had lain in wait for her had been sent by Willow. They had preferred death over her wrath.

But it wasn't her, that's what Buffy kept telling herself. It wasn't really Willow.

A girl vampire with bright red hair and an oversized St. Andrew's sweatshirt vaulted toward her with a savage snarl even as another fang-girl in a large sweater dove at her legs. For a moment, they had her.

Then Buffy moved. Her fists came up and she shattered the grip of the redhead. With the heels of her hands, she thrust the St. Andrew's girl's head back, then slammed the by-now-well-used stake deep into her chest.

As soon as the redhead had exploded, Buffy took care of the other one around her knees.

But there were more. There seemed to be no end to them. And even though she was holding her own so far, Buffy was growing tired.

Seated on her pillow, Willow watched, smiling. Buffy turned to her and held out a beseeching hand, just as Willow had earlier. Panting, she said, "Will, you can stop them."

Willow said slowly, as if the thought was just occurring to her, "Yes."

Hopefully, Buffy went on, "Yes, yes! Just tell them to stop. They'd do what you want. They're afraid of you."

Willow lowered her head. Buffy felt a surge of hope that her sweet, Smurfy buddy was battling the monster that had possessed her.

Then Willow threw back her head and laughed, spreading her arms wide. The features of the other being were laid over her face like a grotesque green plastic mask.

"They should fear me," Willow said, only it was not Willow's voice at all. It was a demon's, and it grated on Buffy's nerves like fingers on a blackboard. "As should you, Slayer."

It snapped its fingers and walked slowly toward Buffy. The other vampires released her and glided away, ringing the perimeter of the room like spectators at a wrestling match.

"You're tired," it said in a singsong voice, the floor echoing its hypnotic rhythm. "Very tired."

Buffy's eyes drooped. An ice-cold wind whipped up around her, sapping the energy from her muscles. Her legs quivered. Her knees began to buckle.

"Your heart is slowing. Your blood is congealing."

Buffy sagged. She could barely keep her eyes open.

Then Willow rose into the air with her arms spread as the wind slapped at Buffy. Her head brushed the ceiling and her hair streamed behind her. Balls of lightning tumbled from her fingertips and crackled as they smashed into the floor around Buffy, setting the floor on fire.

The singing floor began to scream.

The other vampires backed away from the growing flames of the tinderbox wood, looking at one another as if waiting for one of them to jump out a window, so the others could see if it was better to upset Willow or burn to death.

"Know me as the vampire sorcerer Chirayoju," Willow bellowed above the shriek of the wind as it whipped the flames into a brilliant wall of death. "I have come forth from my prison at last. And as soon as you are no longer a threat to me, Slayer, I will rule this place."

"Sunnydale?" Buffy murmured. Now she was sweating from the heat, and suddenly she realized that the threat of the fire had distracted her long enough for Willow's hypnotic voice to begin to lose its effect on her. Her heart was not slowing, it was revving up like she was listening to thrash metal after two particularly thick espressos. And most definitely was her blood not congealing.

"Really, with all these special effects, you could do better," she went on, her voice stronger, her stance more assured. "Conquering Sunnydale would be nothing to brag about to the other vampire sorcerers in Vampire Sorcererland, believe me. They'd take your union card and laugh you right out of the club."

"Silence!" Chirayoju shrieked. It fell from the ceiling, aiming directly at Buffy.

Which would require, Buffy realized, that it pass through the wall of flame.

"Willow!" she shouted. "No!"

The body of her friend continued to plummet. Buffy took a deep breath and looked for a gap in the flames. She saw one about three feet to her left—the flames were only knee-high—and Buffy bounded over to the spot, making sure she still had her Slayage equipment, and jumped over the fire. She felt the heat through the soles of her boots.

Chirayoju landed less than five feet from her and came at her with a series of roundhouse kicks. Buffy ducked them, giving as good as she got, then wincing as the monster cried out in pain, not in its own voice, but in Willow's.

"An interesting dilemma for you, eh?" Chirayoju said. "You must defeat me, but you do not want to kill your friend." It sneered at her, a morphing combination of its own features and Willow's. "You are weak."

"Oh?" Buffy stiff-armed Willow in her changing face. The thing inside her staggered backward. "How's that for weak?"

"You care for her," Chirayoju taunted her, coming at her. "I care for nothing and no one."

"You hear that, you guys? It doesn't care about you." Buffy called. She ticked a quick glance around the room. The other vampires had disappeared. No wonder. The entire building was engulfed in flames, the ceiling included. Any second now, the whole structure would cave in.

With a grunt of effort, Buffy launched herself at Chirayoju, forcing it back into the depths of the room. Yet Buffy's mind registered that Willow was in mortal danger from the flames.

She had no idea what to do. Chirayoju represented a threat far greater than just this tiny combat in a dead garden. Buffy had to stop it. But how to do that without sacrificing her best friend . . .

Above her, two wooden beams dislodged from the ceiling and crashed to the floor behind her. The floor groaned like a dying beast, and then it cracked open. Buffy staggered backward slightly. Another beam fell. Roof tiles shot through the weakened ceiling toward her and Chirayoju like bombs.

Suddenly she rushed Chirayoju, grabbed the demon vampire around the waist, and dove with it out a window.

They rolled in the weeds and the dirt. Then Buffy flung it away from her and resumed her fighting stance.

It was then that she realized her Slayer's bag was still inside the burning building.

Chirayoju seemed to realize the same thing at the same time.

It grinned hideously.

"It ends," it said, advancing slowly, as if savoring

the moment of triumph. Smoke rose from its body. "You will be mine."

"Sorry, I've already got a Valentine."

Her mind raced as she scanned the area for a piece of wood, a branch, anything she could use as a weapon. Finally, in desperation, she reached inside her blouse and yanked the metal chain she wore around her neck. She held the cross before Chirayoju, having no idea if it would have any effect on a Chinese vampire sorcerer.

Chirayoju hissed and stopped short. Buffy almost cheered with relief. It was the same cross Angel had given her the night they met. She would have to thank him again for it. She would have to—

"Where did you get that?" the vampire demanded, gesturing to it.

"Does it matter?" she asked, feeling better as she caught her breath.

"It's mine! Give it back!" it shouted, balling its fists in frustration.

"Yours?" Buffy glanced at the chain. Along with the cross, the disk Willow had taken from the Sword of Sanno dangled from it.

Buffy grinned.

"Oh. *Yours,*" she said. "Then come and get it."

Frenzied, screaming, Chirayoju flew at her.

For a heartbeat, Buffy froze. If Willow was really a vampire, just another hollow corpse filled with some kind of bloodsucking demon spirit—well, that'd be different. It wouldn't be Willow anymore. But as far as she could tell, whatever this Chirayoju was, it was inside the real flesh-and-blood Willow, and she was still in there, too.

For the moment, Chirayoju seemed focused on the

small disk she wore on a chain with her crucifix. Could she just give it up? Maybe . . .

Chirayoju lunged for her. The Slayer dropped her left shoulder, ducked it down and came up under Willow's body, flipping Chirayoju over and back. Claws scrabbled for purchase on Buffy's blouse and arm, dragging deep, bloody furrows across the flesh of her upper biceps.

Buffy spun to face the vampire demon who possessed the body of her friend. The seething sting of the scratches on her arm gave her a new clarity: staying alive was key. Part of the Slayer's job, actually. But unless she was willing to kill Willow, she would die.

Buffy took a deep breath. Then, silently, she apologized to Giles. To her mom. To Dad, wherever he was this week.

Because she knew she was about to fail in that primary task. Buffy Summers knew she was about to die.

Then, in that same moment of clarity, she recalled something that would save her life. Willow's hand. Or rather, her wrist. After Chirayoju had possessed her, Willow's fractured wrist had healed instantly. Almost miraculously.

Buffy smiled. She wasn't going to like hurting Willow, but at least now she knew that Willow would heal. She could defend herself without doing any lasting damage.

"All right, whatever the hell you are," Buffy snapped. "Come on, then. I want my friend back. If that means I have to keep inflicting pain until you decide to forfeit the game—well, let me tell you, I can go all night."

Chirayoju roared and rushed at her again. Willow's red-tinted locks flew back as the vampire sorcerer came at Buffy, more cautious this time, but no less savage.

"I have had entire nations on their knees before me," Chirayoju snarled. "The ancients whimpered in fear at the whisper of my name. So shall you."

The thing circled, looking for an opening. Buffy kept up her guard, and they faced each other down. She found it difficult to look at Willow's face, at the slack emptiness of her features, the hollowness of her eyes. Instead, she concentrated on the gossamer flickering of the grotesquely glowing green face that seemed to cling over Willow's like some sheer Halloween mask.

Only this wasn't Halloween.

Buffy knew from Halloween, and this was way worse.

"The ancients, huh?" Buffy asked, smiling. "Well, then, just for you, the Slayer's gonna have to reach way down deep inside and come up with a real old-school vampire butt-kicking."

That ghost mask stretched itself into a sickening smile. Buffy's stomach lurched as she saw Willow's mouth and cheeks move beneath it, lifted into a tiny smile themselves, as though the ghost mask were touching her face, twisting her features.

"Foolish girl," Chirayoju sneered. "You still do not grasp the truth of this conflict, do you? I have merely been testing you. This fragile shell I now wear has served me well, but it is weak and small.

"You, however, are the Slayer. Your body will be a much more suitable host for my magnificence."

"I could take that as a compliment," Buffy said. "But . . . no."

She shot forward in a high kick. It would have connected well, a solid hit . . . if not for the wind. The wind that sprang up and tossed her through the air as though she were chaff in a summer breeze. Buffy landed painfully between a pair of squat pagodas. When she sat up, she had a hard time catching her breath.

Her left cheek was swollen and throbbing in pain, and she suspected the bone was bruised beneath the skin. Chirayoju wasn't like any vampire she'd ever fought. Maybe it was because she was holding back for Willow's sake, but she didn't think so. There was something so profoundly evil in this creature that it made it difficult for her to concentrate. Not merely evil, but consciously so.

Most vampires were simple predators, their evil confined to their lust for blood and death and terror. This was very, very different. The average blood-sucker barely considered what its prey was, what it might be thinking, what life it might live. Buffy sensed in Chirayoju a horrible intelligence. This ancient, savage thing knew exactly what effect its butchery would have on its victims' loved ones; it understood the questioning of reality that would come from an encounter with it.

Chirayoju was smart. The demon spirit was a vampire in more ways than one. It fed on blood, true. But Buffy realized that it fed on fear and despair as well.

And she wasn't about to give it that.

"Give yourself to me, Slayer," Chirayoju hissed,

and seemed to float across the withered vegetation toward her.

Buffy looked up, felt the sharp pain of a torn muscle in her shoulder. She blew a strand of hair from her face with lips covered in bloody spittle. She was in rough shape, and she knew it.

She lowered her head as the vampire came for her.

She reached for the concrete roof of the little pagoda in front of her and brought it up hard, with all her strength, in a blow that tore her shoulder muscle further. The concrete shattered on the side of Chirayoju's head with a crack. Blood sprayed, and Willow's skull gave way.

Chirayoju dropped to the dead garden.

Buffy's heart stopped. She couldn't breathe. Tears sprang to her eyes.

"Oh my God, Willow!" she whispered frantically. "I'm sorry."

She dropped to her knees in the soft, dead earth and reached for her friend. A hand whipped up from the ground and tangled in her hair, drawing her down, her face forced into the dirt and dead plants. The smell was rich and sweet and laced with rot.

"Now, Slayer," she heard it whisper, "your body will be mine. This form was useful to me, but you are so much more powerful. You aren't like other mortal girls."

Buffy threw an elbow back, slammed it into Willow's gut, then used her leverage to toss Chirayoju off her.

"I've been hearing that my whole life," she grunted, still trying to catch her breath. Buffy looked up at the ghastly double-vision face of her best friend.

Chirayoju's eyes bulged with rage. "You tempt my fury, girl."

"Yeah," Buffy agreed, getting to her feet. "I'm just kinda wacky like that. You and my mom should have a chat."

Wearing Willow's body, cloaked in an armored breastplate, the vampire began to rise again.

C'mon, Buffy wanted to say. *Gimme a second to catch my breath, will ya?*

Chirayoju began to charge. Buffy set her legs, trying to convince her exhausted body that she was truly ready for another round. There was nothing else she could do.

Except to die before she could be possessed . . .

Then a shadow whipped past her and met Chirayoju head on. Claws ripped the air, ripped flesh, and Willow's body was flung backward to the earth.

Buffy blinked.

Angel stood over Chirayoju, his face twisted and feral. The back of his shirt was torn to shreds and long ragged wounds, stained crimson, were already healing.

"You're not going to touch her again," Angel said, his voice that low rumble Buffy knew so well—was so incredibly relieved to hear. "She might not want to do it, but if it comes to it, I'll kill that body you're in to keep you from getting to Buffy."

Buffy's relief evaporated. The Slayer's stomach lurched and a dagger of ice thrust itself into her chest. She reached out a hand as Angel advanced on the demon.

"Angel . . ." she gasped. "No."

CHAPTER 17

Giles felt nauseous. Cordelia wasn't helping.

"Giles, what are we going to do?" Cordelia asked desperately.

Giles didn't tell her that she'd been asking the same question for the past four minutes, barely interrupting herself to breathe. Nor did he mention that his own mind was in as much turmoil as his stomach as he worked feverishly to answer that question.

But he did know that he'd been unnecessarily cold to Cordelia, and he regretted it.

"Cordelia, I must apologize." He sighed. "I've been terribly short with you, and I'm afraid it's because I'm feeling rather useless at the moment," he admitted sheepishly. "You see, I really don't know how to withdraw these spirits from Willow and Xander. I had hoped that if we kept up with

Sanno—Xander—that I might be able to speak with it, to learn enough to stop this insanity."

Cordelia watched the receding figure of Xander. Giles followed her gaze. "And we're losing him, huh. He's getting away from us."

"He's getting away from us," Giles agreed.

"Well, what about your books?" Cordelia asked hopefully. "There's gotta be something there, right? You've got the skinny on every nasty thing that's ever walked the Earth."

"Well, perhaps not all of the nasty things," Giles murmured, then looked at her. "Researching this could take all night, and this is happening right now. Not to mention that until we know where Xander—where Sanno—is going, we won't know where the battle is going to be fought." He looked glumly at the horizon, where Xander was fast disappearing.

Cordelia cocked her head at Giles and frowned.

"What did I say?" he asked.

"Well, only something clueless. I think." Cordelia hesitated, then went on. "You showed us yourself in the museum, Giles. If they're going to have it out, it'll be in that Japanese garden place. Don't you think?"

Giles paused, eyebrows raised. He looked far ahead, where Xander's possessed form melted into the night. It made sense. If he recalled the layout of Sunnydale correctly, they did seem to be heading in that direction.

Which meant they didn't need to follow Xander at all. And suddenly, Giles had an idea or two about possession. It might even be worth giving an old-fashioned exorcism a try.

"I can see the Giles-mind in action," Cordelia declared hopefully. "Usually a frightening thing, but please tell me you've got something."

Giles spun, and turned to walk back the way they came.

"Wait. Where are you going?" Cordelia demanded.

"The library," Giles replied. "Come on, Cordelia, I'll need your help."

"But what about Xander?" she asked, glancing over her shoulder.

Giles stated the obvious. "We can't keep up."

She tried one more time. "But I've always been useless with research."

Giles gestured for her to follow him. "Well, it's time we changed that then, isn't it?"

"We should get your car."

"Agreed." He kept walking.

In the library, Cordelia was too nervous for this sitting around and thumbing through books stuff. She shifted uncomfortably in her chair and said to Giles, "I don't even know how to spell exorcism."

"Look," he said excitedly, as the fax machine rang.

He gestured for her to join him as the paper unspooled. With an excited flourish, he ripped it off.

"'Monsieur Giles, so sorry to hear of troubles in Sunnydale. I have fragments of Appendix 2a of Silver's *Spells*, published much later than your edition. Pages thirty-two through thirty-four only. She writes most excitedly of the sword's movement after the earthquake in Kobe. There was fear of escape of two spirits within. New enchantments were added, disks, I think, and the sword was put in Tokyo Museum. That is all I have at this time. You might try Heinrich Meyer-Dinkmann in Frankfurt, and of course you must have consulted Kobo at Tokyo University. Kindest regards, Henri Tourneur.'"

"All right, that's confirmation that the disks are wards," Giles said.

"All right," Cordelia agreed.

"Do keep looking." He gestured to the two-foot-tall stack of books he'd gathered on the table. "I'll try Meyer-Dinkmann. And it's e-x-o-r-c-i-s-m. I suggest you write it down."

"Giles." She shook her head. "What I mean is I am not getting anywhere. I can't even see the words. All I see is Xander's face when we found him in the bushes. And in the hospital. And now." She swallowed hard. "I can't concentrate."

Giles put down his book and moved behind her. "But we must," he said gently. "I, too, am distracted. But this is what we can do to help him. It's all we can do."

"Then he's in big trouble," she muttered.

Giles was on the phone to Berlin.

"Guten Tag, hier spricht Giles," he began.

"Herr Giles! A pleasure!"

"That could be my job, if I spoke German," Cordelia muttered. "I *like* talking on the phone. But *no,* I have to look up *exorcism.*"

"Ja, ja, vielen Dank," Giles said, and hung up. "Well."

She looked up hopefully. "Yes?"

"Meyer-Dinkmann couldn't put his hands on it, but he's read more of Appendix 2a than Tourneur. It appears that there was an actual Incantation of

Sanno, and it has all the details about how to bind spirits into swords." He looked dazed. "You know, Cordelia, this is rather how Miss Silver went about her research, only of course everything was much slower in her day. Imagine what that woman could have accomplished given a fax, a telephone, and the vast resources of the Internet!"

"Yeah," Cordelia piped. "So where is the Incantation of Sanno?"

"Meyer-Dinkmann said it's been uploaded onto the Net," Giles said enthusiastically. "He said he'd have, ah, downloaded the file for us, but his computer is temporarily down for an upgrade of some sort. But if I understand computers, we can simply access the topic we wish and type in a key word to see if we have any matches."

"Okay!" Cordelia said brightly, saved from the book stack. "Let's do it."

He moved his shoulders as he continued. "I haven't the foggiest notion how to go about it, however. We need Willow."

"We need Willow," Cordelia agreed glumly.

Buffy and Angel caught Chirayoju off guard, and together, were able to hurl the thing, in Willow's body, over the bony, upraised fingers of a dead cherry tree. Buffy fought to catch her breath as the monster landed in the dirt.

"We can't keep this up," Angel murmured to the girl he loved. "We have to finish it." He looked at her flushed, drawn face. "Buffy, we have to kill Willow."

Wildly the Slayer shook her head. "No. No way. Look, why don't you go? It hasn't torched me with that magic fire because it wants my bod. It can't kill me, I can't kill it. Stalemate. We could use some Giles-type help here."

Angel stared at her. "It may not want to kill you. That doesn't mean it won't. I'm not going anywhere."

Chirayoju rose to a standing position and brushed the dirt off its crimson robes with theatrical distaste. "I find this fighting style most plebeian," it said. Its right arm was crooked, and it limped as it moved forward.

Angel scrutinized Chirayoju's movements as it prepared to launch another attack, posturing like a martial arts master. Willow's body was badly injured. He knew Buffy couldn't stand to see her suffer, even if she wasn't Willow at the moment. But Angel would do whatever it took—including destroying Willow, who was *his* friend, too—to make sure Buffy got out of this alive.

"Buffy, you know what must be done," *my love,* he added silently, pitying her. Wishing he could lift the burden of being the Chosen One from her shoulders for just five minutes. But that would do nothing. And she *was* the Chosen One. There was no way she could be anything less, not even for a heartbeat.

Looking very frightened and very young, she lifted her chin in defiance. Her eyes were huge in her face, but her jaw was set and hard. Her shoulders squared. "I won't do it."

"Then I will," Angel said firmly.

"No!" Buffy cried.

Chirayoju the vampire rose straight into the air and made fists of its hands, launching fireballs at them. Buffy and Angel rolled in opposite directions as the balls seemed to track them, then exploded into the earth as the two successfully eluded them. The dry brush and the brittle trees lit up like fireworks.

Buffy murmured, "Okay, maybe it doesn't want my bod."

She frowned, as something occurred to her. "And how come you were so late, anyway?"

Another volley of fireballs careened toward them. Angel leaped on top of Buffy and rolled her out of the way. As she lay beneath him, he said, "Don't tell me you haven't noticed that the rest of Chirayoju's playmates kind of disappeared."

"Yeah. A likely excuse," she said, as he let her up and she assumed a Slayer's fighting stance. "You probably just went out for cigs."

"Gave 'em up," he assured her. "They take years off your life." Then he cried, "Look out!"

Chirayoju hurtled itself from the sky straight at Buffy.

"If you will not give yourself to me, then you will be eliminated! Choose, Slayer!"

Buffy jumped into the air and pummeled the vampire demon with a double kick, then flipped herself backward, catching herself at the last minute with her hands and pushing off them sideways, out of the way of Willow's body as it slammed hard on the ground.

"That answer your questions, Chumley?" Buffy asked. She got in a couple of quick kicks before Angel grabbed it by the shoulders and punched it hard, wincing as he heard a tiny gasp that sounded very much like Willow.

"Please," he heard, in Willow's voice. "Please."

"Stop!" Buffy shouted.

"It's a trick, Buffy," Angel called to her. "It's playing on your feelings. Don't listen to it."

"I'm allowing her to feel the pain," Chirayoju said, pulling itself away from Angel and focusing its attention on Buffy. It didn't even bother to look at him. "And it hurts, Slayer. It hurts more than you can imagine. Certainly more than *she* could—until now."

Tears welled in Buffy's eyes as she panted, fighting to catch her breath. She said unsteadily, "Hurt her any more, and I'll . . . I'll . . ."

Chirayoju laughed. "There is nothing you can do, is there? Except for one thing." It smiled. "I want your body, Slayer."

She sneered at it. "Sorry, I've got a steady."

Suddenly Chriayoju flew away from Buffy and focused its gaze on Angel. It said in a hypnotic voice, "You are my slave, vampire. You will do as I say."

Buffy gaped as Angel's face grew slack and blank. His dark, intense eyes stared hard at the vampire demon. "You will begin to walk. You will walk until the sun comes up. And then you will die."

"No!" Buffy shouted.

Chirayoju smiled at Buffy in victory. It said, "Thus will he die, along with the girl whose body you are killing."

"Angel!" she cried.

"Don't worry, Buffy, you're not like other girls, and I'm not like other vampires!"

Angel flew at Chirayoju and grabbed it around the neck. Angel bared his fangs, preparing to lower his mouth to Willow's throat, growling savagely.

Chirayoju said to Buffy, "I will let him kill her."

"Stop," Buffy said tiredly. "Okay. You win. Angel,

let it go." Smiling grimly, she held out her hand. "Mr. Cheerios, congratulations. You've just won the big showcase on *Let's Make a Deal.*"

"No, Buffy," Angel said.

"Yes, Buffy," Buffy replied unhappily. She said to the vampire. "Let me say good-bye to him."

"No tricks," it said suspiciously, as Angel glowered at it.

"No tricks," she assured it. "But I want something in return, or no deal."

"You dare—" it began.

"Shut up!" Buffy snapped. "You want my help? Then be quiet and listen. You don't attack him or Willow after you take me over. That's my condition."

It paused. Considered.

"That is your sole condition?"

"I'd like to make a list, but I figure that'd be pushing it," she retorted. Her heart was pounding. She was scared, but she wasn't about to let it know that. And there were worse things than being possessed by ancient Chinese demon vampires.

There was always math.

"Agreed," Chirayoju said. "I will not harm Weeping Willow, or the vampire you call your mate."

"Well, not my mate, exactly," she said, reddening as she glanced at Angel. "That sounds so . . . um, primitive."

Angel pleaded, "Buffy, don't do this."

She walked a short distance away as Angel reluctantly let the demon go. Buffy touched the chain around her neck, tried to find the clasp without being obvious about it, and gave it a yank as Angel caught up with her.

Protectively, desperately, he put his arms around her.

"Buffy, you don't know what it's like to be taken over by evil," he whispered. "I do. I can't let you go through with this."

"You don't have a choice, Angel," she said. "Please, just help me."

She lowered her gaze to her fist. "It has a jones for this little disk thingy. Willow accidentally knocked it off the sword just before she cut herself. I figure it helped set Chirayoju free. When it saw it around my neck, it got all hyper."

She gathered the chain up in her fist and pressed it into his. Instantly, a look of pain crossed over his face. Her eyes widened and she glanced down, to see a small wisp of smoke trailing from his closed hand.

"Oh, the cross," she said, remembering that she had been wearing the silver cross he had given her the first night they met. "I'm so sorry."

"It's okay." He gave her a pained, crooked smile. "It's a good kind of hurt."

"Get it to Giles. He'll know what to do. He's like Scotty, you know, on *Star Trek?*" She paused. "Wow. You probably watched it when it first came on in the sixties."

But Angel wasn't swayed by her change of subject. "Buffy, please," he whispered. "Don't do it."

She gazed up at him fearfully. She wondered if she would ever be in Angel's arms again. She guessed he was wondering the same thing, because he looked very, very worried and held her too tight.

"Kiss me?" she whispered. "For luck?"

"I love you," he murmured.

Their lips met. She wanted to fling her arms

around him but she held the kiss, feeling his mouth against hers, a coolness in the fever of her terror. To be possessed by evil . . . she couldn't imagine a worse fate.

Except dying possessed by evil.

She was the first to pull away.

"Okay, Mr. Cheerios," she said jauntily, "I'm ready." She turned to face the monstrous evil as it glided up to her and grabbed up her hand. Its grip burned her as the cross must have burned Angel.

"Remember your promise," she said, swallowing hard. "No running in the halls."

"To the last, your weak and pointless jokes," it said.

"Next stop, Comedy Central," she replied unsteadily.

"Buffy," Angel said. "Buffy, stop. Don't go through with it."

It straightened her fingers and sliced at its own cheek. "My blood," it explained, smearing her hand against the wound.

"Willow's," Buffy said. "It's Will—" She inhaled deeply as something rammed hard through her chest, knocking her completely senseless.

Then she was surrounded by screaming— agonized and hopeless screaming. It went on and on until she thought she wouldn't be able to stand it for another second. Then it grew louder.

She heard Willow cry, "Buffy!"

Then she was burning up, standing inside a firestorm that ate away every inch of her being. She writhed as flames whooshed around her, burning through her lungs, her vocal cords, her ears.

She trembled, freezing, in utter silence. She

looked left, right; but where she was, endless blackness stretched in all directions. She tried to move,
but she was frozen to the . . .

to the . . .

to nothing.

She was utterly, vastly *nowhere*.

Somewhere, very far away, she heard a voice she
once had known very well. With a laugh, it spoke:

"I have won."

CHAPTER 18

top!" Angel roared.

Buffy stopped. Angel stood to bar her path and stared into her eyes. But she wasn't there. Everything that was Buffy had disappeared from her eyes, the spark that was her soul was missing. Still there, he knew . . . from painful experience. But buried as deep as the worst of secrets.

"I vowed to the Slayer that I would not attack you," Chirayoju said, Buffy's lips forming the vampire's words.

Vampire. Yes, but unlike any vampire Angel had ever faced. When it still wore its own flesh, Chirayoju must have been a great sorcerer. That was the only explanation Angel could imagine for the demon's power. It was essentially a ghost, a bodiless demon spirit that, when merged with a human host, made a vampire. Just like him. But nothing like him at all.

"Let her go," Angel demanded, aware that he also had to protect Willow, who was unconscious at his feet. Though Chirayoju's own magical self-preservation had healed her almost completely of the wounds she had received while possessed, she was completely drained of energy.

Chirayoju smiled, and the way its grin twisted Buffy's face, it didn't look like Buffy any more at all. *Which is good,* Angel thought. That would make it easier if he had to kill her. As if anything could make that easy.

The smile broadened, and suddenly a moldy, green face seemed to shimmer into being, covering Buffy's features like a mask, though Angel could still see her through it.

This was Chirayoju's true face, then. Angel's lips curled back and his face changed as well, transforming into the savage face of the vampire within him. Chirayoju had made a mistake. If he'd kept using Buffy's face, Buffy's voice, Buffy's perfect mouth to speak, Angel didn't think he could ever have attacked.

But now he saw the face of the demon.

"I vowed I would not attack, but I said nothing about defending myself," Chirayoju declared. "Stand aside, Angelus . . . yes, I know your name. I plucked it from the Slayer's mind. Stand aside, or you will die your final death."

Without Buffy, he had nothing to live for, but Angel stood his ground. Chirayoju moved forward, prepared to attack, then stopped suddenly. The green ghost face shattered, and Buffy's eyes went wide. For a moment, Angel hoped that Buffy had driven the vampire out of her body, but no, the voice that came from her mouth was still not quite her own.

"I sense . . . something," Chirayoju said. "But it cannot be. Not here."

Then Angel sensed it too. A powerful new presence. He turned, ready to defend himself.

Then he saw who it was.

"Xander?" he called, staring at the new arrival. Xander had a huge old sword in his hands and he marched into the dead garden with a wide grin on his face.

"What do you think you're doing?" Angel asked. "You're going to get yourself killed."

Xander swung the sword up, held it in battle position. It was a very heavy-looking weapon, and yet he moved it as though it were plastic. Angel looked more closely at Xander's face, at his strange smile. And then he knew.

This wasn't Xander any more than the other creature standing in the garden was Buffy. He didn't know who or what it was, but it wasn't the mortal who laughed and joked and called him Dead Boy.

"Another one?" he whispered to himself.

"Chirayoju!" Xander roared, or whatever was inside him did. "Once again you defile the sacred soil of the Land of the Rising Sun! And once again, you will fall beneath my sword. So swears Sanno, the King of the Mountain!"

A powerful wind sprang up suddenly and whipped at Angel. The gale was so strong it almost knocked him back, but he leaned into the wind, trying to figure out what his next move should be. These two were obviously bitter enemies.

"Foolish little god," Chirayoju snarled in return.

"This is not Japan. The soil you stand on now may have been tilled by Japanese hands, but your nation—your mountain—is far from here. You stopped me once, but we have been locked in our bloody battle for many millennia now, and I have the measure of you, Sanno. You cannot defeat me here, on this dead patch of earth. Not when I wear the flesh of one who was already more than human!"

Chirayoju raised its right hand—Buffy's right hand—and laughed deeply. Cruelly. "Time to die, old spirit. The time has come for you to be washed from the earth forevermore!"

As Angel watched them posturing, circling, sizing each other up in the Eastern tradition of combat, he clutched the disk Buffy had slipped him. He realized he was trapped in a horrible dilemma: if he helped Xander, then Buffy might be killed, and vice versa.

Chirayoju's face changed yet again. The sparkle returned to Buffy's eyes for just a moment.

"Xander!" Buffy's voice cried. "No!"

Then it was gone, just as quickly. But Angel had seen it. And he knew that in her mind, in her soul, Buffy was fighting Chirayoju's control. For a moment, while the vampire spirit was distracted, she had taken her body back. She was fighting.

And when the Slayer fought, the Slayer won. In the end. That's why she was the Chosen One. Suddenly Angel had hope. It might be possible to keep them from killing each other after all.

"That's it, Buffy, come on!" he shouted, moving toward Chirayoju, bending against the gale force winds. "Push him out. Take your body back! You can do it!"

Chirayoju sprayed spheres of flame from its palms

and they sizzled through the air toward Xander . . . toward the Mountain King. But the king brought up his sword to stop the flames, and the fire seemed to be absorbed right into the metal.

The sword pointed toward Chirayoju as Sanno stepped forward. Angel jumped between them, eyes darting back and forth between the two ancient spirits.

"Stop," he said. "This battle serves neither one of you. "

He turned to stare into Buffy's eyes, searching for her in there. Finding nothing.

"Out of the way, child," Chirayoju thundered, and raised his hands again.

Angel was about to protest when a blast of fire scorched his back. It had erupted from Sanno's hands, he realized, as he arched with the pain. Then Chirayoju brought fire down upon him as well, and Angel fell to the ground, rolling in the dirt and the dead vegetation to douse the flames.

He grunted in pain as he stared up at Xander's face. The spirit that possessed him clearly enjoyed his own show of power and Angel's agony. It might be a battle of good versus evil, but he didn't think Sanno was much better than Chirayoju. Not after thousands of years of hatred. Sanno wanted to kill his enemy, and it didn't matter who died in the process. The Mountain King was arrogant and cruel, just like a vampire.

Any vampire.

The winds continued to howl all around Angel, kicking up dirt and uprooted plants. Angel slitted his eyes and began to sit up, wincing at the pain of his burns. But the pain was easy to ignore when he thought of what would happen if he didn't do something soon.

Then, over the gale, he heard someone calling his name.

"Angel!" Willow cried again, desperate to understand what was happening all around her. She ached all over, but that was starting to go away. What still hurt was inside: the memory of having been taken over by something not very nice. The brief flashes of reveling in cruelty, of laughing at Buffy and Angel as they had fought her . . .

Then Angel was there, coat flapping in the wind, ignoring the grit that stung her own face and arms. He moved to her and lifted her easily, then ran a few yards to the small gully where water had once run. They ducked behind the cracked wooden bridge that ran over the gully.

Willow didn't even have to ask what was happening. Part of her remembered. The rest of her just knew.

"Are you all right?" Angel asked.

There was an uncomfortable moment between them, even as the battle raged not far away. Willow wondered how long that awkwardness would remain. Both of them were acutely aware that it wasn't all that long ago that Angel had been trying to take her life, rather than save it.

"I'm alive," Willow replied. "Alive is good."

"You remember how you got here?" Angel said quickly.

Willow nodded unhappily.

"Well, something just like it's happened to Xander. That old Chinese vampire's greatest enemy, the guy who defeated him the first time, has taken control of Xander. Buffy's fighting for control of her body, but . . ."

Angel let his words trail off, and Willow felt a chill run all through her body. It was her fault. She'd been so obsessed with being more like Buffy . . . She should never have touched that sword!

But even as the thoughts entered her mind, she knew how foolish they were. There was no way she could have known what was going to happen. No, the only thing she had to concentrate on was how to save Buffy and Xander.

"They're going to kill each other," she said, softly enough that Angel couldn't have heard her over the wailing of the wind.

"Do you remember any of what was in its head?" Angel asked, shouting over the roar of the storm. "Can you think of any way to stop it?"

"No," Willow said, beginning to panic. She shook her head as she stared at the bizarre sight of Buffy and Xander stalking each other, clearly about to launch another attack. She saw the shimmering ghost-faces of the vampire and the Mountain King floating over their features, and that comforted her a little, helped her remember they weren't really themselves.

She turned to Angel, frantic. "Can't you do something?" she demanded. "I mean, come on! I know it's in there, in you! Angelus is in there, and well, he's pretty nasty and you could stop them if you really wanted to! Stop them from killing each other. There's nobody else, Angel. It has to be you!"

Willow stared at him, her eyes pleading. When

Angel glanced away, unable to meet her gaze, Willow sobbed loudly.

"I'm not Angelus any more," he said. "And if I were, all I would do is kill them both, and that isn't really the outcome you're hoping for, is it?"

When she shook her head anxiously, he drawled, "Didn't think so."

"I'm sorry," Willow said meekly.

"Not as sorry as I am."

"So we just let them fight?" Willow asked, wide-eyed.

"What else can we do?" Angel said, turning back to stare at the two figures battling in the moonlight. "I might be able to affect the outcome of this battle, maybe even restrain one of them . . . but not both, Willow, don't you understand? The Mountain King isn't going to stop until Buffy's dead, and even if I could stop him, there'd still be Chirayoju to deal with."

"But what about when it's . . . when it's over?" Willow persisted. "I mean, if the Mountain King kills Buffy, he might just go away, but if Chirayoju wins . . ."

Angel looked at her, and Willow knew she had never seen such sorrow in another person's eyes. "If she wins," Angel said grimly, "then I might just have to murder the one person I love in all the world."

Both of them turned at the sound of Chirayoju screeching in a voice that once had been Buffy's. The vampire sorcerer launched itself at Sanno. Twirling his sword over his head in great, swooping motions, Sanno charged at Chirayoju.

Then Chirayoju leaped into the air, shot flames at the Mountain King, executed a somersault, and landed on the other side of him. Fireballs erupted from the vampire's hands and burned the air as they spat at Sanno, but the Mountain King deflected them with the wide blade of his ancient sword. The orange light reflected off Buffy's features, giving her face combined with Chirayoju's ghastly mask a hellish cast.

Then the two immortal enemies rushed at each other again. Their battle had lasted for thousands of years. Each truly had the measure of the other. But when the battle was to the death, Willow knew there could be only one victor.

As she watched, Buffy and Xander became a blur of fists and kicks and gouts of flame. Willow smelled burning flesh and singed hair. Sanno brought his sword down, slicing the air. The ugly blade missed Buffy's shoulder by inches, the top of her head by even less than that.

Angel turned to her, his eyes narrow and intense. He reached out for Willow's hand and put something into her palm.

"Get this to Giles," the vampire whispered.

Willow looked down, saw the disk and the crucifix, then stared hard at Angel. "What are you going to do?"

Angel smiled. "I'm going to try to keep them both alive." Then he was in motion. He turned and ran at Chirayoju . . . at Buffy . . . and dove at her, face shifting to the savage countenance of the vampire within.

Willow understood then, understood the words he hadn't spoken. He was going to try to keep Buffy and Xander alive, even if it meant his own final death.

But Willow wasn't about to argue. She knew that

Angel was right. There was nothing else for them to do but look to Giles for answers. With a last glance at the fire that burned the air, the blood that spattered the dead garden, the blade that glinted in the light of the full moon, she turned and ran, bent over against the force of the wind.

She ran as if her life depended on it.

As if all their lives depended on it.

In fact, she ran like the devil.

Xander was paralyzed.

He could see. He could hear. But he could not move or feel or speak. Sanno had taken all of those abilities away from him. All he could do was rage in silence against the being that had invaded his body.

Somewhere inside his mind, thunder rolled across an entire world. Almost as if it were coming for him, somehow. As if it would roll over him and obliterate him forever . . . leaving Sanno alone in here, in his body. Somehow he knew that if he stopped fighting, if he just abandoned his body to Sanno, that thunder wouldn't just be in his head anymore. No. It would roll across the surface of the world, starting in Sunnydale. Then the King of the Mountain would be in charge, and anyone who didn't worship the King just might get rolled over too. Or struck by lightning. Or scorched by fire.

It was only that weird intuition that kept Xander from retreating completely. For if he could not control his body's actions, he certainly did not want to bear witness to them. Because his body moved, his arms swung a deadly blade. Sanno was trying to use him for vengeance, but that vengeance was going to cost Buffy her life.

Quietly, Xander realized that he hoped that Chirayoju would win. Then at least Xander would not have to live with the knowledge that he had been unable to stop himself from killing one of his best friends, a girl he cared very deeply for.

When Angel dove at Buffy, Xander felt the tiniest moment of triumph. Somehow, they would all get out of this alive. Or, at the very least, Buffy would. Angel wouldn't let anything bad happen to her.

Chirayoju collided with Angel, and the two crashed to the ground.

"Fool, fool!" Chirayoju shrieked. "What are you doing? I will burn you from the face of the Earth!"

"You swore not to harm me," Angel reminded it, as he grabbed at Chirayoju's punishing fists.

"What is his vow worth?" Sanno demanded as he approached them.

Then suddenly, Chirayoju's features vanished. Angel saw the light in Buffy's eyes. He heard Buffy's voice.

"Angel, stop me now," she whispered. "Kill me."

"Buffy, stay with me," he urged. "Fight him."

He grabbed her hands and threw them behind her back. Her chest pushed against his, and her breath was hot on his neck. He gave her a quick kiss, if only to keep her mind focused on who he was . . . and who she was.

Sanno's eyes lit up.

"The girl has overtaken him?" he asked.

"Yes, I think," Angel replied.

"Then this is the moment of triumph," Sanno declared. "Hold Chirayoju for me, boy. I'll cut off its head."

At that precise moment, the light left Buffy's eyes and she was Chirayoju once more. The demon threw Angel off like a pesky mosquito and snarled at the Mountain King, blasting him backwards with a wave of fire. Then, almost as an afterthought, it used the moment's respite to grab Angel around the neck.

"You would have done it, wouldn't you?" it demanded. It pushed Angel's head to one side and prepared to bite him. "For that, I will destroy you, as certainly as I swore not to."

As Angel struggled, the monster's face congealed and formed over Buffy's. Its teeth lengthened and sharpened into fangs.

"Sanno is correct," it hissed. "My promises are worth nothing. Honor is for those who can afford it."

It smiled in anticipation of the kill, and lowered its teeth toward Angel's neck.

CHAPTER 19

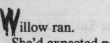illow ran.

She'd expected pain. Aching lungs, bruises on top of bruises, weak and rubbery legs. And she knew the bruises were there, despite whatever healing magic Chirayoju had at its command. But for now, the pain was minimal, completely overwhelmed by fear and adrenaline. In fact, she felt great—alive. The wind whipped her long hair behind her as Willow sprinted across lawns and pavement, jumped low fences and hustled past silent houses, long since dark.

Tomorrow morning she was going to be a wreck. But right now, Willow was focused on only one thing—the only thing she could feel.

Freedom.

She was free. He was gone from her body. It was almost like the horrible flu she'd had in the eighth grade. She'd missed school for a whole week, couldn't even blow her nose her head was so stuffy. The sense of relief she'd felt when the flu was finally gone was only the tiniest fraction of the crazy glee that overwhelmed her now.

Willow ran.

She ran as fast as she could. After all the times that she had thought of Sunnydale as a tiny little burg that barely deserved mention on the map, after all the times she had walked practically all the way across town, now, for the first time, she cursed her hometown as being too big. The school wasn't far away, but it seemed as though she'd never get there.

Then she thought of what would happen if she didn't get there in time. She'd seen what Chirayoju was capable of—had felt it, in fact—and it was obvious that this Mountain King guy wasn't exactly a pushover. Angel was strong, but there was no way he could take both of them on without help. Particularly not while he was trying to keep Buffy and Xander alive.

Buffy. Xander.

Willow's adrenaline spiked even higher, but all the good feeling that came from her freedom disappeared almost instantly. It was her fault. She knew that any of her friends would have argued that with her, but none of them were with her at the moment. She was alone. As alone as she'd been the night she'd been mugged.

That's where it all started.

It was all her fault.

She'd wanted to be more like Buffy, wanted to be tough—a fighter. Wanted, in other words, to be anything but little Willow, everyone's favorite brainy Smurf. All that had somehow led to her becoming possessed by Chirayoju, though she didn't know exactly how. Still, it had to be true. When she cut her finger on that blade, somehow the vampire's captive spirit had sensed her, tasted her blood, felt how vulnerable she was. It had attacked her, violated her in ways much worse than any simple mugging.

And then Buffy had come and fought for her. Had been hurt. For her. Then she had done the thing that made Willow feel like throwing up. The thing that was even now gnawing a guilty little hole in her gut. Buffy had offered herself up to Chirayoju in Willow's place.

"Oh, God, Buffy, I'm so sorry," Willow whispered.

Incredibly, though Willow was already at her top speed, she began to run even faster. The little disk clutched in her palm felt warm there, and she prayed that Giles would know what to do with it.

They were a team. She understood that now, more than ever. Each did his or her part, whatever they were called upon to do. Right now her job was to get this thing to Giles as quickly as possible. After that, it would be in Giles's hands.

"Please, please, please, please," she chanted under her breath as she ran. But Willow had no idea whom she was pleading with: her body, or Giles, or someone else who could make all this right. Maybe all of them.

Maybe anyone who'd listen.

Willow ran.

Her heart pumped so fast and hard that her chest constricted and she wondered if this was what a heart attack felt like. But when she glanced up again, she saw the school. She had never been happier to get to Sunnydale High.

Willow stumbled going up the front steps, catching her foot on the long Chinese robe in which she found herself dressed. She skinned her knee on the concrete. But she picked herself up and kept moving. The front door was locked, of course. Giles hadn't expected anyone to be following on his heels.

She pounded on the door and began to scream his name. Barely able to hear the sound of her own voice, Willow shrieked her throat raw. The side of her hand hurt, and she started to slap the door instead. Anything. Whatever it took.

The door opened. Cordelia stared at her.

"Oh my God, Willow, what's . . ."

Willow fell into Cordelia's stunned embrace, barely noticing the other girl's astonishment. Then Cordy hugged her a little, which surprised Cordy as much as it did Willow.

"What is it?" Cordelia asked, staring at her. "Your clothes. Is that armor? If you're here . . . oh, my God, what's happened to Xander? And Buffy?"

"Still alive, I think," Willow panted, then moved past Cordelia and started down the hallway toward the library. "But not for long if Giles can't do something."

Cordelia hurried up next to her and helped her along, gripping Willow's forearm and putting her other arm around her shoulders. "I think we may have something," Cordelia said simply.

"For all our sakes," Willow rasped, "you'd better."

* * *

In the library Cordelia looked up worriedly and said, "What was that? Are we having an earthquake?"

"Hmm, not a welcome thought, that. Seeing as the garden has a bit of a bad history with earthquakes," Giles muttered.

"Take a look at this," he added, showing her the fax. "Can you find this for us? On the, um, computer?"

Willow shrugged. "If it's on there, I can find it."

Giles picked up the sword disk and scrutinized it. It gleamed in his hand and he murmured, "It's a shame that simply replacing this disk wouldn't bind them once again. Of course, we would also have to manage to get that sword from Sanno . . . Xander . . . somehow."

He must have felt both Cordelia's and Willow's eyes on him, for he looked up from the disk and cleared his throat.

"So, to the Net."

"To the Net." Willow cracked her knuckles.

While she was working, Giles received another fax:

Giles-sensei,

My deepest apologies for my earlier behavior. It was very rude of me to criticize your methods of working with your Slayer. I feel a great bitterness in my soul that I failed in my own duty to Mariko-chan. It is difficult for me to accept responsibility for her death. My sense of powerlessness now colors my life, and I felt great jealousy when I spoke to you because your Slayer is alive. I am very ashamed.

As a token of my regret, I offer this: intrigued by your studies, I have found the Legend of the Lost Slayer, as detailed on a scroll which was discovered late last year in Osaka. I am sending you the complete story, but the short version is this:

In 1612, there was a Watcher who was a samurai. Because he failed in his duty, he was ordered by his lord to commit seppuku. Where did his duty lie, to his Slayer or his lord? He chose his lord, and his Slayer was left without help. She was killed three months later.

I think that your young American girl is fortunate to have such a caring Watcher as you, Giles-sensei. I thank you for this lesson, and again, I beg your pardon.
Kobo

Giles swallowed hard, moved by the old man's confession. There were many kinds of demons in the world, and many ways to be bound by them. In his own way, Kobo had been blooded.

A short time later, they were in Giles's ancient auto, trundling toward the site of the climax of this ancient battle. Willow only hoped that everyone was still alive.

"Y'know, Giles, I was thinking," she said. "I mean, if you can do this thing, put the demon into the sword, why can't we pull the demon out of Angel the same way?"

Giles ran a red light and Cordelia murmured, "Yay."

"It had crossed my mind. But we're not sure how well the spell will work. Even if it does, it may only be because we're using an object that's already enchanted. Not to mention that, of course, the only result of removing the very thing that makes Angel a vampire would be that Angel would no longer be immortal."

"But Buffy's not immortal," Willow said helpfully. "That wouldn't be too bad."

"What I mean, Willow, is that Angel would be dead."

"Okay, that would be bad."

"This is all so insane," Cordelia said suddenly. "Why do I keep getting myself involved with you people? I'm going to get myself killed!"

"You just can't help yourself?" Willow suggested helpfully.

Cordelia smiled weakly. "Maybe not. So, are you okay?" she asked.

Willow blinked. Surprised and happy that Cordelia would bother to ask. "I guess so," she answered. "Actually, I'm pretty much one big bruise, but I think I'll be all right. If I ever get over the guilt of having started all this."

Cordelia frowned and Giles shot Willow an angry glance.

"What's happened is no more your fault, Willow, than it is Buffy's fault that we all live in the Hellmouth," Giles said sharply.

Willow thought about that. "I don't know how

Buffy does it," she replied. "I mean, she's got to live, right? She has to have a life, but she's constantly putting herself and everyone she loves in danger by being the Slayer. Not that she means to put us in danger," she added loyally.

Cordelia turned around in her seat to look at Willow. "We're in danger just living here. I'll never admit it if you tell her I said it, but I'd hate to think about what Sunnydale would be like if we didn't have a Slayer in town."

"Willow, Buffy merely does her best. That's all any of us can ask of her, or one another. Thus far, I think we've all done rather well," Giles said.

"Yeah." Willow nodded. "Thus far."

But she was comforted by their words. And she agreed with them. Buffy did her best to protect them all, but in the end it was their job to protect themselves. They all had to deal with living in the Hellmouth in their own way. They all had their own roles to play in the fight against darkness. It was a team effort.

"Thanks, you guys," she said.

Cordelia rolled her eyes and offered a little scowl in return, and Giles was already off elsewhere, deep in thought. Which was okay. They were doing what they did best.

Willow stared out her window at the stars.

Stared out and saw a reddish glow against the sky.

Beneath the car, the earth trembled.

The three looked at one another.

Cordelia said, "If it'll make this heap go faster, I'll get out and push."

CHAPTER 20

Angel landed atop a granite pagoda, which shattered beneath him, sending a good-sized shard of stone tearing through his abdomen. He groaned loudly, rolled over, and tried in vain to sit up once more. His face had long since transformed into its more feral, vampiric appearance, and it felt like ice now to him, cold and dead.

Angel stared down at the shiny granite shard protruding from his belly, cursed under his breath, and gripped it with both hands. He yanked it out, roaring with the pain of it, and then held a hand over the hole. A ripple of pain passed through him as he forced himself to his knees, but Angel ignored it.

His own pain meant nothing as long as Buffy was in trouble. Right now, she was in very serious trouble.

"You think that little girl's body can stand up to the King of the Mountain?" Sanno roared through

Xander's mouth, with a voice that didn't sound anything at all like Xander anymore.

With that, the Mountain King swept the great sword around once more and brought it down at an angle that would easily have decapitated Buffy. But Chirayoju was fast . . . Buffy was fast.

Only when Sanno laughed, as he did now, could Angel hear Xander inside him. That laugh was keeping him from killing the boy. That, and the fact that without Sanno, he didn't think he had a chance at all of defeating Chirayoju. Which was the dilemma, of course. He needed help to stop even one of them, but neither of them was interested in doing anything but killing each other.

"I have conquered foreign lands, Mountain King," Chirayoju thundered as it sent another ring of fire spouting at Xander. "When the bones of your host are ground into this earth, into the false garden of your homeland, I will be ruling nations!"

Using Xander's arms, Sanno brought up the sword and the fire was turned harmlessly away, as if it were a weapon as solid as the blade. Which, in a magical sense, Angel guessed it was.

They moved at each other again.

Angel tried to stand, tried to stop them, but a wave of pain overcame him, and he stumbled slightly. He needed just a few seconds to focus. To orient himself. But they were a few seconds he did not have.

Chirayoju's fist was aflame with a magical blaze— Buffy's hand was on fire!—and it drove that burning fist into Xander's face, scorching flesh and boiling blood with a smell that made Angel's mouth water and made him want to retch all at the same time.

"No," Angel grunted, started stalking toward them.

With a roar of pain and fury, Sanno drove his sword home. Its point punched through Buffy's shoulder just below the collarbone, and Angel wasn't sure, but he thought he saw her shirt tent out in the back, as though the blade had passed all the way through.

"No!" Angel screamed, and picked up speed, hand still clamped over his healing belly.

They stood that way, frozen for a second, maybe two. Then Sanno ripped the sword out, slamming his—Xander's—upper torso into Buffy's body and sending Chirayoju stumbling back, left arm hanging limply by her—its—side. Blood ran freely from the wound, and Angel stared at it as he approached. But already the blood was drying up. Already the wound was healing. By sorcery, or because Chirayoju was a vampire, he didn't know. But the speed of it was amazing.

He glanced at Sanno, saw that Xander's face was also healing, and with that amazement running through his mind, he launched himself the last few feet toward Buffy. In her eyes, Chirayoju's spirit burned. Her lips stretched into a disgusting laugh, and that ghostly face that the sorcerer had worn earlier returned, even as it reached out for Angel.

Angel clasped his fists together, brought them around from waist level and up into Buffy's face with all the strength he could summon. There was a loud crack, and Buffy's body flew backward several feet, her head snapped back and to one side.

"Well done, young one," a deep voice that was not Xander's said behind him.

Angel turned quickly as a powerful hand clamped on his shoulder. Behind him, the King of the Mountain grinned with Xander's face, but more and more, Sanno was taking over and Xander seemed almost to be disappearing into himself.

But then that smile disappeared, and for the first time Angel saw the true arrogance of an ancient god, or whatever manner of being this was that had once been called a god. He saw the cruelty and the conceit there, and Angel stiffened, prepared to fight again.

"Arigato gozaimasu," Sanno said. "I thank you, stripling. But now, keep out of my way!"

Then the King of the Mountain lifted Angel from the ground and threw him into the air. Angel landed hard on his back, and though his rage increased even further, a tiny spark of dread was born in his heart, a sort of hopelessness unlike anything he had ever known.

Somehow, he had to stop them both from fighting to the death. But he had no idea how to go about it.

"Come then, Mountain King. I will tear the throat from your host body, and drink down the boy's blood, and your spirit with it," Chirayoju sneered as it regained its footing, its guttural grunting twisting Buffy's perfect, soft mouth into something horrible, something Angel could barely stand to see.

"You will spill no more blood this night, vampire," Sanno declared, sword held at the ready.

"You're right," Chirayoju crowed, then slid toward Xander—toward the Mountain King—with the grace of a dancer, despite the arm that hung limply by its side . . . by Buffy's side.

Buffy's mouth contorted into a repulsive grin. "I won't spill a drop," it said from within her. "I wouldn't want to waste it. No, I will taste the blood of your host, and then I will gather the small army already in my thrall, and I will walk the night of this new land and my power will swell with each risen moon."

"You will walk only in the spirit world, parasite. I will see to that," Sanno proclaimed, and launched himself at the vampire again.

Chirayoju rushed to meet him.

Buffy was cold. She imagined she could remember what it was like to be buried in the frozen earth. To be dead, immobile in her own flesh. It must be something like this, she thought. But of course she could not remember it. And she was grateful for that at least.

But this wasn't the same. Not exactly. For as she floated inside the limbo that was her own mind, she could see cracks in her prison. Glimpses of the outside. There were moments when she felt a phantom pain, the tingling of her fingers, the thudding of her heart. Moments when she saw through her own eyes and heard with her ears.

She gathered her energy, reached into the deepest reserves of her mind, into the fabric of everything that made her herself. Buffy Summers. The Chosen One.

The Slayer.

And when dawn finally broke, what was Chirayoju but another vampire. More powerful than others, maybe. Older. And there was that whole magic thing, sure. But he was still a vampire.

Buffy knew what to do with vampires.

She focused her anger, her hatred, and her duty,

concentrated on her revulsion and her thirst for vengeance until they became like some kind of mental weapon, a blade of her own. A blade that sliced from within. Then she surged up through her consciousness, and she attacked! Chirayoju screamed inside her mind.

"I hope it hurts, you son of a . . ." she started to say.

With her own voice. Her own lips.

Then she was wrenched back down again, down away from the surface, away from the body that she'd successfully navigated through seventeen years of living in America.

Buffy should have given up then. She knew that. Every ounce of strength had gone into that last effort, and it had given her only a moment of triumph. No matter how strong she was, no matter how brave, no matter how persistent, even she might have lost all hope in that moment, were it not for one thing.

Chirayoju was afraid.

She didn't know quite what it feared. It had to do with the sword, and with the millennia it had spent as a captive inside the sword. But the King of the Mountain had already stabbed her—stabbed *it*— once, and there had been no reaction. But still, Chirayoju feared that sword, as if there was still some possibility that it might be trapped there again.

Chirayoju was afraid.

In the secret chambers of her mind, Buffy smiled.

As smoke from the burning Japanese farmhouse roiled toward the combatants, Chirayoju glared with hatred at the Mountain King and thought of the girl whose body it inhabited with loathing. She was fighting to reassert control of this form. For that she would pay.

While the ancient spirits raged, the fire from the farmhouse had spread. Flames raged around the battleground as the desiccated plants of the garden fed the blaze.

A wind whipped up, fanning the flames. Fireballs shot like arrows from Chirayoju's fingertips and were diverted by Sanno's sword, helping to spread the blaze ever faster.

As Angel watched, the winds whipped up and seemed to lift Chirayoju from the oval of garden that was not aflame, the patch of earth which had become the arena for this ancient battle. Buffy seemed to fly then, with the magic of the vampire sorcerer propelling her along. She hovered above the place where the tiny farmhouse had been, where the fire burned brightly.

Then she dropped into the flames.

"Buffy, no!" Angel screamed.

But it was only a moment before she reemerged, hair ablaze, skin blackened and smoking. Then the flames were out, and already Chirayoju's magic was working to repair the damage; new pink skin began to show through.

In Buffy's hand, Chirayoju held a long, gleaming *katana*. The sword reflected the light of the fire and of the full moon above. For a moment, Buffy's body just hung in the air.

Then the wind swept down with pummeling force and carried Chirayoju with it. It dropped to the earth in front of Xander . . . in front of Sanno, and the two spirits clashed swords.

"Buffy," Angel whispered.

Giles screeched to a halt. Before the car stopped rolling, Cordelia and Willow were out and running to the rise above the sunken garden.

"Oh, my God!" Cordelia cried.

Silhouetted against a backdrop of fire, Xander and Buffy were fighting with swords. Metal clanged against metal as they savagely battled, hacking and slashing with every ounce of their supernatural energy.

Angel saw the three of them, waved, and began to run toward them.

"Willow! Cordelia! Help me," Giles called.

They both ran back to the car and took large sacks from him. Inside Willow's sack were salt, water, and white paper, all symbols of purity. Cordelia carried Claire Silver's book and a printout of Sanno's Incantation. Giles brought a white bandanna on which he had written the Chinese character for the Japanese word for the life force: *ki*. And the disk.

Giles joined the girls at the crest and began pouring salt in a sacred circle. "Cover it with the paper," he said, and they quickly laid the pieces of paper inside the circle.

"They're blowing away!" Willow shouted, grabbing at the sheets as they were lifted by the wind and went sailing toward the fire.

"Here. Use rocks," Cordelia said, gathering some large pebbles and handing some to Willow. Impressed by Cordelia's quick thinking, Willow did as she said.

Once the paper lined the circle, the two girls stepped out and Giles sprinkled the water over the field of white.

Then he stepped into the circle and lifted the bandanna to the east and intoned, "Oh, great ancestors of the lords of Japan, I call upon you to cast the spirits forth from these mortal beings!" Bowing, he put the bandanna against his forehead and knotted the ends.

Angel ran up to Willow. "What's going on?" he asked, staring at them with a mixture of doubt and hope on his face.

"We're going to get the spirits out of Buffy and Xander," Willow explained. "Then we'll bind them in the sword with the disk."

"Great rulers, I call upon you to heed me!" Giles cried.

Xander rushed Buffy. She deflected his sword thrust and somersaulted over his head with a horrible, maniacal laugh.

"It's not working," Cordelia fretted. "It's not working!"

"Yet," Willow said hopefully.

Chirayoju faltered.

For a moment, Buffy felt as though she could break out of her prison and take her body back. She cried, "Yes!" and hoped that someone could hear her, sense her.

Help her.

Sanno looked at the crest of the hill. Willow swallowed as he seemed to stare through her at Giles.

"Mortals, do not interfere," he said.

"I have the ward," Giles told him. He held the disk high. "You can use it to bind the vampire and—"

"It is too late. It is unnecessary," Sanno said, but his attention was focused on the disk.

"He's lying," Angel murmured to Giles. "He was pretty interested in that when Buffy had it."

"Yes." Cordelia nodded. "He's lying for sure."

"How do you know?" Willow asked her.

Cordelia smiled grimly. "Believe me, I know when guys are being bogus. And that is *one* Mountain King who is not telling us the truth."

"Because it will bind him, too?" Willow asked hopefully.

They both looked at Giles, who murmured, "Perhaps. But we must get them out of Xander and Buffy before we deal with that issue."

Below them, the battle raged.

CHAPTER 21

Giles shook his head and dropped his arms to his sides.

"It isn't working!"

Angel stared at him, trying not to panic at the rage and helplessness that was welling up within him. All along, he'd been battling the feeling that he could do nothing to affect the outcome here. He'd fought at Buffy's side time and again, and nearly always he had felt secure in the knowledge that he had helped. He was a vampire, after all. He was strong and very hard to kill. The perfect companion for the Slayer, in an odd way.

But all night long, as the battle raged, the despair had grown greater in him as each moment ticked past. As each of his attacks was brushed aside by beings far more powerful than he. Angel could do nothing. He had held on to one small hope: that he could keep Xander and Buffy from killing each other long enough for Giles to arrive with a solution. He'd done that.

And now . . .

"What do you mean it isn't working?" Cordelia shrieked. "It's got to work! You're doing everything the book says to do! It's got to work!"

Giles ignored her now. He had begun chanting the Incantation of Sanno again, as if repetition was going to make it suddenly work when it hadn't been working before.

She stared down the small incline at Xander, slashing away at Buffy, fire burning from his hands and the wind making his hair sweep back off his forehead.

Cordelia didn't know exactly what it was she had with Xander. But she didn't want to lose him.

Not like this.

Cordelia Chase began to cry.

Without thinking, Willow stepped in close to Angel and reached for his hand. He clasped her fingers in his own without even glancing at her. Together they looked down at the two battling warriors, at the elements scorching and scouring the dead garden, and neither of them spoke a word.

Willow shivered and realized that she could barely recognize her friends from up here. They stood inside a circle, almost like an arena, made of blazing fire. The garden had long since given way to flames for the most part, and it was already starting to burn down to nothing but cinder and ash. There had been very little there to burn in the first place.

Xander and Buffy wore ugly, frightening masks, one white and the other sickly green, that shimmered just in front of their faces. Their bodies hadn't changed, not really, but just the way they carried themselves, the way they moved, they didn't look like Buffy and Xander anymore.

They weren't Buffy and Xander anymore.

Willow was over it being her fault. She had to be. No way could she have known what was going to happen when she touched that sword, when she was "blooded." And Willow had learned her lesson, no question about that. She'd learned that she should worry about being the best Willow she could be, and let Buffy worry about being Buffy.

If Buffy lived long enough to worry about being Buffy.

And that was it, wasn't it? That was why her heart hammered in her chest and her stomach felt like a ball of ice. Because the lesson wasn't over yet, was it?

It wasn't her fault. But that didn't make it any easier.

And she still felt useless.

Completely, and totally . . .

Willow stared at Xander and Buffy. Something was happening. Giles was finishing up his latest rendition of that radio-saturated top-ten hit, the Incantation of Sanno. And something was happening.

For a second, Buffy and Xander both faltered. The wind died. The flames fizzled. Then the moment was gone. Xander—Sanno—raised his sword and brought it down swiftly, but Chirayoju spun out of the way, using a move that Willow just *knew* the sorcerer had stolen from Buffy's mind. She had had enough information stolen during her own possession to know what it was like.

It was over. But for that moment . . . that split second . . .

"Am I hallucinating, or did something just . . ." Giles muttered.

"Giles!" Willow shouted. "Do it again!"

Giles turned, opened his mouth to ask for elaboration, but when he saw the look on Willow's face—on all their faces—he began the chant again immediately.

For a stunning second, Buffy was in charge. It wasn't so much that Chirayoju was gone as that it had been banished far back into her mind, just as she was now.

The vampire sorcerer controlled her body again. But it was anxious now, unfocused. Confused.

Buffy liked confused.

All right, you evil SOB, she thought, *let's try this again.*

The Slayer concentrated her energies, reached out, and gathered up all the things that made her the Chosen One, every personal moment, every intimate memory. They were her weapons and her armor, all the things that made her *her.* Her individuality was her strength. It hadn't been enough before, when Chirayoju was filled with confidence, at the peak of its strength.

But she didn't think it was at the peak anymore. Someone . . . Giles or Angel, maybe . . . someone was doing something to throw it off. And then there was that sword. Chirayoju was afraid of the sword, Buffy knew that. It had been trapped there before, and the thought of being . . .

. . . oh boy, Cheerios. I am so not going to be your favorite girl after this, she thought.

Gently this time, so that it would not sense her, she tried to glide upward, tried to inhabit her body. To see through her own eyes.

And suddenly she could see. Xander, with that ghostly face in front of his own, bringing that huge, razor-sharp sword around for another thrust.

"Chirayoju, you lose!" Buffy screamed with her mind.

And with her mouth! The word came out of her mouth! She had her body again, before the vampire sorcerer even knew that she had taken over. It would toss her back quickly, she knew. But she only needed a second to do what she needed to do.

"Do it, Xander!" she shouted. "Do it!"

Buffy threw her arms wide, left herself wide open for the falling blade, and waited for the cold rush of its point sliding through her chest and toward her heart.

Xander had been submerged completely. The King of the Mountain had taken him over and driven him under so far he had not even been aware of his possession. For him, it had been like a particularly deep sleep.

Seconds ago, he'd awakened in his own body, staring at Buffy, who was bruised and burned and . . . healing before his eyes, even as fire scorched her again. He'd felt the weight of the sword in his hands, felt the aches of his own bruises as he let the sword's point fall to the dirt so he wouldn't have to hold it up anymore.

"Buffy," he had whispered hoarsely, "what's . . ."

And then the Mountain King had surged up within him again.

But this time Xander didn't go away. This time he saw it all through his own eyes, though he was powerless to act. Powerless, that is, until the precise moment when Sanno began to bring the sword around into a thrust that would have cleaved Buffy's heart in two.

In that moment, Xander Harris had all the power he would ever need.

"No!" he roared, and his muscles were his own again.

Too late to stop the thrust, he could only redirect it. The blade impaled Buffy through her lower abdomen, sliced cleanly through. It was the second time she'd been stabbed with that sword, Xander seemed to recall from a horrible dream he'd been living only seconds earlier.

But this . . . this was different.

With Xander's mouth, Sanno, the King of the Mountain, screamed.

With Buffy's mouth, the vampire sorcerer Chirayoju wailed in agony.

Xander tried to move, but he was frozen. His entire body was locked in place, the blade stuck inside Buffy and she wasn't moving either. It was, he thought, in a weird moment of clarity, like being electrocuted. Some kind of weird energy danced from Buffy to Xander and back again, a circuit had been set up between them.

No, Xander couldn't move his body, but neither could Sanno. Nobody was in the driver's seat now.

Buffy felt the pulling start, felt a horrible urge as blood rushed to the spot on her belly where the sword intruded. It was sucking at her, somehow.

Inside her mind, Chirayoju screamed again, and then she knew what was happening.

The sword was dragging the vampire's spirit back to its prison. Dragging . . . but dragging at her as well. And if Chirayoju wouldn't let go, it would take Buffy instead.

Yesssss! Chirayoju hissed inside her head.

I don't think so, Myron, Buffy thought. *You crashed this party, bud. I'm not going anywhere.*

"Oh my God!" Cordelia cried. "Look at them! They're, like, frozen, or something!"

"Buffy," Angel whispered.

Willow tried to breathe. "This is bad."

"Not necessarily," Giles began, interrupting his chanting for a moment.

Angel saw Buffy move, just a bit. Half an inch. Obscured by smoke and what little remained of the fire. But when Giles stopped chanting, she—or Chirayoju—had started to move again.

When he turned on Giles, Angel was in full vamp mode.

"Giles, shut up and chant!"

He was relieved when Giles did as he demanded. He'd apologize later, if there was a later. For now, Angel thought he understood, just a little, of what Giles had been about to tell them.

"Come on." Angel grabbed Willow and Cordelia by their hands and started running down the incline toward the burning circle of embers that had been a garden, once upon a time.

"Angel!" Cordelia pulled on his wrist. "Angel!"

"What?" He tugged at them both to get them to keep up with him.

"I'm barefoot!" she screeched.

Angel reached around and grabbed both girls around the waist. Then, one under each arm, he sprinted across the ashes into the circle where Xander and Buffy were still joined, paralyzed in their weird portrait of battle. Of murder.

"Willow, get behind Xander!" Angel barked, putting them both down. "Cordelia, you get behind Buffy. When I tell you to pull, pull on them as hard as you can!"

Willow frowned, puzzled. "But won't that just start it all over again?" Willow asked.

Angel turned to meet her anxious gaze. "I'm going to be holding the sword. If Giles's spell is working, which it seems to be, then maybe they'll be trapped with it."

Cordelia stared at him. *"Maybe?"*

"Just do it!" Angel said angrily. "It's the only chance they've got."

"Okay," Cordy agreed instantly. "Just . . . Willow, be gentle with Xander, okay?"

Angel held the disk in his hand and stared at the odd inscriptions. He had no idea if this was going to work, but no time to worry about what might happen if it didn't.

"Wait, Angel!" Willow wrung her hands and chewed her lower lip as she looked uncertainly up at him. "What if Chirayoju and Sanno are trying to escape? Won't they try to go into you?"

"I've already got a demon in me, Willow." He flashed her a self-mocking smile. "Remember? There isn't room for another."

"But what if the sword tries to pull you in, too?" Cordelia asked.

Angel didn't want to think about that, and he didn't reply. He glanced at Willow, who always seemed so fragile, and saw so much strength there that he vowed never to underestimate the girl again. Then he glanced at Cordelia, and he realized that the same was true of her. As annoying as she could be, it was mostly just the way she had learned to be. But inside . . . well, she was here, wasn't she? Ready to do whatever it took.

"Ready?" he asked.

Both girls nodded.

"One . . . two . . . pull!"

Angel grabbed the blade, its edge slicing into his palms. Xander and Buffy were torn away from the circuit, falling to the ground with Willow and Cordelia. Angel felt the electricity of the magic surge through him, into him . . . tugging at him.

Chirayoju and Sanno were there, inside the blade, and they were fighting still. As they had been for millennia. As he figured they would be until the end of time. And he had no desire to join them in the land of their hatred, the world inside that blade.

Fighting the pull of the sword, Angel held it up by its blade and stared at the hilt. He took the disk and placed it back into the slot from which it had fallen. Just as he realized he had no way to hold it in place, he felt a sharp tug at his sleeve.

Buffy.

Really Buffy, this time. Weak, pale, trembling— holding onto the bloody wound at her belly, the wound which had not closed completely when Chirayoju had been yanked so unceremoniously from her body—but Buffy just the same. She held up to him a piece of cloth she had torn from the bottom of her shirt. Angel smiled and tied it around the hilt of the sword, holding the disk in place.

Still, the blade seemed charged with the hatred that lived inside it.

Buffy just wanted to sleep for about six months. That, and have somebody sew up the wound in her gut. Every inch of her felt bruised, the wound stung sharply, and yet, oddly, the places where she had been seriously injured before Chirayoju's magic had healed her felt all tingly and new.

But it wasn't enough that she'd been put through the wringer physically. She'd also ruined a brand-new top.

Then Angel looked at her, his eyes searing with his concern for her, and nothing else seemed important.

"I'm okay," she said. "A quick trip to the ER, and I'll be doing back flips in no time. Now, give me that," she said, gesturing to the sword.

Angel handed her the heavy blade. Buffy held the Sword of Sanno with both hands above her right knee, took a breath, and then brought it down hard. Anyone else would have broken their leg. But Buffy Summers was the Slayer. The Chosen One.

The blade snapped in two.

"Now they'll be fighting forever," Willow said as she stepped up to where Buffy stood with Angel.

Xander and Cordy were right behind her, holding each other. "Sounds like another couple I know," Xander said dryly.

So, *he* was back to normal.

"Angel." Giles panted as he rushed down the hill. "Thank God. You did it. You saved them."

"Buffy put the final kibosh on them," Angel said.

Willow pointed at Giles. "But if Giles hadn't kept chanting . . ."

Buffy reached out to Willow, took her hand, squeezed it, and then dropped it again. She looked around, got a bit dizzy, and held on to Angel for support.

"Looks like we all had a part to play tonight," Buffy said. "If any one of you hadn't been here, this might have turned out very differently."

"Yes." Giles pushed up his glasses and wiped the beads of perspiration from his brow. "It might have turned out to be the longest night mankind has ever known."

"It certainly feels that way." Cordelia sniffed. "I just want to go home and . . . by the way, Summers, where's my car?"

"I'm sure it's around here somewhere," Buffy replied, snuggling into Angel's embrace, wincing at the pain in her abdomen.

"Buffy." Willow reached for her friend. Buffy nodded back, giving her an "I'm going to be fine" look.

Xander cleared his throat. "Y'know, not that I'm not doing a little happy-to-be-alive dance—which, for those of you who don't know it, is generally done with little in the way of actual pirouettes—but I'm a little bothered by this whole Chirayoju thing."

"Only a little?" Willow looked at him, a small smile on her face.

"No, really," Xander argued. "I mean, don't we have enough *local* vampires? Now we have to start importing them?"

"C'mon, Xander, haven't you heard?" Buffy

asked. "We live in the Hellmouth. This is, like, Disney World for vamps."

"I'd hate to see Mickey," Willow muttered.

"You're missing the point, Will." Xander pointed at a certain young Slayer. "To the vampires, Buffy *is* Mickey."

And they went on that way, mixing their cartoon metaphors and generally making Buffy's headache worse, until they had to split up to get to Giles's and Cordelia's cars. Buffy paused then and took Willow aside, away from the others.

"Are you okay?" she asked, when she and her closest friend were out of earshot of the others.

"You've got a hole in your stomach, and you're asking me if *I'm* okay?"

Buffy looked at her gravely. "Will. Are you okay?"

Willow smiled sheepishly, shrugged a little Willow shrug, and nodded.

"I'll be all right," she replied. "I still think I should learn to fight a little better, but I doubt after the past week I'll ever start thinking that being the Slayer would be a *good* thing. No offense."

"None taken," Buffy said, grimacing in pain. "Besides, if I'm going to be laid up for a night or two, Giles may need a little help out on patrol. And you know Xander . . . he's a little distracted by that case of Cordy on the brain that he's come down with. Somebody's got to look out for him."

Willow grinned, then helped Buffy over to Giles's car.

In the back of Giles's ancient four-wheeled monster, on the way to the emergency room, Buffy fell soundly asleep in Angel's arms, a bittersweet smile on her face.

Bittersweet because she knew, even as she drifted off, that in the morning he'd be gone. But not forever. Not even for long. It was the curse of the Slayer, and the gift of her love for Angel, that the night would always come again.

And in the front seat, next to Giles, Willow felt a curious lightening inside her, as if the heaviest of burdens had been lifted. Giles must have noticed, for he cocked his head, half taking his eyes off the road, and said quietly, "Willow?"

"You know," Willow said, "it's a lot of work and everything, fighting the forces of darkness on such a regular basis. But I think if we all stick together, we just might win."

Giles smiled. He was the luckiest of men.

And the most fortunate of Watchers.

"Bravo," he whispered, and drove on.

About the Authors

Christopher Golden is the best-selling author of the epic dark fantasy series *The Shadow Saga*, as well as the X-Men trilogy *Mutant Empire* and the current hardcover *Codename Wolverine*. With Nancy Holder, he has written several other Buffy projects, including the *Gatekeeper Trilogy* and *The Watcher's Guide*. He is currently at work on a series of YA mystery novels for Pocket Books. Please visit him at www.christophergolden.com.

Four-time Bram Stoker Award–winner Nancy Holder has sold thirty-six novels and over two hundred short stories, articles, and essays. She has also sold game-related fiction, and comic books and TV commercials in Japan. Her work has been translated into over two dozen languages. She and Christopher Golden have written four Buffy-related books together, the most recent of which was *Blooded*. She is the author of *Gambler's Star: The Six Families*, book one of a science-fiction trilogy for Avon Books, due out in October 1998. She lives in San Diego with her husband, Wayne, and their daughter, Belle.

BUFFY

THE VAMPIRE

SLAYER™

THE WATCHER'S GUIDE

The official companion guide to the hit
TV series, full of cast photos, interviews,
trivia, and behind the scenes photos!

By Christopher Golden and Nancy Holder

POCKET
BOOKS

Published by Pocket Books

1492-01

"Well, we could grind our enemies into powder with a sledgehammer, but gosh, we did that last night."

— *XANDER*

BUFFY

THE VAMPIRE

SLAYER™

As long as there have been vampires, there has been the Slayer. One girl in all the world, to find them where they gather and to stop the spread of their evil ... the swell of their numbers.

Based on the hit TV series created by Joss Whedon

 Published by Pocket Books